RED PLANET

RED PLANET

RED PLANET

Peter Telep

Based on a story by Chuck Pfarrer
Screenplay by Jonathan Lemkin and
Channing Gibson

ACE BOOKS, NEW YORK

This is a work of fiction. Names, characters, places, and incidents are either the product of the author's imagination or are used fictitiously, and any resemblance to actual persons, living or dead, business establishments, events, or locales is entirely coincidental.

RED PLANET

An Ace Book / published by arrangement with
the author

PRINTING HISTORY
Ace mass-market edition / October 2000

The Penguin Putnam Inc. World Wide Web site address is
http://www.penguinputnam.com

Check out the ACE Science Fiction & Fantasy newsletter
and much more on the Internet at Club PPI!

ISBN: 0-441-00762-7

ACE®
Ace Books are published
by The Berkley Publishing Group,
a division of Penguin Putnam Inc.,
375 Hudson Street, New York, New York 10014.
ACE and the "A" design are trademarks
belonging to Penguin Putnam Inc.

PRINTED IN THE UNITED STATES OF AMERICA

10 9 8 7 6 5 4 3 2

acknowledgments

I am grateful to my editor, Mr. Tom Colgan, for thinking of me, and to the other kind folks at Penguin Putnam, most notably Elaine Piechowski and Samantha Mandor, who supplied me with information crucial to completing this manuscript.

I owe a particularly heartfelt thank-you to my agent, John Talbot, who continually walks point for me, despite the hazards lurking in every shadow of the publishing business.

My webmaster, Richard Bowden, and all of the folks who have helped him build my website are most certainly in my debt. Visit www.earth-netone.com to see the work of many talented artisans.

For Nancy, Lauren, and Kendall—
three women Mars can't have . . .

prologue

CHANTILAS, BUD
CHIEF SCIENCE OFFICER
UNITED STATES SPACECRAFT *MEDEA ONE*
LOG ENTRY DATE: 23 November, 2050
MISSION TIME: DAY 181

The Earth of my childhood. Crystalline blue. Teeming with life. The most perfect, self-regulating organism imaginable.

We went out into space. We turned around. We looked back. We saw it. You would think we would behold and learn something.

We didn't.

Why?

I keep searching for answers in the past.

It was 1961 when we first went into space. Gagarin made one orbit in April, and Shepard went up in May. President John F. Kennedy instituted the Apollo program that same month. We vowed to put a human being on the moon before the decade was out. Four months shy of our deadline, Neil Armstrong took one small step.

There were about four billion people on the world that day.

Then, at a rate scarcely comprehensible, we began to poison and populate our planet. By the year 2000, six billion of us swarmed the globe. From then on, we increased by one hundred and twenty million people a year and pumped out our toxins beyond measure. We cut down our forests faster than they could be replenished, tainted our soil with landfills and fertilizers, and choked ourselves with so many industrial emissions that they turned our rain to acid. In ninety-five percent of our developing nations, we discharged untreated urban sewage into rivers and bays. Anything that could not be trademarked and sold at a profit we annihilated without a thought.

During this time, middle school students in Henderson, Minnesota, noticed deformed hind legs on frogs they had caught at a nearby pond. They began the Minnesota New Country School Project. They made a difference in their hometown. Won a battle. But those bright, beautiful kids had no idea of the war's immensity.

We killed all the frogs.

Every frog on the face of the planet.

We had killed species before, even a genus or two. But this time we had wiped out an entire phylum. Frogs breathe through their skin and react faster to toxins in the environment. This should have been a warning. But we failed to notice because we could not pinpoint exactly what had killed them. Was it the acid rain, climate changes, ozone depletion, habitat destruction, a worm parasite, or even the introduction of nonnative species to their environments?

Maybe we were afraid to learn the truth.

Or we just didn't pay attention.

So here we are. Halfway through the twenty-first century with over half the environment destroyed. Twelve billion of us back home now pile up in cookie-cutter homes, apartments, condos, duplexes, tents, grass huts, lean-tos, caves, and in the shade of dying trees.

It took us one hundred years to go from the industrial revolution to putting a human being in space.

It took us nearly another century to poison and populate the planet so seriously that if we do not find somewhere else to live, we will die out as a species within the next two generations.

I ask again, how did we get here? Was it only greed? Are we being punished?

Or was it self-mutilation, a rebellion against ourselves for our own frailties?

I'm reading here in Ecclesiastes 1:4, "One generation passeth away, and another generation cometh: but the Earth abideth for ever."

I want to believe that. I want to believe that out there on that small, red planet lies at least one answer.

one

She knifed through space at forty-eight thousand kilometers per hour, never once betraying her previous life as a much slower lunar cargo ship. She had been painstakingly modified so that she could whisk her six wayfarers on a round-trip voyage that would take them nearly four hundred million kilometers away from their homes. Thirteen massive spheres formed part of her T-shaped bow, and each rotated to produce near-Earth gravity at their equators. A single orb remained at the center of the group, with the others packed in tightly at each vertex of an imaginary cuboctahedron to illustrate what engineers and mathematicians called "cuboctahedral packing."

One inventive CNN reporter had taken to describing *Medea One* as "a bunch of marbles glued together with a two-hundred-meter-long bundle of stogies stuck in one end. Slide a couple of hula hoops over the stogies, slap a windmill of solar panels on her stern, and you had yourself an interplanetary spacecraft that got the worst gas mileage of any vehicle ever manufactured."

While public relations officers from the Space Exploratory Office had protested that rather unflattering description of a spacecraft with such a profound mission, they had recognized that most citizens were not up on their geometry. Cuboctahedral packing or not, *Medea One*'s design complemented her purpose. Sphere functions ranged from crew quarters to garden to multipurpose laboratory to elevated flight deck, where Lieutenant Commander Kate Bowman now sat intently in her pilot's chair, listening to a message from Spacecraft Communicator John Skavlem. "*Medea One*, Houston. You have acquired orbit. Welcome to Mars and congratulations on a successful outbound."

Bowman rose, and despite having nearly six months to prepare for the moment, she gazed slack-jawed at the image dominating the flight deck's viewport.

Mars.

Really Mars. Right there. Not an enhanced simulacrum relayed from orbital telescopes or probes, but the planet itself; mottled browns and reds bleeding north and south toward shimmering ice caps.

Mars. Fourth planet from the sun. Home to the largest shield volcano in the solar system. Home to a great rift valley spanning the distance of New York to California. Home to a complex network of ancient channels formed when liquid water once flowed on its surface.

Home to humanity.

Perhaps.

The Romans had regarded the deity Mars as the father of their people, and Bowman liked to muse that humanity was leaving mother Earth to find solace in father's arms.

Bowman prayed that he had a forgiving heart.

With a nod of reassurance, she rubbed her eyes, raked fingers through straight, dark hair that barely touched her shoulders, then shifted toward the guidance and control touchboard. "Almost there."

"Commander, I don't care what they say about you. You're not even thirty, and look where you've come in your life."

She raised a brow at Captain Ted Santen, an olive-skinned fighter jock about her age, who wore his game face even while sleeping. But reaching Mars had affected even him. "Lieutenant, what *are* they saying about me?"

Too many stories lay hidden in his grin.

NATIONAL SOLAR OBSERVATORY, SACRAMENTO PEAK
ALAMOGORDO, NEW MEXICO

Solar astronomer Dr. Joseph Byntana tugged nervously on his graying beard as he observed the images filtering through the third generation Richard B. Dunn Solar Telescope (DST), the finest instrument of its kind on the planet. With zero point two arc-seconds resolution, the DST could detect some of the most intricate surface features of the sun. Two mirrors formed the scope's heliostat, and those mirrors followed the sun and redirected its light back to Byntana in the optics room. The scope itself lay partially hidden underground, stretched the length of a football field, and weighed over two hundred fifty tons.

All of which was to say that Dr. Byntana did not doubt for a second the validity of what the DST had revealed. "Hey, Too? Have a look at this."

Dr. Too Lee, a forty-two-year-old solar astronomer visiting from China, set down his handheld computer, then crossed from a bank of monitors feeding him data from the Advanced Stokes Polarimeter, a device that, along with others, he and Byntana used to study the sun's complex magnetic fields. Too's face blanched with mild surprise as he glimpsed Byntana's screens. "Looks like major precursor for sure. Soft x-ray emission detected."

"Been picking it up for about seven minutes now," Byntana answered, feeling a tingle at the nape of his neck. This day could represent the most exciting moment of his career. Typically, when two solar regions of high magnetic-field strength approached each other, they would pass uneventfully, like many of Byntana's days. But the two Byntana now observed had passed close enough and in just the right way to produce a highly volatile, s-shaped region called a "sigmoid."

An alarm beeped from the spectrograph's touchboard behind them. Too darted to the panel. "Impulsive stage for sure. Way past one MeV. Detect radio, hard X ray, and gamma ray. Detect coronal-mass ejection."

Byntana's throat lumped. He whirled back toward his screen and gaped at the largest solar flare he had ever seen, a flare releasing energy equivalent to millions of one-hundred-megaton bombs exploding simultaneously. Byntana had examined old photographs of an event that had occurred in 1973, the largest solar flare ever recorded, but that flare's eruptive prominence paled in comparison to the one before him. "Jesus. . . . It's over a million kilometers long. It'll shut down every comm satellite on this side of the planet."

"Good news," Too said. "It is directional. I believe most of it will miss us."

"So where's it headed?"

In one sweeping gaze, Flight Director Matthew Russert took in the Flight Control Room, the "ficker." For the first time in many weeks, the ficker buzzed with an activity that made him feel like an eighteen-year-old instead of a fifty-one-year-old balding man with a slight paunch and high cholesterol.

Still, Russert's rejuvenation might come at a terrible price.

He hustled down a short staircase and into a rectangular chamber devoid of the consoles and large screens that his grandfather, a propulsion engineer, or "PROP," had used during his own tenure with the space shuttle program. Instead, Russert and the nineteen other controllers wore barely discernible headsets with Projected Image Monocles flipped down over their dominant eyes. When so moved, Russert could issue a voice command and project an image on the common viewer, otherwise the PIMs kept his teams well-informed through their Heads Up Displays.

At the moment, a controller sat at every station, each monitoring data through PIMs or dictating it to their handheld computers. Tomo Jax—the flight dynamics officer, call sign "FIDO"—seemed especially wired, leaning into his desk as though he were Sisyphus pushing the rock. Mission Operations Directorate Manager Kathleen Crete craned her head, caught Russert's approach, then darted from her own station. Ms. "MOD" guarded herself behind an implacable demeanor that had served her well during her recent divorce. She'd gotten everything. Or so rumor had it. Not much younger than Russert, she had always regarded him politely, but had never gone out of her way to chat. And that had been just as well since the petite brunette served as liaison between the ficker and JSC MOD management, basically the brass. Lately, news from her had rarely been good: save humanity, but come in on budget.

"Flight?" she called.

"What do you have?"

Crete pursed her lips, hesitated. "They're asking that you wait for a positive trajectory."

Russert raised his index finger, then steered himself toward Science Officer Andy Lowenthal's desk, with Crete tight on his heels. "Andy, I gotta know, and I gotta know now."

Lowenthal, a long-bearded genius who wore the spare tire of a decade's worth of epicurean repasts, gave Russert that same look he made every time they ordered cheap pizza. "We're still correlating with Alamogordo. This isn't something we wanna be wrong about."

"Understood, Andy, but if we're right—"

"Hang on. Getting something." Lowenthal stared intently into his PIM and nodded as he skimmed the incoming data. "All right. Alamogordo confirms that it's directional. Most of it's gonna miss us. Bad news is it's directional—and most of it's going toward Mars."

"Flares this big are rare," said Russert disgustedly, drawing Lowenthal's nod. "Course they happen on my watch. Time?"

"Emissions usually take about eight minutes to reach Earth. Mars is in aphelion. I'm thinking about fourteen minutes."

Russert grinned crookedly over the time. It would take twenty minutes for a warning to reach *Medea One*. He turned to his left, where Capcom John Skavlem sat at his desk, his youthful face framed by a crew cut gone prematurely gray. "Sorry, Flight."

Sighing in frustration, Russert moved off and bowed his head. He imagined an enormous tidal wave of energy rolling through space toward a little boat parked in orbit around a red planet. The wave hit, smashed the boat to smithereens, then carried off the debris as twelve billion souls railed against their fate. The loudest cry came from Jessica, the sixteen-year-old gem of Russert's life, the daughter for whom he would sacrifice anything.

"Flight? You okay?" asked Skavlem.

Russert shook off the nightmarish screams and looked up. "What're we doing? We have flare protocols. Let's run 'em."

two

Robert Gallagher floated through the access tube connecting the crew quarters sphere with the Flight Deck. Rivulets of sweat lined his narrow face, descending from his equally sodden crew cut. He had been pedaling the exercise bike as though he were gaining on the leader during the Tour de France, but he had failed to sweat off any of his anxiety.

With a slight push, he tipped himself upright in the three-meter-wide conduit and drifted toward a small porthole. Mars hung there, an immense, dilated pupil against an iris of stars. Fettered shadows crept across the massive plains and valleys of Hellas Planitia, and Kepler Crater finally rolled into view. Or maybe Gallagher had not seen those surface features at all. True, he had studied Martian geography, but the challenge of picking out features in all

that unfurling gloom and through six centimeters of permaglass would have even the rockheads back home
squinting and consulting their topographic maps.

"Holy shit," Gallagher whispered as the enormity of
the moment struck him. He touched the permaglass,
traced the planet, and felt even more taken aback as he
noticed his reflection superimposed over the dusky orb.
His forty years barely showed, and he had been accused
of abusing his boyish charm by more than a couple of
girlfriends. Now he hovered like a little blond kid enrap-
tured by the one colossal present Santa had squeezed
down the chimney.

*Robert Gallagher. One of the first human beings to set
foot on another world.*

He had been saying that to himself for the past two
years, since the day he had received the call. He had put
on his rebreather and had been on his way out of his Daytona Beach duplex to hook up with two old submariner
buddies when Rita Didorsa from the Space Exploratory
Office had called on the vidcomm. Dressed in an expensive blouse and skirt and looking for all the world like a
first lady, the young black woman had raised a knowing
smile. "We were wondering if you wouldn't mind going
to Mars. We think you have just the right amounts of in-
dividuality and self-reliance to be an effective crew member on our first manned mission."

After he had pried himself off the ceiling, Gallagher
had uttered a simple, "Sure. What'll it cost me?"

Didorsa had chuckled. "No. We're paying you. I doubt
you'll worry about money anymore."

Gallagher had known SEO officials were interested in
him. They had already put him through a week-long
process of personal interviews, thorough medical evalua-
tions, and orientations that had tested his boredom—but

until Didorsa had called, he had had no idea how they'd planned on exploiting his talents.

Robert Gallagher. One of the first human beings to set foot on another world.

During a press conference, a journalist from the WB Network had asked Gallagher what he planned on saying when his boot hit the soil. "Well, that one small step thing's been taken. And I won't be first out. So I don't know whether it's that important."

Over one hundred reporters had frowned.

"I'm sure he'll think of something," Lieutenant Commander Bowman had said.

Her voice now reverberated over his headset. "All right, gentlemen. We have stable, circular orbit at twenty-two thousand kilometers. We have three laps around, ninety minutes each. In four and a half hours, we'll launch the MEV. Bowman out."

"Confirm that," Santen said. "Moving into light side. Polarizers activating."

A brilliant shaft of light cut through the permaglass, and Gallagher slid on his sunglasses, a perfect complement to his loudest Hawaiian-print shirt. He had donned the shirt to piss off Santen, who had packed standard utilities and uniforms as unimaginative as he was.

Gallagher's anticipation drove him away from the porthole. The Flight Deck's open hatch lay ahead, and he glided up and into Command and Control. Bowman and Santen sat before a curving bank of illuminated touch-boards and data screens, though the whole array served as a mere supplement to their PIM headsets. They could pilot the ship through those panels, through a Virtual Cerebral Interface, or through simple voice commands. The ship's artificial intelligence would read their pulse, blood pressure, respiration, and mood, then decide upon the best way to deliver data. Were Bowman tied up in a delicate manual maneuver that, say, raised her blood pressure, stressing her out, the computer might choose to deliver supplementary data through voice reports rather than force her to glance at a screen. The system solved the problem of data overkill, and Gallagher admired it for that. He had asked SEO engineers if he could take it apart, study it, have some fun. He had never seen four geeks grow more pale.

Bowman glanced over her shoulder, offered an easy grin.

"Are we *there* yet?" Gallagher asked, gripping the back of her seat and steadying himself against the Flight Deck's gravity. "It's not like I haven't been waiting four hundred million kilometers for this moment."

She shook her head, opened her mouth, and—

Two touchboards directly in front of her winked out.

Warning messages in bold, crimson letters rippled across overhead screens. NAVIGATIONAL SUBSYSTEM THREE OVERLOAD. REROUTE IN PROGRESS. NO RESPONSE TO REROUTE. SECONDARY SYSTEM OVERLOAD. CAUSE OF ANOMALY UNKNOWN.

Sliding to the edge of her seat, Bowman beat a fist on the two dead touchboards, then regarded another data bar with yet another glowing warning: MULTIPLE PROTEIN PROCESSOR OVERLOADS IN PROGRESS. SOURCE: EXTERNAL CONTAMINATION.

"Houston, *Medea One*," called Santen. "Experiencing multiple guidance and navigational failures." He checked another screen. "Interference. Can't get off a signal."

"Let me check it out," Gallagher said, pulling himself next to Santen.

"Mr. Gallagher, remove yourself from my flight deck."

Gallagher looked to Bowman, but her rapid resetting

of the two systems ruled against sparing him a glance.
The guidance system touchboard glimmered back to life.
Bowman stage-whispered a "yes" even as the system
died once more. "Single event upsets. All over the board.
Latch up. Free-flow. We're gonna lose chips. Shut it
down."

Santen's jaw dropped. "Shut it down?"

Before Bowman could answer, two Klaxons resounded, their rapid beeping driving her out of her chair
and to starboard, to the air recycling and life-support
touchboards. "Shut it all down," she finally answered.
"Only way to save the systems. Looks like we got S-E-P,
some kind of massive flare. Computer. Give me intercom." She paused. "Gentlemen, correction, we'll launch
MEV on *this* pass. In fact, in five minutes."

"We can't deploy now," Santen argued, typing rapidly
on a touchboard, the screen up top popping with shutdown confirmations. "MEV'll be affected same as us."

"Aeroshell might help," Bowman said. "Either way,
you're going. Or we got a billion dollar entry vehicle that
we can't get out of the garage." She stormed back to Santen's station, swiped his hands away with her arm, and
finished the shutdown herself.

A third alarm kicked in, high-pitched tones blaring a
premature dirge for the dying ship.

"Proton flux," Bowman said, reading data pouring in
from the ship's spectrometer. "*Multiple* event upsets. Radiation alert. Captain? Gallagher? *Bye.*"

Santen bolted out of his chair.

"Gallagher, I mean it," Bowman warned.

He resigned, nodded. "See you back there."

"Right." She waved him off, consumed by her touchboards.

Gallagher hustled after the copilot, feeling his boots

lift from the deck as the artificial gravity fluctuated. Klaxons echoed through the entire ship, and he grimaced over the thickening stench of melted electronics.

Bud Chantilas had already donned the tight-fitting thermal undersuit laden with sensors. Now he stepped into his twenty-one-pound, navy blue, environment suit, or e-suit, struggling to get his left arm into the damned Kevlar sleeve without straining that deltoid again. The fiery pain singed a little before he straightened and the arm slid in. *If that's the worst of it, then I'm all right. Not bad for sixty. Not bad at all.*

In truth, he had a sprout-fed body that men half his age envied, a body he would now subject to the ungodly forces waiting in Mars' upper atmosphere. He buckled the Y-shaped life-support vest, then pulled the suit's gelatinous hood over his head. Autolocks snapped into place, and the hood morphed solid and transparent. He checked the wrist panel for status: systems green. Pressure up to eight point three pounds per square inch. He floated off, back toward the airlock's permaglass door.

The Mars Entry Vehicle hung out there, beyond the anteroom's airlock, affixed by explosive bolts to a long mooring track that jutted out into the two-hundred-meter-long cylindrical bay. Unlike any lander ever constructed, the MEV boasted an icosahedral aeroshell that, like *Medea One*'s cuboctahedral packing, made it seem more like a geometry experiment than a spacecraft. Chantilas had tried to explain the design to the media when the MEV was still under construction. "Your basic icosahedron has twenty triangular faces that meet in groups of five at each of twelve vertices. What that really means is that the object resembles a kind of funky top, or the result of someone trying to construct a sphere out of a handful of triangles. You want simple? Describe it as a coppery gem cut by an overzealous jeweler." One reporter had quoted Chantilas, and the crew had teased him about being more poet than scientist. Then reporters had begun asking him about the teasing, and Chantilas had tossed them a quote from Percy Shelley: " 'Poets are the hierophants of an unapprehended inspiration, the mirrors of the gigantic shadows which futurity casts upon the present, the words which express what they understand not, the trumpets which sing to battle and feel not what they inspire: the influence which is moved not, but moves. Poets are the unacknowledged legislators of the World.' "

Their vacant stares had told Chantilas that they did not entirely understand the reference, but they soon jumped all over the last part about him becoming politically active. "No," he had told them. "I want to *help* people."

Chantilas grinned inwardly over the reminiscence, until Gallagher and Santen soared into the lock's antechamber. They went directly for the transparent tubes containing their thermal and e-suits. "Mr. Chantilas?" Santen cried in his military baritone. "Stand by on the lock!"

Chip Pettengill rubbed sleep grit from his eyes, finished zipping up the fly on his cotton slacks, then walked directly into the bulkhead. "Son of a bitch!"

No, the gravity in the crew quarters sphere had not suddenly shifted. Pettengill's nerves had. He took a deep breath, rubbed his sore nose, and assured himself that it would not swell. The crewcut alone had already done a fine job of ruining what his girlfriend had called his "sinister good looks." No more curly blond locks. Just stubble.

Now where the hell is the satchel? There. On the deck.

He scooped it up as the sphere's gravity failed. "Be nice if she explained why the goddamned ship is falling apart. Thought saving humanity was popular with the politicians. Didn't we spend the big bucks on this ride?"

Pettengill swam up toward the ceiling, then booted off, arrowing toward the octagonal hatch. *Great. Now I can get spacesick again. Love it. Shit. Look at me. I'm a skinny bastard, a terraformer. This, I don't need.*

The two things that Quinn Burchenal hated most in life had occurred simultaneously. You did not interrupt one of his catnaps, and, by God, you did not do it with a wailing alarm. Ask any one of his ex-wives, and they'd tell you that he had broken at least two of their alarm clocks and had even managed to destroy a 3D wake-up system that lured you out of bed with soft tones and a scantily clad lover who promised to reward you for "being an earlier riser." That one deserved to be broken.

With his jaw set to prevent him from swearing and his face knotted into his usual mobster's scowl, he muscled his husky frame through the conduit and bobbed into the anteroom, carried by ghostly currents.

"Suit up, Mr. Burchenal," Santen said, having already done so himself.

"You're good. You notice things like that," Burchenal returned with a smirk, then crossed to the intercom's touchpad. "Kate? You can cut that caterwauling. I'm up from my nap." He started toward his suit's storage tube, remembering the dream he had just had of being back in the climate-controlled indoor track where he and his Arabian were enjoying a Saturday afternoon. He loved that damned horse as much as the mission. And despite making facetious appeals to SEO brass, he still could not take his horse to Mars.

Burchenal stepped into his thermal, looked up, and found Gallagher floating there, already helping him with the buckles. As usual, the guy wore his how-the-fuck-did-I-get-lucky-enough-for-this-mission grin, all bright eyes and too-damned-clear complexion. Burchenal had pores the size of Martian craters, or at least his insecurity told him so. Gallagher assisted with the e-suit, double-checked the fittings, then Burchenal returned the favor. He winced a little as the suit's autocatheter pushed through the thermal and slid into place.

In the meantime, Pettengill had darted in, and Santen busied himself by setting up the lean, thirty-two-year-old's suit. Ignoring Pettengill's protests, Santen and Chantilas stuffed him into the protective skin and banged his helmet home.

"All right, gentlemen," roared Santen. "Sound off on taccom two."

Gallagher, Pettengill, and Chantilas checked in over their intersuit comm system. Burchenal finally offered his own tired response.

Chantilas returned to the airlock's control plate. "Opening lock."

Twin permaglass doors swished aside. Burchenal followed the others through the lock and onto the MEV deck. With their legs dangling in zero G behind them, they clambered up a ladder bolted to the bulkhead. At the top, they gripped the railing of a catwalk, then crossed to the mooring gate, a rectangular bridge leading to the MEV's primary hatch.

"Hey, Burchenal? How do you stay so calm?" asked Gallagher.

"Dunno. But it does take a lot more than a solar flare to impress me."

•   •   •

Kate Bowman chewed her lip as she scrutinized the MEV's mooring release system. 3D schematics flashed across the screen, rotated, then zoomed in to ID the damaged triggers. Each time she tired to repower the system, another processor melted into lifelessness. She wanted to scream, but clung tightly to her anger, a rotten, ugly thing that she refused to expose to anyone, even herself. *I'm not that weak. Remember that day over the Adriatic Sea? This is the same. Fly navy. Fly forever.*

All right, she had the idea. Now she just needed the damned ship to go along with it. She plugged the command into her last active touchboard. Green light. "Gentlemen, it seems I won't be joining you and will maintain manual release for the MEV from the Flight Deck."

"Commander!"

"That's right, Santen. *I'm* the commander. You are go for Mars descent. On my signal."

three

Though not particularly spacious, the Mars Entry Vehicle would have been regarded as a penthouse suite to those who had flown the original Apollo missions. Six high-G couches with crew names stenciled on them fit tightly against the bulkheads of the circular hold. A single swivel arm affixed to the side of the couch supported a command station that included a touchboard and miniscreen. In the event of an emergency, any crew member could perform a manual lockout and assume control. And because of that feature, Gallagher had been forced to spend six seemingly interminable months training in a simulator for something he would probably never do.

After a longing glance at Bowman's empty couch, Gallagher plopped into his own and wriggled through the straps. Burchenal sat across the compartment, brooding, nodding, doing a strange rubbing thing with his lips. Chantilas sat like a wizened monk, eyes closed, gloved fingers laced and resting in his lap. Pettengill's gaze darted to and fro, and, noticing that, Santen flashed him a cocky look. "Just take it easy, little man. I'll get you down."

Pettengill smiled. "Fuck you."

One hundred and ninety days ago, they had all been professionals. But, Gallagher reasoned, this is what happens when you take six bright people and stuff them in a can for about six months without checking said can's expiration date. "Oh, that kind of language and behavior would never happen," engineers and former astronauts would say, furthering the conspiracy. . . .

"Commander?" cried Santen, gaze riveted to his command station, one hand steadying the unit's swivel arm. "We're green across the board."

Gallagher cleared his throat. "Private channel to the Flight Deck," he ordered his suit's taccom.

"Channel open," came the lovely female voice he had selected from over a dozen samples.

"Hey, Commander? Promise you won't leave if we don't like it there?"

He waited, wondered what she thought, then her faint reply finally came through: "I promise." She followed up with a curt report over the general frequency. "Captain Santen, you have control authority of the MEV in three, two, one."

"Shit," Santen hollered. He punched his command station, and the unit tilted to reveal warning messages and a blinking touchboard.

Burchenal hemmed. "Hey, Santen? Waiting is not a good plan."

The copilot looked lost for a second before he shouted, "Crew secure?"

They answered in turn, as they had practiced, with Gallagher chipping in the final "secure."

Santen drummed twice on his board, then shoved it away and clutched his couch, chin tilted up in defiance of the forthcoming gravitic war.

Gallagher dialed into a bit of Chantilas's peace by closing his eyes, pulling in a deep breath, then surrendering himself to the couch.

Peace lasted exactly six seconds, then successive, rhythmic explosions thundered through the MEV. Gallagher clutched his straps.

". . . the fuck?" Pettengill cried, his question butchered by the booming.

The stars gleamed through a triangular porthole. Explosive bolts had been detonated, and the MEV deck's cylindrical housing had divided and now tumbled away from the ship like two steel rinds to expose an icosahedral fruit.

"On the clock," said Santen. "Five seconds. Three. Mooring release!"

Another quake struck the MEV, though it rattled nerves more than bulkheads. Barely perceptible but still there, the sensation of free fall tingled up through Gallagher's legs. The stars outside shifted. The MEV had blown free.

"Jets functioning," Santen reported with a sigh. "Setting us up for the burn."

Gallagher knew the rest; after all, he had gone through the simulation eleven hundred times. The MEV's AI would flip the lander around, point eight small maneuvering jets at exactly the right angles, then fire those jets for exactly twenty-seven minutes to decelerate from orbital velocity. Mars's gravity would then drag the MEV downward for two hours in a slow, controlled arc.

Once the MEV hit atmosphere, its aeroshell would protect the crew from temperatures in excess of fifteen hundred degrees Celsius. Within eight minutes, atmospheric drag would slow the craft down to about eight hundred kilometers per hour. At that time, Santen would have the option of landing via chutes and gas bag deployment or, with conditions right, he could opt to bring her down in a nice, picturesque vertical landing caught by a remote camera that he would jettison a minute or so before touchdown. After all, everyone back home wanted to see action.

"We're in the pipe," Santen cried. "Autoburn sequence in ten seconds."

Gallagher appreciated the way Santen sang the report. The pilot's swelling confidence allayed at least one of his ten thousand fears.

"Everybody take a breath and hold it," the pilot instructed. "Here we go . . . mark."

"Wow. That's not so bad," Pettengill said.

Burchenal snorted and shook his head, jowls wagging. "We ain't moving."

Jolt number one sent Gallagher slamming into his harness. Jolt number two sneaked up from below, driving his stomach into his throat.

"Burn's a go," Santen announced. "Son of a bitch is late! I'm going manual after cutoff."

"Whatever," Pettengill said. "Just land. That's what you do, isn't it?"

"It ain't that easy, my dear assistant," Burchenal said. "With a bad angle and an incorrect burn—"

"Yeah, yeah," Pettengill groaned. "We already got an incorrect burn. Hope megapilot can compensate." His eyes narrowed on Santen, whose own eyes widened as he skimmed his command station.

"All right," Santen muttered. "All right."

For the next twenty-two minutes, only Santen's voice broke over the freight-train rumble of entry. His confidence had returned to a respectable level, and he issued his reports evenly, doing a marginally successful job of bolstering spirits. Gallagher noted how the fire in Pettengill's eyes had cooled and how Burchenal's expression betrayed his absence. The man had levered himself into his saddle and booted his Arabian into a canter. At the moment, his life had nothing to do with plummeting toward a reddish-brown valley cut by ancient water flows.

The vibration came on slowly, warmed up into a steady knocking, then jarred the needle toward an eight or nine on the Richter scale as the MEV stabbed the Martian atmosphere.

"Temp's way up," Santen said, voice quavering as much as the vehicle. "Past two thousand C. We won't burn up, but our angle sucks." He thumbed the touchboard. "And we are manual. Two chips down on the nav. And there, we've lost the third. But no contamination in the hold. It's seat of the pants, gentlemen. I'll eyeball us in."

"I love it when my pilot says that," Pettengill spat. "Where's my little bottle of whiskey?"

"Would anyone like to join me in a prayer?" asked Chantilas.

"No!" Burchenal and Pettengill cried.

"What the hell," Gallagher said. "I mean, yeah."

UNITED STATES SPACECRAFT *MEDEA ONE*
MARS ORBIT
MISSION TIME: DAY 182

Bowman slammed her elbows on the touchboard, rested her chin in her hands. Twenty-one onboard systems still refused to shut down and continued obeying the looping commands of processors damaged by the flare's emissions. Free-flows rippled across her boards. Systems popped, flickered, started up and shut themselves down. The MEV deck's airlock had opened and shut eleven times already, and she remained but minutes away from performing an autopsy on a comm system that breathed no more than static.

A crimson glitter flashed at the corner of her eye. There. Red light. Fire warning.

Bang. The alarm went off.

And, of course, automatic fire control had already been shut down.

Working the touchboard with a fury that would have drawn queries about her caffeine consumption, Bowman pinpointed the source: CONTROL PANEL #AQ97-BX3, BULK-HEAD 221, SPHERE SIX. CAUSE: SURGE PROTECTION FAILURE.

Decision time. She could attempt to reactivate the fire control system in that sphere, but then she would run the risk of frying that unit's processors since flare emissions still raged over the ship. No. She would go down there and fight it herself. She might need auto fire control later on. And on the way, she would manually cut electrical power to as many spheres as she could.

Leaving the thrumming alarm and flashing touchboard behind, Bowman ducked into the first access tube, charged through, then rushed down a ladder bolted to the wall of another tube. She emerged in Sphere Three, Hydroponics. She raced down a path between tomatoes and cucumbers hanging from long, vertical nutrient tubes, then found the sphere's main panel. She yanked open the door, worked the touchboard. One by one, overhead phosphos and sun lamps winked dark, yielding to the pale red stain of emergency lighting.

Another marathon through another access tube.

Sphere Four, Flower Garden. Orchids wandered up curved bulkheads. Seven different colors of roses stretched off toward the opposite exit in a great quilt of color. The panel lay just beyond them, and Bowman reached it, heady with the flowers' scent.

"Take this with you."

"Our relationship won't survive this mission."

"You don't know that."

"Yes, I do. I'll be gone for too long."

"This rose is us. If you don't take it, then maybe you don't believe in us."

"Maybe I don't."

Swearing off the cold memory, Bowman cut power, then sprinted toward the next access tube. She bridged that gap in just a handful of heartbeats and burst into Sphere Five, Crew Rec. Interactive art glimmered on panels exceeding ten meters, with the famous journey through the double helix flashing a prompt to continue beneath the massive, translucent coils. She smiled inwardly as she noticed Gallagher's selection on a panel in the back, a hands-on journey over the landscape known as woman, with the shapely silhouette of a thigh curving up toward the sphere's apex. The main panel hung near the thigh, flashing through a veil of smoke. Three commands later, art faded to shadows daubed in red.

The lights in the next access tube repeatedly dimmed, the smoke growing more dense, and by the time Bowman reached Sphere Six, Main Lab, she felt the fire's heat surge from the murk ahead.

Stealing little breaths and blinking off tears, she clawed through the smoke, found the extinguisher mounted near the entrance, then whirled back to spot flames licking their way up a bulkhead. Much of the ship's wiring had been coated with *gvhada*, a new flame-retardant material, but something in the lab must have broken, spilled, then swallowed a spark from the panel's surge. She keyed on the extinguisher. The big light on its handle flashed green. She closed her fist on the trigger.

And found herself hurling backward through the air, propelled by the foamy gel and realizing the hard way that you first needed to adjust the damned pressure. She slammed on the bulkhead and gasped as the impact rattled up her spine.

But the gel had found its mark. Flames wisped out. She rocked the extinguisher sideways, tapped down the pressure setting, then rose and fired once more, killing the last of the flames.

She coughed and grimaced, but it felt damned good to prevail.

"Fire, Sphere Seven," the ship's AI reported coolly in its masculine voice. "Fire, Sphere Seven. Smoke, Sphere Eight. Smoke, Sphere Eight."

As the computer finished its report, Bowman took off for the next access tube. More smoke there, primary lights off. The flare's emissions spread through the ship's veins like heroin. Down one ladder. Down a second. Twenty long strides through the next tube—

And the maintenance level/MEV deck swept up and away, fully illumined. Master breaker panel on the left. She floated for it. Closed the first breaker. The second.

She sensed something. Looked up. With a hum and crackle the surge hit, blew the rows of phosphos so violently that they stole her breath. A torrent of glittering fragments fell, collided, and rang out like windows shattering in a hurricane. She sprang for the bulkhead, found minimal cover, and caught a fire/smoke report flashing on a nearby status screen. Bad news. Half the spheres had been affected.

With an arm raised against the remnants of falling glass, Bowman crossed the deck and headed toward the anteroom. She rolled the latch on her suit tube. Thermal suit. Easy one. Now the hard one: the e-suit. Right leg. Left. First seal. Second. Hood up and over. Cloudy view. Hiss of oxygen. Globe tight and transparent. She bounded back to the maintenance level, steered herself to the main touchboard, and pulled up hatch status. Sixteen open, three closed. She tapped in the command to open the remaining three. Nothing. Then, through her suit's powerful external mike, came a faint rumble. The 3D schematic on the screen supplied the picture. All hatches open.

Resignation tightened her lips as she plugged in the command she hated the most: LIFE-SUPPORT SYSTEM DE-ACTIVATE.

No sound but her breathing. Darkness save for the light of the main touchboard. The ship had died, but she still burned.

A pair of safety carabiners hung from their retractable lines on the wall near the main hatch. Bowman clipped both lines to the steel loops on her suit, pulled out some slack, then crossed the hatch's panel. You needed a code to go out for a little space walk. Bowman fed the computer its numbers.

"Warning. Primary hatch activated," came a tinny voice from the hatch's AI. "Atmospheric venting will occur in twenty seconds. Override lockout in ten seconds."

She tightened her grip on the tethers, locked her boots into tracks on the floor—

"Hatch override locked out."

—and held her breath. Waited.

The doors rumbled apart, unleashing a surreal mael-

strom excerpted from a Jean Cocteau film. Long tongues
of flames, beakers, handheld computers, bottles of as-
pirin, boxer shorts, spare data squares, razors, liters of
soda, test tubes, slippers, tampons, several Hawaiian-
print shirts, pencils, a pair of coffeepots, and a bottle of
Old Spice cologne hurtled by. A flock of black-and-white
photographs of an Arabian horse collided with Bowman's helmet, as did two die-cast models of NASCAR
racers and a third model of an Ohio-class nuclear submarine. *Rivinsky's Dictionary of Terraforming Terminology*
ricocheted off Bowman's shin, along with a bottle of
Geneva "Muscle Bulkers" and a King James Bible.

And then came the garden. Cucumbers, tomatoes, fifteen varieties of lettuce, herbs, sprouts, cabbage, and
onions dragging a thousand flower bulbs that had ripped
from their stems. Even as the flurry of color enveloped
Bowman, the last of the air escaped. The remaining bulbs
hung in zero G, inertia carrying them toward the hatch,
while out there, in space, the air crystallized in an enormous white plume sagging with debris.

The fire/smoke reports scrolled up on the display,
glowed a second or two, then vanished. Bowman kicked
off the wall and glided to the main hatch, looked away
from the dizzying void, then hit the seal button.

Breathing now. Just breathing. Trembling. Darkness.
Fumbling for the suit light's switch. Alone. Dead ship.
Millions of miles from home.

MARS ENTRY VEHICLE
NORTHERN HEMISPHERE, MARS
MISSION TIME: DAY 182

Gallagher beat a fist on the hatch's emergency release,
and the door exploded outward. To either side gas bags

hissed and deflated around the MEV. The icosahedron had begun to unfold, but one-third of the vehicle lay mangled and buried in the ruddy brown soil. For a second, Gallagher's vision cleared, and a light pink sky sewn with pale blue tendrils rooted him to the hatchway. He pried himself forward, tripped over something—a rock presumably—then inspected the powdery sand with his helmet pressed face-first into it. Bile burned Gallagher's throat as he rolled over, the sky now swirling in pastels. "It wasn't supposed to be like this."

And those, he realized, were the first words uttered by the first human on Mars.

four

With the air toxin count especially high that week and the jet stream looping by 1601 NASA Road, Gallagher had taken the extra precaution of donning his hooded jacket, gloves, and rebreather before shuffling across the parking field. A mantle of thick, gray clouds had already descended upon all sixteen hundred acres of the facility. Flashing blue lights set into the pavement jogged off through the nebulous pathways and led Gallagher to a rectangular, two-story office building and media relations center constructed especially for the *Medea One* mission.

Security Officer Jim Krecitz manned the airlock, his white hair flapping in the fetid wind, his voice muffled by his own rebreather. "Morning, sir."

"Stuck out here again, Jimmy?"

The potbellied guard worked the lock's touchpad before answering. "Wouldn't call it stuck. Get to say hi to y'all. And I got these new pills that help with the exposure. Actually been feelin' pretty good of late."

"Well, Jimmy, if all goes well, you won't be taking those pills anymore."

"I wish you well. But I don't think that'll happen. Not in my lifetime, anyway."

Gallagher nodded soberly, then passed through the lock. Once the air exchange had been made, the inner doors hissed opened.

Perhaps four hundred journalists had filed into the broad, horseshoe-shaped briefing hall, some of them seated and conferring with one another, others standing in smaller throngs along the wall. Scores of camera people shouldering knapsacks and brandishing holo- and conventional cameras staked out positions near the dais, podium, and beneath the twenty-by-sixty meter vid screen that loomed over the place. Cameras flashed and the murmuring rose as Gallagher removed his rebreather, jacket, and gloves, then descended the staircase. He shifted past the center aisle and took a seat beside Burchenal, who tipped his head fractionally and handed him a small, wireless mike that Gallagher clipped on his collar. Pettengill, Chantilas, Bowman, and Santen had already taken their reserved seats, and Gallagher could not help but picture them as bored monkeys in mission jumpsuits. From the beginning, he could not shake off the feeling that he and the rest were just a science experiment, an experiment to figure out why another experiment had gone wrong.

"This thing was supposed to start at nine," Bowman said with a groan.

"Well, now that the most important member of the

crew has arrived, we can get started." Santen raised his
werewolf's grin.

"All right," said Chantilas. "There's Harry. The can-
dle's lit."

Senior Scientist Harold Ernest hoisted his sixty-six-
year-old frame up the three steps to the dais, then adjusted his clip-on tie as he scuffled toward the podium.

"You should think of yourself as an antibody," Ernest
had once told Gallagher. "You don't exist until there's a
problem."

Gallagher had nodded politely, had thought a fuck you,
then had told the man how much he appreciated his ad-
vice.

Lights dimmed. Gallagher straightened then relaxed,
just minutes away from falling asleep with his eyes open.

"Good morning. I'll spare the introductory remarks,
though I'll be accused of being long-winded anyway.
And let me add that we've kept the nature of our mission
classified until now for a number of reasons that I'd be
happy to address later. First, though, a little history lesson. We must understand the past so that we may effec-
tively forge our future. Now then, as many of you know,
in twenty-twenty we began a series of unmanned flights
to Mars, picking up on where our colleagues had left off
earlier in the century."

Specks of light rippled across the immense vid screen
behind him, burned brighter, formed a star field that suddenly streaked as the image panned right to follow the
Mars Polar Lander III sailing through space like a shiny,
copper bug impaled by antennae and towing a Frisbee-
like aeroshell.

"We had determined that Mars harbored no life. Although beginning with the same resources as Earth four
billion years ago, Mars had not supported any life beyond

the microbial stage in the last three hundred million years."

Even as Ernest finished, images illustrating the four-stage history of Mars congealed on the screen. The planet spun, differentiating into a thin crust and small, nonconvective core. Thousands of meteors impacted the surface, weakening the crust and unleashing lava flows that flooded into many of the basins. Water pushed on in great channels, and the atmosphere grew thick. After a few seconds of that—seconds that represented perhaps millions of years—the planet cooled rapidly, flows hardened, and water froze beneath the surface. Finally, the atmosphere thinned, and the crust thickened. Gallagher yawned as a Mars he recognized finally materialized from all of that computer animation.

"Now, ladies and gentlemen, up until thirty years ago, Mars was in its fourth stage of history, one of slow decline. Volcanic activity probably reached a maximum about one billion years ago, and slow erosion was wearing away the volcanic and impact features. Ironically, this slow decline stage is what makes Mars so ideal for terraforming. We decided that if we could raise the temperature of the planet by only four degrees, via carefully placed polar explosions, the resultant melting of the ice caps would increase the density of the atmosphere, enabling greater heat retention and melting the icecaps further. We also needed to increase the oxygen content of the atmosphere.

Resultantly, a series of probes were sent, each releasing further and further genetically manipulated lichen and algae designed to withstand the rigors of the Martian environment while augmenting the oxygen content of the atmosphere. In the last twenty-eight years, we have sent over two thousand two hundred probes."

The screen lit with one such probe, the camera following as it punched a hole in the Martian atmosphere, then burst in an aerosol deployment over the surface. The image zoomed in on the living rain as it collected in puddles, streams, tributaries. The liquid darkened then bloomed into algae, colors vibrant against the dull sands. Black hogbacks rolled down into burnt sienna valleys. Blue ridge lines wandered toward greenish black basins. Crimson escarpments lorded over orange lava plains.

"The average temperature of Mars has increased two and a half degrees over the last three decades. The oxygen content's begun to increase as well."

Hogbacks, ridge lines, basins, and plains shrank as the camera pulled back to a satellite's viewpoint. Splotches of color shied back into the soil, as though the symbiotic relationship between the algae and lichen had been broken.

"Eleven months ago, the oxygen on Mars suddenly began to decline. Soon after, remote sensors on the planet ceased functioning. We've studied the telemetry. We have no idea what's gone wrong. The algae is vanishing. We need to know why. Humanity's very destiny may lie in the answer." Ernest cocked a furry gray brow at Gallagher and the others.

"All right, movie stars," Bowman stage-whispered. "Asses up."

They tiptoed forward in the shadows as Ernest continued:

"Ladies and gentlemen, we are about to embark on the greatest mission of human exploration. By using a number of Heavy Lift Launch Vehicles and a modified close-lunar cargo ship, we have created a vessel capable of journeying to Mars."

Medea One pulled out of her spacedock at the aging

but heavily used International Space Station, then lumbered silently across the screen, spheres spinning in a grand recital of engineering, sunlight glinting off her rings and solar panels.

Gooseflesh fanned across Gallagher's shoulders, and he called himself an idiot. Then he realized that he had a license to be giddy. How many people on his planet could say, "I'm going to Mars." Six. Period.

Medea One faded to reveal a massive hangar. Inside, over a hundred clean-suited techs worked on five geodesic domes connected by triangular passages; the whole affair resembled a miniature metropolis supported by titanium ribs.

"There she is, ladies," Santen whispered. "Mars Hilton."

"Three months ago, Hab One, an unmanned living environment, was launched," Ernest explained. "Our astronauts will live and work in this shirt-sleeve environment for up to two years. This facility is nothing short of a miracle. And in just nine days, *Medea One*, our first manned mission, will be sent to Mars."

Bowman led the way onto the dais. Gallagher lined up as he had been told, then, of course, realized that he needed to use the bathroom. Too late. Spotlights set into the dais's floor focused on them.

"Ladies and gentlemen, I give you the first men and woman to travel to the next planet in our solar system."

The old man's gesticulating drove the journalists into a frenzy. Gallagher blinked off another round of camera flashes as the applause came so loudly that he swore he felt it on his cheeks. The spotlights dimmed, then a single one focused on Bowman.

"Lieutenant Commander Katherine Bowman will supervise the flight component of our mission. Commander

Bowman is a former navy pilot with over twenty-two hundred hours in space. She will be assisted by air force pilot and Mission Specialist Ted Santen."

Yes, the big jock enjoyed the spotlight. He waved, winked, then pulled in a deep breath to expand his chest.

"And we're pleased to have Doctor Bud Chantilas come out of retirement to serve as our Chief Science Officer. Bud brings a view as a generalist few can offer, with a Nobel prize in chemistry. He was off getting another Ph.D., this time in . . ."—Ernest consulted his handheld computer—". . . theology when we asked him to join us."

The light found Pettengill. He squinted, forced a smile, and Gallagher knew the terraformer hated every moment of this.

"Doctor Chip Pettengill, who until recently has held an assistant directorship in the Terraforming Office, is an expert in extremophile and crytoendolithic biology. And next we have Doctor Quinn Burchenal, late of Western BioTech and the only member of our team with a Mac-Gregor in bioengineering. The good doctor is a renowned geneticist and biological systems expert. We've lured him away from the private sector to join us."

Burchenal summoned up the barest of nods, an effort for him, probably. Gallagher had seen him on networks before, the genius with more degrees than God touting BioTech's latest discoveries. Burchenal's experience with the press clearly showed. He stood there, inert, his face hatcheted from a piece of oak.

"And finally, we are also joined by Robert Gallagher."

"The janitor," Santen muttered to Bowman, but he had turned on his microphone, and the comment echoed throughout the briefing hall.

Gallagher switched on his own mike and leaned forward to eyeball Santen. "That's technically *space* janitor."

The journalists ate that up and belched with laughter.

Santen opened his mouth—

And Gallagher beat him to the punch. "When the toilet breaks two-hundred-and-fifty-million miles from the nearest hardware store, they call me. Actually, they called me now, 'cause then would be too late."

Big laugh to that. So big that Ernest raised his hands to quiet the group. "To be more precise, Mr. Gallagher is the Mechanical Systems Engineer, and his credentials are as outstanding as his colleagues'. We're glad to have him along." Ernest stole a breath, then followed quickly with, "We stand on the threshold of the most triumphant moment of the millennium. Science has brought us here, and science will take us further."

Gallagher scanned the sea of faces. All the grandeur and bullshit aside, if he and his comrades did not succeed, the kids and grandkids of every person in the room would not make it to the next millennium. He bore the burden proudly, a terrible burden, nonetheless.

five

MARS ENTRY VEHICLE
NORTHERN HEMISPHERE, MARS
MISSION TIME: DAY 182

In one distinct jolt, the entry into Mars' atmosphere came back to Gallagher as he lay on the soil:

Thirty-five thousand feet. Another round of explosive bolts. One massive jerk. Drogue chute deployed, and three, two, one . . . the main canopy whooped open. Sudden deceleration pinned Gallagher to his couch, his eyelids fluttering, pupils rolling back, world growing dark around the rim.

One minute. Two. G-forces letting up.

"Ah, we're still off target. Terrain's crappy," Santen said.

Chantilas snorted. "Find a new LZ."

"No time. Deploying bags."

Announced by a triplet of booms, the gas bags burst from the MEV's sides and inflated to envelop the entire craft.

"Five hundred feet!" Santen cried. "Three. Here it comes."

Gallagher's throat and stomach found his knees as the MEV rebounded off jagged terrain, rebounded again, again, and again—like a carnival ride operated by a toothless old man nursing a near-empty bottle of Jack Daniel's.

Another memory struck Gallagher. *Chantilas. My God. Chantilas!* The science officer's seat had been ripped from the bulkhead.

"Mr. Gallagher? Little help," Santen ordered.

Gallagher sat up, waited for the dizziness to pass, then rose and stepped gingerly back to the hatch. Santen stood there, his arms bracing Chantilas, who winced against the pain. Gallagher threw one of Chantilas's arms over his shoulder. They shifted away from the MEV, then Gallagher lowered Chantilas onto a fairly smooth patch of ground. The science officer lay on his back, eyes shut, and his breathing came in ragged spurts.

"Bud, you with me, man? We made it. We're on Mars."

"Lift me a little. I want to see it."

Water-ice clouds collected in the Martian sky, their dozen shades of blue eclipsing a dozen shades of pink. The clouds assumed a blue hue because their ice particles were one-thousandth the thickness of a human hair and appeared bright in blue light but almost invisible in red. Gallagher had inspected thousands of photos and 3Ds of the Martian sky, but not a one of them did it justice.

On the other hand, the landscape offered the predictable assortment of gently rolling hills heavily freckled by rocks; hills whose mottled tint reflected the abundance of iron oxides. A few two- or three-meter-high outcroppings marked a treacherous obstacle course weaving off toward two peaks in the distance, the one on the left slightly taller and more pointed than its brother on the right. Those peaks should be obvious landmarks, but Gallagher did not recognize them. "Bud, any idea where we are?"

"Not yet."

"Check your suits for damage," Santen said. "Help one another out."

Gallagher seized Chantilas's wrist and tapped a button, ordering the suit's AI to perform a six-second diagnostic.

"Who took the first step?" Chantilas asked weakly.

"What?"

"The first one on Mars. Who was it?"

"Uh, me, I guess."

Chantilas managed a smile. "Congratulations, son. You're history."

"Bud, I'm sorry. I wasn't thinking. That was your step."

"Forget it. Get me over to that rock. I want to sit up. Then fetch me the triage comp, if you would?"

Seeing that Chantilas's environment suit had checked out, Gallagher lifted the man and eased him toward the meter-high rock ahead. With Chantilas propped up, Gallagher headed back to the MEV and fetched the triage comp, a small, high-powered medical scanner and database. He handed off the comp, then hurried back to the MEV's hold to make a cursory inspection of the damage.

And wished he hadn't.

He emerged from the hold as Santen finished tapping in commands on his handheld. "Report?"

"Comm's dead. No power for the redundancies. AMEE's screwed up. Launch system . . . well, I can't even get to it."

Burchenal marched up, appearing as glum as Gallagher felt. "Science package is KO'd, too. We can't analyze the soil, the atmosphere, nothing."

Santen averted his gaze. "Shit."

"No more mission," Pettengill moaned, then kicked up a cloud of powdery dirt.

"Mission's not over yet." Santen leered into a thought.

"Oh, really? You miss something? We lost the science gear. We can't do what we came here to do."

Santen broke his thought to glare at Pettengill. "Quit whining."

"Hey, Ace, you're the one who parked us in the rocks."

With two steps Santen placed himself squarely in Pettengill's face. "Hey, shithead, there are *always* risks."

"Right now, locating Hab is what matters," Chantilas cut in, then lapsed into a fit of coughing.

The standoff continued, Pettengill flushed, holding his ground, Santen equally colored, his gaze shifting to Chantilas.

"If Bowman were here . . ." Gallagher began.

"All right," Santen said, tone softening as he lifted his computer. "I think we're somewhere down range. Comp, give me original HAB LZ, pulling back to incorporate surrounding grids. Three-sixty pan."

The book-sized computer's screen flashed data, brought up several topographic maps, picked one, then panned and pulled back. Santen studied the map for a few seconds before asking the device to zoom in on the Hab's landing site. Burchenal, Pettengill, and Gallagher slid out their own HHCs from hip pockets and patched in to Santen's data. "Based on the last uncorrupted nav state, I'd say we're in this sixty-by-one-twenty-kilometer ellipse."

Gallagher gawked at the area highlighted on his screen. "We are *so* lost."

"No," Burchenal insisted. "All the mission data's in here. We just need to close in on the downrange variables. Tighten up the ellipse. It's about the math." With that, he spoke in a rapid monotone to his computer, asking for said variables.

A wry grin nicked the corners of Gallagher's mouth. "This is it. That moment they told us about in high school, when one day we'd use algebra, and it'd save our lives."

"Shut up," Burchenal barked.

"Heard that a lot in high school, too."

As the three math whizzes engaged in a conversation about coefficients and aerobrake friction, Gallagher jammed his HHC into his pocket and crossed to Chantilas, who stared at something on the triage comp's display. "How're you feeling?"

Chantilas ignored him.

"Bud?"

"Leave me."

No room for argument in that tone.

Gallagher wandered off, cerise vistas calling out to him. Still hard to comprehend. Mars. Another planet.

Of course, I could die here.

Spurred by the thought, he reached for the HHC, called up the Hab details, the topographic map, studied them, asked for the panorama around the Hab site, studied it, looked up at his own location.

Son of a bitch, there it was.

Tingling, he charged back for the group. "Hey, guys?"

"What?" Santen asked, eyeing him sternly for the interruption.

"I don't think it's about the math. I think it's about the picture."

Santen furrowed his brow. "What picture?"

"This one." He thrust out his HHC.

The trio gathered around to scrutinize Gallagher's screen. Burchenal took one look and cursed. "We're not in that picture. If we were, we'd know where Hab was." His eyes bugged. "See, Mr. Gallagher, we're trying to figure that out."

Gallagher ignored the man, picked up a rock, then tossed it back in the sand. He pointed his HHC at the rock, then ordered the computer to project a holo of the panorama. The image wrapped around the rock like a shimmering, opaque ring creating a miniature landscape with the rock at its axis. He tipped his head toward the rock. "Say that's Hab. About thirty degrees in the distance. It sees this mountain with the funny top. At about one-hundred-and-eighty degrees, it sees this set of peaks, one a little larger than the other." Gallagher pulled away from the group and pointed to the horizon. "Now, I see that mountain over there. And those peaks over there." He pivoted twenty degrees. "And then this other peak, maybe."

It took a moment for Santen and Pettengill to catch on, but Burchenal's expression, well, that was priceless.

"See, if I'm right, then our location puts us on a line, say there," he said, swiping his finger through the air. "Which leaves the angle to the Hab about here." He dug his boot in the soil, made a karate chop to indicate the direction.

Santen regarded his HHC. "Space Janitor First Class Gallagher, good job." Then he ordered his HHC to calculate the coordinates based on the images it scanned as compared to those from the Hab's panorama. In four seconds the data came through. Santen made a face. "It's about an eight-hour walk."

Pettengill rolled his wrist, shook his head at his suit's readout. "Our thermal batteries will be dead in about six hours, then we start freezing. And I got only seven hours, twenty-eight minutes of air. I guess *about* is the operative word here."

"Let's go," Santen said. "We'll leave everything. Salvage it all later."

Gallagher fell in behind the others as the pilot led them toward Chantilas, who now clutched his abdomen.

Santen hunkered down before the wounded science officer. "We gotta go, Chantilas."

Face waxy and pale, Chantilas lifted his chin, a simple act producing a severe grimace. "Unfortunately, I'm staying here."

"What're you talking about?" asked Gallagher, circling behind Santen to crouch down and place a hand on Chantilas's shoulder.

"That's the thing about your spleen. It's quite susceptible to blunt abdominal trauma. Once it ruptures, blood loss is massive. And rapidly fatal."

"There's emergency medical equipment at Hab," Burchenal pointed out. "You can walk us through it."

"Trying to carry me will slow you down," countered Chantilas. "We'll all suffocate before we get there."

Gallagher wrenched Santen's arm. "We have to get him there. We have to help him."

"Gallagher," Chantilas warned.

"Santen, c'mon . . ."

But the pilot stared through Gallagher.

"He has to say no," Chantilas said, voice creased in pain. "But I'll spare him the words. I'm not going."

Stricken, Gallagher looked at the man, the mentor,

the father away from home. He could not imagine anyone else who deserved to be here more. But this fate?
Why?

A dreaded moment. Grave faces hovering over Gallagher.

Then, visibly unnerved by the silence, Chantilas took
in a deep breath. "You all know what to do. Survive and
carry on with the mission. It won't be easy. You'll need
faith. The same kind of faith humanity placed in us. Now,
please . . . get going. I can assure you that within ten minutes, shock will set in. My pressure's already falling. I'll
feel clammy and cold, and five or so minutes later, I'll be
laughing at you assholes from above."

Santen trudged away. "He's right, gentlemen. Move
out."

Gallagher stood, watched the others break off, then
met Chantilas's faltering gaze. "Bud, I want to—"

"It's okay. I got to see Mars . . ."

If Gallagher stood there for another second, he knew
he would break down. He ran off, soil crunching under
his boots.

"Keep looking for that rock," Chantilas rasped.

The reference halted Gallagher. He turned back slowly,
gave a weak salute that fell into a wave, then double-
timed to catch up with the group.

Yes, it's okay, Bud Chantilas thought as the four figures in
the distance vanished over the ridge. Short of breath, of
life, his gaze lowered to a nearby stone. He traced a finger around the stone, digging an orbit in the sand, then
ventured off to draw a series of graceful lines around the
rock, his last Zen garden.

Funny thing. He had had a premonition about his own
death that had driven him into his Bible, to Psalm Thirty-

nine, verse four: " 'Lord, make me to know mine end, and the measure of my days, what it is; that I may know how frail I am.' "

The cold spread through him now, its icy fingers groping for what little warmth they could find.

I have done good work, he thought. *I can go.*

꠵

six

Gallagher tentatively crossed into Main Lab, careful not to touch any of the equipment that lay across the work-tables or hung Velcroed to the wall. Burchenal had a thing about that, a very intense thing.

"Give the soil analyzer one last calibration test before we stow it," the scientist said from a far table. "Then let's eat."

Pettengill lifted a tablet-shaped unit. "Already done. It's dead on. And I made sure the battery's at max." He placed the analyzer into its silver case and lowered the lid. "Man, it's finally real. Not just another drill. We're gonna blaze the new frontier."

"We're not here to blaze trails," Burchenal answered, his tone burred by cynicism. "We're here 'cause oxygen levels are diving, and they need eggheads to figure out why before the whole Mars program belly flops. Slightly less glamorous, don't you think?"

Seeing Pettengill squirm for an answer, Gallagher came to his rescue. "I need help with AMEE. Final diagnostic before I load her up."

Burchenal's nod released Pettengill, and the lean terraformer followed Gallagher into the access tube.

"Makes sense they chose Chantilas to take the first step on Mars," Pettengill said, making idle conversation, as was his wont. "Burchenal back there, he's all about the science, not the beauty."

"Thought you were, too," Gallagher said.

"Not like him."

"Well, I agree with you. Chantilas is a good choice. Been to space more times than anyone. Big-time scientist. Theology scholar. The guy's your basic larger-than-life legend."

"Yeah, but doesn't part of you still wish it could be you?"

Gallagher chuckled inwardly. "Wouldn't want all the attention."

Santen rounded the corner of an adjoining access tube and brushed shoulders with Pettengill, who offered a sincere "Sorry."

"Just watch what you're doing," Santen growled. He marched on, trailing a frosty haze of self-importance.

"Life's just like high school," Pettengill said, glaring after the captain. "You and I aren't part of the in crowd."

Though Gallagher considered that only half true, he decided to play along. The guy obviously needed a friend. "Hey, you watch my back, I'll watch yours."

"Yeah, screw him. We were handpicked for this team just like he was. Besides, you've done jock stuff before. You did Antarctica—"

"Fixed subs at McMurdo," Gallagher qualified. "No big deal."

"You were a mechanic on the NASCAR circuit, too."

"Did that for two years just before this. My ears are still ringing. I miss Daytona, though. The night life."

They came into Ship's Hold, a sphere resembling a massive warehouse with hundreds of storage compartments of varying size charging up toward the dome. Gallagher paused before a wide, two-by-four-meter door, keyed it open, then he and Pettengill hauled out an ungodly heavy steel case about the size of a coffin with AUTONOMOUS MAPPING EXPLORATION AND EVASION stenciled on one side.

Gallagher opened a smaller compartment beside the first and withdrew a spacesuit sleeve with a flexible screen and small touchpad set into the wrist. The sleeve mimicked the controls on his own e-suit. He keyed for power. "Wake up, sweetie."

The case came to life, extending six tri-jointed legs and a narrow, beaklike head. Its back thrummed as sharp corners rounded off into layers of bony, metal plates. More shields sprang up around its neck with the *sring* of knives being pulled from metal sheaths.

After a beep, the screen on Gallagher's wrist tuned to "AMEEvision," a fish-eye panorama through the bot's eyes. Gallagher whistled.

AMEE whistled back.

"We're buddies," Gallagher said.

Pettengill hunkered down for a better look at the mechanized arachnid. "They never told me how she navigates on Mars when there's no magnetic core to get bearings."

Gallagher thumbed a switch, then patted the small, pyramid-shaped drone that sprouted from AMEE's back.

"She's got a portable scout. Flies around and feeds back MPS data so she can calculate our position." He circled in front of the bot. "Let's check your infrared, cutie." He motioned to Pettengill, who went to the sphere's power panel and killed the overhead phosphos.

The sleeve screen depicted an infrared image of Gallagher and Pettengill, crimson blobs representing invisible radiation wavelengths from about seven hundred fifty nanometers to one millimeter, on the border of the microwave region.

"So AMEE's a techie, too," Pettengill concluded as Gallagher hit the lights.

"Robust real-time response to the environment. Little known fact: she did her first tour as a Green Beret."

"Bullshit."

Gallagher would prove it to him. Three taps on the touchpad gave him the mode menu. He chose one, then pulled a pen from his breast pocket and proffered it to AMEE. "Here."

One of her forelegs telescoped out, as did a pincer from its end. She took the pen with the grace and ease of a human.

"What's she gonna do? Write me a letter from the front?" Pettengill quipped.

Wearing an assured smile, Gallagher shook his head. "AMEE? Gut him like a fish."

The bot's arm flashed.

Even as Pettengill recoiled from the attack, it was over. He stared down at the ink mark extending from the navel of his thermal suit to his sternum. "That's real funny. Lucky for you I have a sense of humor."

"Lucky for you they removed her knife," Gallagher amended, then pulled the pen from AMEE's grasp. Three more taps on the touchpad. "Now she's back to techie mode." He winked at the machine. "Okay, baby. You're all set." One final whistle. She returned the same. "Back in your box."

She folded in on herself like a turtle.

Gallagher straightened. "Let's load her into the MEV."

After stowing AMEE safely away, Gallagher and Pettengill met up with everyone else in the kitchen for their first dinner aboard *Medea One*. They complained about the food, then the conversation assumed a more reflective tone when Bowman asked Gallagher why he had chosen to come along.

"Whoa," Gallagher said, lowering his forkful of glazed chicken. He thought about the question. Thought about it some more. "I went cross-country once with my cousins in a motor home. This didn't seem so bad."

"That's right," Burchenal said. "You don't turn down a phone call like that. Reason I'm here."

Gallagher shook his head, glanced back to Bowman. "You?"

"I spent my entire life training to fly the biggest, fastest thing you can fly. This is it. It's the best job in the world." Her gaze favored Santen. "He's here because he got the second best job in space. He's a little pissed about it, but he still came."

Santen winced and found something particularly interesting in his steamed carrots.

"I was never supposed to come," Pettengill volunteered, clearly vying for a little attention. "Some of you might not know this, but I came because my boss couldn't. He failed the medical. Heart arrhythmia. So here I am. They tapped me on the shoulder, told me I was going to Mars. Thought I'd be an assistant director of terraforming till the day I died."

"What about you, Bud?" Gallagher asked.

Chantilas drew in a deep breath, taking a moment to meet each of their gazes. "Psalm one-oh-seven, verse twenty-three: 'They that go down to the sea in ships, that do business in great waters, these see the works of the Lord, and His wonders in the deep.' So I figured, how much wonder for those in space?"

Gallagher loved the answer, and he loved the way it made everyone else shift uncomfortably in their seats.

"You're going to Mars because of a *poem*?" asked Santen.

The veteran leaned back in his chair, considering. "I'm going to Mars because of a poem? Basically . . . yes."

UNITED STATES SPACECRAFT *MEDEA ONE*
EN ROUTE TO MARS
MISSION TIME: DAY 13

Exercise equipment had been mounted to the "floors," the "walls," and the "ceiling" of the rotating sphere, not that Pettengill could distinguish between any of those references. He approached Bowman and Santen, both rabidly pedaling stationary bikes, wireless electrodes reporting their vitals back to the machines. "So, required exercise. Haven't had this since grade school. Wasn't all that preflight training enough?"

Santen blew sweat from the top of his lip. "Not in your case. You must have been doing some kind of reverse thing."

"You're done," Bowman told the captain.

"I'm not done," Santen corrected. "I was going—"

"No, you're done."

The copilot ceased pedaling, rolled his eyes, then swiped a towel across his face and head. "Yes, ma'am."

Pettengill tensed as he watched Santen leave. *That's right, you bastard. You know better than to argue.* Then he felt ridiculous as he faced Bowman. "Didn't have to do that."

"Flying this beast is only half my job," she explained, wrapping a towel around her neck. "The other half involves getting the crew in place, in shape, to do what they have to do. Strange thing is, flying's the easy part."

He cocked a thumb over his shoulder, resentment bubbling out before he could cap it. "I just hate all of those guys. I feel like I've spent my entire life being the one who was hassled in phys ed. I lost the first girl I ever cared about to some ass who could throw a football farther than I could. It's like women are hardwired to think guys who are proficient at sports will be better providers. It's not like we hunt and kill our own food anymore." He crossed to Santen's exercise bike and scowled at it, fully possessed by the past. "That ass sells cars for a living now. *Cars.* I'm working on a project that may save humanity, and he sells cars."

"That was what, twelve, fourteen years ago?" Bowman asked. "You kept track of him? What happened to her?"

"Who?"

"The girl."

He had been staring at Bowman but had seen only Mr. Ass spouting logical fallacies about his dealership's service department.

The girl. What had happened to her? He shrugged.

"Little competitive," Bowman said through a smile. "Who's hardwired for what, Cro-Magnon Guy?"

His face warmed, and a grin found his lips before he could stop it.

"We'll start with bungees," she told him. "And try to quit being pissed off that you weren't chosen for dodge-ball, will you?"

"I'll try. Twenty years of hating the bullying bastards is a hard habit to break."

seven

AMEE's nanotech repair crew had nearly finished restoring the final servo. She felt the microscopic machines crawling through her metallic bowels and instructed them to commence operations on her right, middle limb, which had inadvertently extended during entry and had smashed against the bulkhead. She had run forty-three thousand, one hundred twenty-one survival algorithms since the crash, and she could finally initiate main sequence programming.

The repair crew communicated their damage assessment and concluded that the leg could not be repaired and should be replaced. Another survival algorithm blazed through her protein processor.

All remaining servos now whined. Calculations to compensate for the damaged leg completed, and the appropriate commands went out to her remaining limbs, which extended from her shell, lifted off the MEV's hold, then ignited her sensor eyes. She scanned the environment for the operator called Gallagher. No visual or infrared confirmation. Another operator lay out there. No life signs detected. She accessed an audio file. Whistled. No response.

Intent on making contact with her operator, AMEE crawled toward the hatch, picked her way over the wreckage, then impaled the rock-laden sand with her talons. She panned the horizon and emitted another whistle. Then she activated the drone, which spun up in its housing to two thousand rpms. The program's clock cycled down. Rocket motors fired.

The drone screamed away from AMEE's back, reached two hundred meters in its ascent, then rolled northeast and began wheeling overhead, its sensor inspection uploading directly to AMEE's memory. Like her own, the drone's visual and infrared inspection did not identify the operator, but it did provide telescopic images of footprints leading away from the site. As per its protocol, the drone broke from its circle and whirred off to chart latitude and longitude. In the meantime, AMEE plotted the footprints' course, then ambled off, evading rocks and vaulting over a network of furrows as intricate as her own circuitry.

Gallagher and Pettengill walked point for a while. Two ridge lines back, Santen had called up Chantilas's vitals on his HHC and had shared the grim report. A legend had passed on.

Up there, from one of those peaks, Gallagher thought, *you're really laughing at us, laughing at how alone we are against this landscape. Quote me something, Bud. Something that'll make me feel better . . .*

"Hey, take it easy," called Pettengill, now lingering behind.

"You all right?" Gallagher asked.

"Little tired. But I'm okay. Just slow up."

"Should've put more time in on the treadmill," Santen said as he pounded on by the terraformer.

Pettengill muttered a curse.

Santen froze. Whirled. "What'd you say?"

"*Gentlemen,*" Burchenal said, emphasizing the word as a reminder. He checked his HHC. "In point of fact, Captain, Pettengill has used up less oxygen than you have."

The fighter jock summoned his blackest look. "Whatever." He regarded his own handheld. "We're making good time. Should reach Hab soon." He spun on his heel and took the lead.

Everyone followed but Pettengill.

"Don't do this," Gallagher said, pausing, his gaze alternating between the others and the blond-haired rebel. "How would we ever explain—"

"I'm not being sophomoric. Look around. It's weird. There's nothing here."

Gallagher made a lopsided grin. "It's Mars."

"No, I mean there's not one sign of the algae we sent up." He hustled toward Gallagher, and together they hastened to catch up with the others.

"Think about it," the terraformer said, still engrossed in his epiphany. "Even if all the algae died, there should still be something. A dried algal mat. Traces on the lee sides. Something."

"He's right," said Burchenal. "We sent up fifty-two varietals. Blue-green, black, orange. Anhydriobiosics, chemotrophs, even a thiobacillus that could grow autotrophically on elemental sulfur. Not only are they dead, they're all just gone, like they've been scoured off the rocks."

"Don't mean to point out the obvious," Gallagher began. "But maybe there was never anything in this valley."

"I've supervised the terraforming project for over five years," said Pettengill. "This area was covered with blue algae as recently as a month ago. Valley before this one should've been blazing with orange-red chloroflectic."

"Least we know what happened to the oxygen," Burchenal said, booting a rock. "There's nothing here to make it."

"Talking's just sucking up air," reminded Santen. "We still have to conserve, guys."

The pilot enjoyed getting the last word, and for once no one would argue. They plodded on, in silence, the sun uncharacteristically small in the mauve sky.

A short while later, at the crest of a small rise, Santen and Burchenal paused to check HHC maps.

"Now something that makes sense," sang Burchenal.

"Debris apron," Santen observed. "Delincatcd valley fill. Depositional fan. We're on course."

The hike resumed, and Gallagher found himself testing the point three eight gravity, taking larger strides and weighing but sixty pounds on the surface. However, the exertion increased his respiration, so he fell back into his steady shuffle.

Surface gravity, as Gallagher had learned, fluctuates much more radically on Mars than it does on Earth, where gravity and topography are largely uncorrelated because of something called isostatic compensation, basically the fact that the light, outer parts of the Earth are floating on a more fluid, denser interior than the ones on Mars. Here, gravity increased in the Tharsis region, particularly over volcanoes like Olympus Mons, while the area chosen for Hab exhibited few if any fluctuations. And that was just fine by Gallagher. He would hate to wake up one morning, having acclimated to point three eight, and feel a sudden and irrepressible weight on his shoulders that had little to do with guilt.

More walking. God, how long had they been traveling? Shit. Just forty minutes. And the proverbial eternity.

Santen and Burchenal set a blistering pace up a long hill, its craggy summit about twenty paces away. Gallagher wanted to shout, "Slow Down." Didn't. Couldn't waste air. Looked back.

Pettengill's boots dug deeply into the dirt as he swung his arms, trying to create a bit more momentum. Poor guy. Gallagher thought of helping, but he figured Pettengill's pride would not allow that. He turned back, itching with fear for the terraformer.

What to do? How to keep busy? To distract one's self from the height of the mountain, the length of the sea, the damned distance to the Hab?

He imagined the small of an old girlfriend's back; the sweat steam billowing off Aunt Tanya's peach cobbler; the softness of his pillow as it hugged his head; the good, clean feeling after a hot shower; the tiny smile of his sister's three-year-old daughter; the relief of a crisp, cold beer flooding his throat after a workout; the taste of meat sauce, of salmon, of pepperoni pizza, of peanut butter; the glow of the waxing moon on a windy night; the feel of his legs on solid ground, of the rocks crunching underfoot, of the aches in his joints, of the thermal suit strangling his body, of his shallow breathing, of his defeat in trying to forget. Oppressive Mars. All around. Uncaring, unmerciful, utterly indifferent.

"Tell me about your father."

"Why does the SEO need to know about my father?"

"It's just part of the profile."

"Don't wanna send any psychotics to Mars, that it?"

"You're not on the witness stand, Mr. Gallagher. Why not play along? Says here that he just retired from a senior-level engineer's position at Exotech."

"That's right."

"Get along with him?"

"Just fine."

"Guess he's proud of you."

"My mom's the one going nuts. Built a goddamned sat-net site to me. It's really embarrassing."

"But not your dad."

"What are you looking for? You think I got some kind of complex? My dad did the best job he could."

"Do you love him?"

"Of course I do. He's my dad."

"If you were him, tell me one thing you'd change about the way he raised you."

"I wouldn't change anything."

"Not a thing?"

"Not a thing."

"You're a very lucky man, Mr. Gallagher, having been raised by a perfect dad. Unfortunately, he tells a very different story."

"Hey, isn't that a breach of client-patient confidentiality? Wait a minute. You interviewed him?"

"Of course. Six out of twelve billion people are going to Mars. We, as you said, need to be careful. You didn't read the release?"

No, Gallagher had not. Too many papers. Give them a

quick glance and sign. And, as he quickened his pace, drawing nearer to Santen and Burchenal, he wondered what his dad had told that SEO psychologist. Gallagher had never mustered the nerve to ask his father.

"Hold up," Pettengill cried. "Hold a sec. Just a sec. Let me catch up."

eight

Nearly an hour and a half had passed since Houston's last contact with *Medea One*.

Flight Director Matthew Russert massaged his temples as he listened to Capcom John Skavlem continue his dire hails: "*Medea One*, Houston. Do you copy? *Medea One*, Houston. Do you copy?"

Russert had known Skavlem for ten years, and during that time the capcom had displayed nothing less than consummate professionalism. However, neither of them had ever lost a manned spacecraft, and the heavy bulwark guarding Skavlem's emotions had begun to falter. Russert questioned how long his own barriers would hold.

An indicator in his PIM flashed: report in from Flight Surgeon Rose Palladino, who monitored crew activities, coordinated the medical operations flight control team, provided crew consultations, and advised Russert of the crew's health status. The report listed each crew member and their vitals at the moment before communication disruption. Pulse and respiration rates were up across the board. No surprise there. And no surprise that she had no further data.

Medical emergencies on board *Medea One* posed a significant threat to the mission, given the lag time in communication. If a crew member suffered a traumatic injury, Houston would learn of it twenty minutes after the occurrence. Palladino would need a few precious minutes to coordinate with her people, then call back to the ship—which would receive her instructions twenty minutes later.

Realizing that a "golden hour" existed between the time a trauma patient suffered an injury and the time that patient reached surgery, a golden hour that, once exceeded, severely decreased the odds of patient survival, Palladino and her staff had insisted upon every crew member being trained not only in basic first-aid skills but in the necessary skills required of full-fledged paramedics. If crew members could stabilize a patient on their own and get that patient to the infirmary, onboard diagnostic systems could assist controllers in helping the crew perform simple or even complex surgeries.

But with no communication, Russert and his people could do no more than speculate on possible damage and the kind of help those people might need.

Report now in from GNC Reshard Talford, the most respected Guidance, Navigation, and Controls systems engineer on Russert's staff. Coincidentally enough, the slightly built black man charged toward Russert. "Hey, Reshard. Just reading your report."

"We've run the flare protocols and got with the people at Lockheed, who feel pretty confident that the hull should've protected the crew from most emissions. They also could've used the safe room. E-suits would've provided additional protection."

"Good. And on your end?"

"We predict multiple event upsets. Irreparable damage to some chips. PROP concurs. And we talked to Joey. He says we can expect electrical systems overloads, possible fuel cell damage, AC and DC power bus problems, and he won't rule out sphere fires, given the vehicle manifest."

"What about EECOM?"

"Right behind you, Matt."

"Well, shit, that's what I like about this team," Russert said, craning his head. "Y'all are a bunch of mind readers."

Greg Sudmanski's silk tie hung loosely, and the sleeves of his coffee-stained shirt had been rolled up to his elbows. Though bleary-eyed, he spoke evenly. "Thermal control will be compromised. How severely, we're still not sure. Joey predicts fires. So do we. Could have degradation and or system aborts to cabin atmosphere control, avionics cooling, and the supply and wastewater system."

"So basically every system on board will be affected in some way by flare emissions."

"You can't build a spacecraft that can withstand a solar flare of this magnitude," Sudmanski said, in a tone even more agitated than Russert's. "What would you do? Design bulkheads of twenty-inch-thick lead against an event that might occur once in a hundred years?"

"Of course not," Russert conceded. "We'll just play the cards. We've already got everybody and his mother back in that simulator with Alamogordo's report. Once the checklists are in, we'll go over them a hundred times if we have to."

"Flight?" That from Science Officer Andy Lowenthal. "Got all thirty-six dishes of the Deep Space Network pointed at Mars."

"Very well."

Lowenthal stood and lumbered forward as his gaze traveled across the room to Public Affairs Officer Mylssa Wong. He cringed and leaned in toward Russert. "The PAO wants a word."

Russert nodded. No doubt amateur astronomers had detected the flare, had plotted its trajectory, and had spread the word that a massive disturbance had blasted straight for the Mars team. And no doubt the media demanded answers.

As Russert braced himself and retrieved his blue "diplomat's" vest from his chair, Kathleen Crete intercepted his path. "Ms. MOD, I was just—"

"On your way to see Ms. Wong?" Crete guessed with an affected smile. "Let's the three of us get together and talk about our statement."

"What's there to talk about? We've lost contact with *Medea* because of flare emissions. That's the truth, and that's what the public needs to hear."

"We'll need to provide some assurance that contact will be reestablished."

"I've played the game, Ms. MOD. We'll assure them that the SEO will remain hopeful. Nothing more."

UNITED STATES SPACECRAFT *MEDEA ONE*
MARS ORBIT
MISSION TIME: DAY 182

Commander Kate Bowman would not see the surface of Mars. She knew exactly how astronaut Jim Lovell had felt over his missed opportunity to walk on the moon. Still, Bowman retained the distinction of being the farthest woman from home.

Which raised her spirits for the better part of a

nanosecond before she returned to a stoic commitment to the work. The repairs. Her beast. Her job to fix it.

She had cracked open a half dozen electroluminescent panels, which now tossed down a steady glow over the maintenance level/MEV deck. She fished out another of the menu-sized panels, cracked it down the center seam, and the twin rectangular sticks warmed with blue light. She swam down to the main touchboard console and placed the panel just beneath her set of digital multimeters, which hung off their Velcro straps like bizarre ornaments on a spaghetti wire Christmas tree. Bowman had removed the access panel on the console and had set up a half dozen jumpers in a feat of jury-rigging that would have raised brows.

After a final check on her leads, she warily placed her index finger on the touchboard, as though she were testing its heat. Hope remained as long as she did not press the button and activate a systems-wide reboot. If she did so and nothing happened . . . only one way to find out.

Two phosphos that had not blown out glowed to life. The touchboard itself blinked on, and status reports stitched through data bars on her screen. Red bar graphs dissolved to green. A half dozen screens behind her reflected self-tests in progress.

Bowman took a deep breath. Gave a slight chuckle of relief.

Everything died.

All right. Panic is a state of mind. It is controllable. *Check the leads. Check them all.*

There. Bad placement. Adjust. And reboot.

Lights dimmed, burned steady, and then, then . . .

Safe reboot in progress. Rotation servos back on-line. Roses, books, dirty socks, and a hundred other objects hanging in midair thudded to the deck. She steadied herself as gravity stood on her shoulders for a moment, then lightened its load. All right. Now she had power to begin restoring other systems. She accessed the life-support menu, ordered a purge of emergency reserves, listened for the hiss. There it was. But two valve ports remained jammed and required manual release. She scooped up the atmosphere wand from the console, then jogged off—

Through a disaster area. Soot streaked the bulkheads. Debris lay everywhere in miniature traffic jams. Glass broke under her boots. Two access tunnels hung under drapes of darkness.

She reached the two valves in the access tube between spheres ten and eleven, rolled them open to a pair of bellows, then checked the readout on her wand. Almost there. Thirty seconds. She leaned back on the bulkhead.

Disembodied voice: "Call the ball, Nova Five."

Night. Rain over the Adriatic Sea. Gray deck. Bobbing. Weaving. I got this. I'm on top of my game. I'm ahead of this aircraft. I will make the right moves before the situation demands them.

Gray deck. Bobbing. Weaving. See the lights. See them now. Know what to do. Stay ahead. Fly my needles.

Too fast now. Too fast. I'm behind. I'm behind. Two degree glide slope. Flat. Increase angle of attack. Hold what I have. Power.

Wave off? No wave off! Hook dragging. Dragging. Power! Power! Flame out.

Breathe. Just breathe.

Bowman checked the atmosphere wand, then tapped her wrist. The transparent helmet clouded over, became soft, and she rolled it back. One breath. Another. Slight stench still in the air. "EECOM," she muttered. "Can't live with us, can't live without us." Bowman enjoyed the humor and truth in the life-support team's motto, and thank God their system still worked. That done, she bolted for the Flight Deck.

And there, a thin thread of light cut through the main viewport. In a few minutes the ship would glide into harsh beams as though emerging from a cold cavern. Bowman dropped into her seat, fired up the touchboard. Eleven systems were just plain dead, some of them only redundancies, but all would need to be locked out. The comm system required chip replacement and rebooting. The propulsion systems had sustained major damage. She knew she would need help from the teams back home. And her orbit? Shit, that didn't look good.

With the drop site approaching, Bowman hastened across the deck and keyed open the optical scope panel. Power on. Outer door open. Scope extending. Route image to main viewer.

Browns, oranges, reds, and pinks smudged across the screen until Bowman rolled a trackball and focused the image. She pulled back, started a wide search for the MEV, rolling past the heavily scored surface until the original drop zone coordinates lined up: Chryse Planitia, in the heavily cratered uplands just outside of Ares Vallis. Nothing. She zoomed in, scanning the surface to about one-meter resolution. Ten minutes of searching produced no sign of the MEV.

Another zone. Downrange. Moving in at an extreme angle that would remind laypersons of a spy satellite's image. Tracking now, the ship becoming less oblique.

There. Coruscation. Her fingers flew over the board.

The Mars Entry Vehicle resolved into view. Profile. Major structural damage.

Bowman stiffened as the angle slowly shifted and revealed even more of the shattered icosahedron.

Then something else caught her attention. She gasped.

A figure lay slumped against a rock. She zoomed in once more, squinted at the man, couldn't identify him.

But the others. Where were they? She squinted at the panel. If footprints lay in the sand, they also lay beyond the camera's resolution.

She searched again for any sign of activity. Just the MEV, with a lone astronaut eternally sitting shiva for its occupants.

No, maybe they got out. Went to Hab.

Another inspection of the entry vehicle argued against that possibility.

But an argument remained, and Bowman would see it through. She would be over the Hab site in about six minutes. Until then, she would affect repairs to the comm system.

And hope.

nine

Thirty-one minutes of air left.

Thirty-one minutes of life left.

Plenty of time for Gallagher's entire existence to play out like a maudlin documentary before his eyes.

But now he would much rather lock himself into the moment, despite the fatigue, despite everything. *No distractions this time. No memories. Just this valley, these rocks. Those two guys ahead.*

Another glance back at Pettengill proved disappointing. The terraformer scuffed thirty meters behind, plowing through rocks instead of steeping over them. He had fallen twice in the past seven hours, had, as expected, cursed off anyone's help, then had sworn at himself.

"Crew? Check in," Santen requested, his voice as steady as the day they had lifted off from Cape Canaveral. Military brainwashing? Perhaps. But comforting at the moment. Someone had to lead, and Gallagher quite enjoyed the luxury of following, much to his father's chagrin.

"Well, my legs feel like mozzarella sticks, but I'm here," said Burchenal.

"Thanks, Mr. Burchenal. A simple 'here' will do. What about you, Pettengill? You ever gonna catch up?"

"Just check in, Pettengill. That's it," Gallagher urged, his gut tightening. "And I'm here, too, Captain. Be nice if you didn't haze him. You're not this mission's DI."

"I'll chalk that up to a long hump," Santen said. "But you get out of line once more, Mr. Gallagher, and I'll drop you."

"You guys don't stop, and *I'll* renegotiate my referee's contract," Burchenal said jovially, his attempt to undermine the tension a tad too obvious. "You'll get stuck with some minor league scab who'll probably let you kill one another before he steps in. Don't get me wrong, though. That has crossed my mind."

"I asked for a simple check in. You idiots wanna waste more air, go ahead," said Santen.

No one did.

The march resumed, four Boy Scouts earning demerit badges for bad attitudes.

Another hill, steepest one yet. A mother of a hill.

Damn you, Mars. You and your hills and shitty carbon dioxide atmosphere. We'll kick your ass. Smoke cigars and laugh with Bud about it later. You have no idea who you're dealing with. No idea. Do you contemplate your own existence? Come on. If you have a voice, use it.

Rock underfoot. *Push. Oh, shit. Down. On my butt. Whoa. Whoa. Whoa!*

Gallagher rode the express slide down, rocks tumbling between his legs then up and over his groin.

"Got ya," Pettengill cried, seizing Gallagher's arm and burrowing his boots in the sand.

A dust cloud wafted over them as Gallagher sat there a second and recouped. "Thanks."

"Just watching your back," answered Pettengill.

Santen's voice broke over the taccom. "Hey, down there. Report."

"Uh, sir, I fell on my ass, sir," Gallagher said in his best goofy private's voice. "Sorry, sir."

"Well get your ass up here. You're gonna like this."

Gallagher and Pettengill exchanged bug eyes, then Gallagher rolled over, sprang to his feet, and hauled up the slope.

Panting, he hit the crest, where Santen pointed to something in the valley below, something about five hundred meters off and firing dazzles of reflected sunlight:

Hab.

"Twenty-six months of food, water, and air," Santen cried, betraying his own excitement.

Burchenal checked his air supply. "We made it."

Pettengill finally reached the top and caught sight of the distant gem. "Well, shit," he gasped. "It's about time."

And, like plane crash survivors coming down from an icy mountain or Bedouins catching sight of their first oasis in a month, the four dashed madly down the hillside.

Gallagher shifted his weight onto his right foot and vaulted into a five-meter step, landed, skid, then rebounded into another. He felt powerful, godlike, pictured himself razoring through the air like a comic book hero, sans leotard.

And with every flying leap, he shed another doubt and let it wither in his dust.

He would not die on Mars. *I told you we would kick your ass. You have nothing on us.*

Santen and Burchenal matched each other's strides, and the sight of those two hurdling the regolith on invisible springs took Gallagher aback. No simulator could, well, simulate that.

"God, I love this place," Pettengill hollered as he swooped down next to Gallagher. "Watch this!" After three modest strides, he bent his knees and took to the air.

Drunk on the weaker gravity, Gallagher followed the terraformer's lead, jumped as though from a trampoline, and flew maybe six, seven meters before skittering across the dust.

Santen and Burchanel reached the base and navigated their way through a sharp-edged collection of talus and scree.

Five steps later, Gallagher and Pettengill booted through their comrades' dust trail, and Gallagher could almost smell the dirt. A red carpet of rock and loose soil unrolled before them, leading to Hab. Gallagher felt so intoxicated now that he imagined a welcoming committee of centerfolds who would help them out of their gear and massage their aching muscles. He chuckled off the thought, then frowned as up ahead, Santen came to a sudden halt.

Followed by Burchenal.

Followed by Gallagher, who reached them, took one look, and felt the lightning of the scene strike him inert.

Pettengill stepped ahead of Gallagher. Froze.

A series of titanium ribs jutted from the soil like the remains of some giant mammoth who had died and lay there for thousands of years.

From Gallagher's vantage point, those ribs were the only clear indicators that the Hab had actually existed.

Geodesic outer shells, internal walls, floors, all of it . . . gone. He staggered forward, barely feeling his boots, the strong anesthesia of shock flooding his chest.

"What the hell happened?" exclaimed Burchenal. He hustled over to the wreck, vanishing behind a rib.

Pettengill's mouth opened. He started to say something, caught himself, tried again, opted for a word: "Jesus . . ."

Santen spun to face Gallagher. "You saw it, right?" he demanded.

"Saw what?"

"The goddamned telescopic images we took of this place en route!"

"Yeah, so what?"

"It was here. Right fucking here. Intact. Waiting for us. What happened?" He faced the ruins. "What happened?"

For once in Santen's life, he did not have a handle on the situation. The comfort of control had been utterly, irrevocably removed. Worst thing you could do to a control freak.

Still wearing his horror mask, Santen wrenched out his HHC and hurled it at the ruins. Then he stormed off toward a slope in the east.

"Look at this," Burchenal said, waving them over.

Gallagher hurried behind the first pair of ribs. Burchenal squatted near an area strewn with titanium crossbeams and smaller poles. "Our water supply was right here," he said. "Life-support system as well. Foodstuffs are gone. Just some fabric items, foam, paper goods, some other crap. That's it. Where did the rest go?"

Leaning against one of the ribs, Pettengill broke into dark laughter. "*They* took it."

"They as in—"

"Don't even go there," Burchenal said, cutting Gallagher off.

"I was gonna say the Chinese," Gallagher corrected. "They've wanted in on this program from the start. Their guy didn't get picked, and they've been pissed ever since."

"He could be right," Pettengill said. "But what did they do, sabotage Hab? How? What kind of bomb leaves this kind of debris? And if they hurt us, they only hurt themselves. No, that's ridiculous. Then again, who cares? We're gonna die."

Gallagher checked his O2 supply: sixteen minutes left.

Sixteen minutes of life left.

UNITED STATES SPACECRAFT *MEDEA ONE*
MARS ORBIT
MISSION TIME: DAY 182

They were all dead.

Or at least they would be shortly.

What would you do if you discovered that the entire crew had died and you were the only one left?

Save the ship. Get home.

But first Bowman needed to complete repairs to the comm system. Her first diagnosis indicated a five minute replacement of chips, but upon visual inspection, she realized that the wireless transmitters between subsystems would also need replacement—a minimum eight hour job.

At least the work had helped to deflect some of the grief, though during every spare moment between tests, her thoughts returned to the crash site and to Hab, which had inexplicably been destroyed.

Worse still, *Medea One*'s orbit had become much more

oblique since Bowman's first inspection, making subsequent searches with the scope far more difficult. Even if the crew had survived the MEV crash and had trekked to Hab, they would still run out of air and die.

Fighting back the tears and damned proud of herself for not shedding a single one, Bowman activated the comm, waited for each of the new transmitters to register systems status, then tingled in small triumph.

"Ground crew, *Medea One*, copy?"

Pause. Double-check taccom frequencies. Okay.

"Ground crew, *Medea One*, copy?"

Bowman trembled with the desire for just one of them, any one of them, to still be alive. She tried again. And again. Every thirty seconds. Different frequencies. After ten minutes, her shoulders slumped.

And she knew.

Each face glistened in her mind's eye: Santen's sharp-angled self-assurance, Pettengill's tentative smile, Burchenal's cynical smirk, Chantilas's wide-eyed wonder, and Gallagher's boyish pout. She had spent more time with them than any other people in her entire life. They were family. Lost family.

Hollow now, her throat lumped, Bowman switched to another frequency. She took a breath and groped for composure. "Houston, *Medea One*. We have experienced a massive proton field upset. Comm system down until now. MEV launched with crew of five. Radio contact zero. Visuals show crash site near Shalbatan Vallis. One body. No motion. No other signs of life. *Medea One* systems at below seventy percent. Orbital path degraded by fire-control air purge. Telemetry and video data to follow." Two keystrokes, and the upload began. "Overhead inspection of Hab One indicates total destruction. Source unknown. Repeat. Hab One is destroyed. End of transmission. *Medea One*, out." She pushed her headset's mike under her chin and muttered, "If anyone can hear me."

MEDEA ONE MISSION CONTROL
JOHNSON SPACE CENTER, HOUSTON
MISSION TIME: DAY 182

"I know I haven't been home, sweetheart. Just please understand. I have six people up there who're depending on me." Russert listen to himself rationalize his workaholism, and he wondered if he appeared as pathetic as he sounded. He gazed longingly at the vidcomm screen.

Jessica crinkled her nose in disgust and tossed her head, blond locks swinging out of her eyes. "Know what, Dad? You got one daughter here who depends on you, too." She averted her gaze and *tsk*ed. "I'm not an idiot. I know you're the flight director and everybody needs you and it's real prestigious and the money's decent and you gotta be there and if you left the whole place would fall apart and rockets would be crashing into Mars. But all I wanted was a goddamned ride to the mall." She looked up now, her wounded face boring into his heart. "You promised. You blew it. And all I can say is . . . LOSER!" She hung up.

He sat alone in his office, surrounded by the photos and models that represented the choices he had made, choices that at the moment seemed terribly wrong.

His ex-wife would attest to that.

Successful people knew how to balance family and career. Why had he failed so miserably?

John Skavlem's agitated voice boomed through his headset. "Flight?"

"Yeah?"

"We've made contact. Need you in the ficker."

Yes. At least one thing had gone right. "On my way." He burst from his seat, took one last look at the replica of *Medea One* on the corner of his desk, then left.

Personnel scrambled in the hallway outside, and by the time he reached the Flight Control Room two minutes later, he felt physically and mentally exhausted.

Skavlem played the message for him, and with each sentence his already wounded heart sank a little more. "Oh, dear God . . ."

Still in a daze, he mumbled a command, and ship's telemetry and video data faded in on the common viewer. The camera flew them through a transparent schematic of *Medea One*, damaged systems outlined in bloodred. The image dissolved to Bowman's scope recordings of the MEV crash site and the skeletal remains of Hab One.

"I can't believe it," soughed Andy Lowenthal. "The flare was one thing. But this . . ."

Russert balled his hands into fists. "All right, ladies and gentlemen. We still got one living, breathing astronaut. I don't care what it takes. We're getting her home."

ten

As in many households, the kitchen aboard *Medea One* quickly became the central gathering place, and Gallagher relied on most of the crew being there at 0800, 1200, 1900, and 2200 hours Zulu time. Conversation ran the usual gamut and then some, with Burchanel frequently arguing for humanity's past scientific successes and Chantilas rebutting with carefully crafted statements of scientific empiricism that blended all sciences into great acts of luck, fate, faith, or God. Santen would occasionally wade into the argumentative waters and cast out his sincere belief that were it not for military-industrial complexes, there would be no modern society and the scientific advances that accompany it. While Gallagher expected Bowman to agree with such statements, being a military pilot herself, she neither defended nor dismantled them; she would only lean back and quietly observe. Contrarily, Gallagher would like nothing more than to partake in these conversations, but they so often drifted into the unintelligible discourse of Ph.D.s that he felt equal measures of boredom, frustration, and intimidation.

Inspired by Chantilas's frequent quoting, Gallagher found one of his own, a truism of the first order uttered by a physicist named Dyson: "A good scientist is a person with original ideas. A good engineer is a person who makes a design that works with as few original ideas as possible. There are no prima donnas in engineering." A decent mantra for a mechanical systems engineer, one that Gallagher had tossed into the mix, not realizing that Burchenal, Pettengill, and Santen would spend forty-five minutes deconstructing the simple quote.

Now, as Gallagher padded into the sphere, still rubbing sleep grit from his eyes, he wondered what hole in his education today's chat would address.

Pettengill, Santen, and Chantilas sat at the table, and as Gallagher swiped a juice from the fridge and joined them, Pettengill blurted out, "It's not there. Yesterday, I could see it. Today, it's gone. I couldn't find it."

"What's *it*?" asked Gallagher.

"He's talking about Earth," Chantilas replied.

Santen made a face at Pettengill. "What? You afraid the Earth vanished? I don't think so."

Pettengill returned the face. "It's just weird not seeing it, y'know?"

With a slight snicker, Santen rose. "Hey, get used to it." The captain and his ill humor strode out.

"I didn't expect this, that's all," Pettengill said. "It's not something they ever told us—Hey, one day when you look out a porthole, Earth will be gone. I guess it's just real now. We're a long way from home."

"Do you like bacon?" Chantilas asked, cocking his salt-and-pepper brows.

Pettengill drew back his head, confused, then answered as though speaking to an insane man. "Uh, yeah . . ."

"I do, too. Except we don't have any. Not even turkey bacon. So when I want some, what I do is, I imagine that I'm sitting down to breakfast in the restaurant of a five-star hotel, and the waiter's lifting the cover off a sizzling plate of bacon. In all its bacon glory. And I can taste that bacon. I can taste it right now. Can't you?"

"Yeah," Pettengill moaned, nose twitching, mouth falling open in ecstasy.

"Okay. Now, do that with Earth." Chantilas paused, waiting as Pettengill crossed the mental bridge. "Make sense?"

"Makes me hungry."

Chantilas grinned. "Me, too." He palmed Pettengill's shoulder, offering the terraformer that calming, gentle look that reminded Gallagher so much of his own grandfather.

Pettengill muttered a thanks, then started for the hatch. "Well, the God of Biology awaits me in the lab."

"Say hi to Mr. Burchenal for us," Chantilas said. He eyed Pettengill's ghost in the hatchway and added, "Some people aren't at home among the stars."

Gallagher half-shrugged. "I'm probably more at home here than anywhere else. Yeah, I still miss it, but . . ."

"You don't miss the people?"

"Some I could live without."

"Me, too. But we're here for all of them: the presidents, the prostitutes, the bank robbers, and the bricklayers." Chantilas lifted his coffee mug, frowned at the contents, then slid back his chair. "Up for a little walk?"

"Sure."

"Let's take a couple laps around the campus. Two weeks of Russert and the rest of them constantly on your back gets old pretty fast. Nice to just walk."

They started into the access tube, and Gallagher stole a quick glance at the veteran. "Can I tell you something, and you don't get pissed?"

"Don't tell me, and I'll keep that promise."

"You know what I mean. What I wanna say is, you remind me a lot of my grandfather."

"Good-looking man?"

"Of course. He taught me to sail when I was a kid. Made me learn the stars in case all the GPS satellites fell out of the sky at once. He said anyone who put his life in the hands of anything run by batteries was a jackass."

"Sounds like quite a guy. A real Yankee."

"Yeah. I miss him. Died when I was thirteen." Gallagher summoned a clear picture of the man, the glistening, freckled pate, the coral blue eyes soaking up his environment, the cigar stub clenched between his teeth, the garish Hawaiian-print shirt tented up by a paunch he boasted took thirty years to build. "He didn't like easy answers or quick fixes. He wouldn't own anything he couldn't repair himself. And, oh yeah, everything automatic sooner or later fails automatically, usually during or immediately before a crisis. He had a lot of damned sayings. And he wouldn't have approved of this."

"Going to Mars?"

"He would've been okay with going, but not for our reasons. He would've been pissed that we killed off half the living things on Earth. That after we all but destroyed one planet with pollution and global warming, we're trying to bring another to life so we can do the same damned thing. He'd say we're asking for more trouble."

"What do you think?"

Gallagher threw up his hands. "We don't know if this'll work out."

"Say we didn't try. We just finished poisoning the Earth, and everyone was dead in a couple of generations. Then what was the point? Music, art, beauty, love? All gone. The Greeks, the Romans, the Enlightenment, the Constitution, people dying for freedom and ideas? None of it meant anything? The Sistine Chapel? The great pyramids? Hemingway's *The Sun Also Rises*? Fitzgerald's *The Great Gatsby*? The Beatles, the Stones, the Doors? Great old films like *On the Waterfront*, *Bridge Over the River Kwai*, *Ben-Hur*, *West Side Story*, *The Godfather*? Has this just been one terrific waste of time? I'd rather go out making a mistake than live in a world that bleak."

They shared a few moments of contemplative silence, rounded a bend, then Gallagher returned to Chantilas's last statement. "'Music, art, beauty, love,'" he quoted. "You said you're here because of a poem. I get that now. But what I don't get is why you quit being a scientist. You went back to school to study God?"

"I just realized science couldn't answer any of the really interesting questions."

"Like . . ."

"Like questions that involve values fundamental to an adequate understanding of our world, values that can't be expressed by equations or experiments. In them, you see the hand of God." He read Gallagher's confusion and clarified: "Acknowledgement of basic values. Love, kindness, joy. Science doesn't have much use for these. Look, ugly theories are wrong. We know it by insight. Science doesn't want to accept that. We live in a moral world and have moral knowledge that tells us that love and truth are better than hatred and lies. But it's modern to think that this is little more than genetic imprinting or a tacit communal cultural agreement. That's not a world I cared to live in anymore."

"One time I asked my grandfather if God existed. He played me Brahms's Third. Then he asked me what good it was, or was it just vibration."

Chantilas nodded. "Yes, what good is the study of aesthetics?"

"Anyway, my grandfather said that if a man could listen to Brahms and not believe in God, he was a fool."

The veteran's gaze lit. "Think I would've liked your grandfather."

They turned right, strolled down an intersecting access tube, then neared the Main Lab's hatch. Gallagher peered in, spotting Burchenal in the rear of the lab, the man's face an eerie vermilion in the screen light. Pettengill stood behind him, looking somewhat irritated.

"See them in there?" Chantilas asked. "Maybe they'll find some answers. Maybe they won't. But what they need to realize is that there's something bigger than them, bigger than all of us. There's a reason the planets go around the stars in exactly the same way electrons go around the nucleus of the atom. It's not an accident. There's a design at the bottom of all this. God's watching over them, over you."

"Yeah, he is," Gallagher agreed. "Just wish he wasn't laughing."

"There's another one—humor. Tell me the equation for it. The formula. What are the variables?"

Another face seared into Gallagher's thoughts, a hard face with a sandy complexion and brows arrowing toward a pug nose. "My dad would try to answer that."

"Never heard you mention your parents. What about him?"

"He thinks he's God."

"Hard-ass," Chantilas concluded.

"Stainless steel."

"Judging everyone else."

"Mostly me.

"Well, sometimes even screw-ups do okay in the end." Chantilas's expression grew serious, then he smiled broadly.

Gallagher shared the look, then, as they quickened their pace, he thought he would touch on something, well, a bit more touchy, figuring he already had Chantilas talking. "Some people say you were sent on this mission as a kind of—"

"PR stunt," Chantilas finished. "I'm the space program poster boy."

"I think maybe they sent you to watch over us. Be like a guidance counselor."

"Personally, I go with the poster-boy theory, though I do have the white hair of an archetypal wise one who helps the heroes. Either way, I'm grateful for the chance."

"To be first on Mars."

"To serve humanity as a scientist, while the theologian looks for God in a new place."

"You didn't come on this trip because of science at all. That's why they let you come, but you're going to Mars to prove to yourself that God exists."

"Why not? Maybe I'll pick up a rock, and it'll say so on the bottom: made by God. The universe is full of surprises."

"That'd be a big one. But maybe God's more subtle than you think."

Chantilas lingered at a porthole, staring wondrously

through the permaglass and into the starry void. "I won't be disappointed if I don't get an answer. Only if I don't try. You see, I keep getting this feeling that we're supposed to find something or learn something that's important about ourselves and our place here. It sounds pretty nutty when I say it, but it's a truth I can't escape. The answers are out there. And there's a voice calling me to them. Calling all of us."

"Whose voice?"

"I'm not sure. Maybe it's Mars."

"You're right. You sound like a nut. But don't worry. I won't tell 'em."

"You don't need to. They're already convinced."

"Well then, I won't tell 'em we had this conversation. And when we get to Mars, I'll help you look under all those rocks."

Chantilas beamed. "Thanks. Could use the help."

eleven

Seated on a reef whose back had been polished smooth by the Martian winds, Gallagher leaned down, picked up a rock, and turned it over. "Made by God. Sorry, Bud. It ain't here."

The status panel on Gallagher's wrist conveyed even greater bad news: his e-suit's thermal battery had already died, as had the others', and he now had only thirteen minutes of air left.

"Maybe we got what we deserved," said Burchenal, settling down beside Gallagher. "We ignored science and truth on one planet and poisoned it beyond repair. Then we tried to get science to save us on another. Maybe it's the inconsistency that did us in."

"Maybe we just know too much," Gallagher suggested. "Bud told me something that Mark Twain said about how we can't recognize the beauty of a rainbow the way a savage does because we stand, we look at it, and we know *why* it's produced."

"I disagree. We can appreciate its beauty even more because we understand the refractive dispersion of sunlight in falling water droplets. We understand the amazing processes of nature."

"But do we look at it as a beautiful rainbow, or do we view it as a process of nature?"

Burchenal pointed at a broad depression about thirty meters away. "See that? What is it to you?"

"It's a place where the ground dips. Call it a hollow. What have you."

"See, I know exactly what it is, and thanks to science, I can marvel at its beauty better than you can. That's what we call the datum, our reference for sea level. If there was a sea. Or when there was a sea. You can tell because the sand was created by what's called the fluvial process, where water breaks rocks into smaller and smaller pieces. To you, it's a dip in the ground. To me, it's a book that records a billion-year-old story. That's not just reductionism, though some would argue it is."

"So you find beauty in knowledge. Maybe we oughta be looking for knowledge in beauty."

"Whoa, Gallagher, for a toilet repairman, that's pretty goddamned profound." He leaned forward, eyes glassy. "Here's another one: we're the first men on Mars. Even if it won't last long. And hey, you want me to shut up so you can die quietly?"

"Nah, keep talking. Makes me forget the time. Just let it sneak up on us."

"Yeah. And if nothing else, we go out like men. We're not dying some ridiculous, freak death like the soldier who does four tours and earns a half dozen purple hearts.

Then he goes home, slips on his kid's skateboard and buys it right there in the garage. That kinda irony makes me want to puke." Burchenal's voice hardened. "Some final entry to have in your bio, huh? Disappointed twelve billion people, not counting the ex-wives."

"They'll be disappointed, but the dream won't end here. Congress will come up with another trillion or so and send another team."

"Or they'll pour money back into temporary fixes and write off the whole Mars project. Politicians love living in denial; it's a gated community just outside D.C."

"Don't make me smile," Gallagher cautioned him. "I don't wanna feel too much now. And hey, other than Bud, you think they chose us 'cause we're all single with no kids?"

"I know they chose me because I got the only Mac-Gregor in bioengineering, which means absolutely dick right now."

It hit Gallagher that they had not heard from Pettengill and Santen for several minutes. He glanced back at Hab; neither of them lurked among the ruins. "Where's Pettengill?"

Burchanel slapped palms on his hips, pushed himself up from the reef, then surveyed the jagged horizon. "Pettengill? Santen?"

A handful of seconds passed.

"Must have gone over the ridge and toward that canyon, out of contact." Burchenal sat. "Guess that was good-bye."

"I thought I could just stay here and talk it away," Gallagher said quickly. "But I don't think I can. I don't think I can do it. I mean, I gotta do something. We gotta do something, right?"

"What?"

• • •

Pettengill had followed Santen's footprints up and over the first slope, then he had tracked parallel to a ridge running above a wide channel that, according to his HHC, drained into Chryse Basin. Presently, he neared a section of channel that had obviously suffered a great landslide. Two hundred meters ahead, a sheer cliff dropped off for nearly a kilometer. Ever the scientist, he inspected the rhythmically layered sediments on the channel's opposite wall. Those layers suggested a quiet depositional environment like the one provided by standing water. Had flowing water produced the channel? Had it at one time stopped flowing?

You're going to die in a few minutes, you ass. You want this to be your last thought? Or is this how you deal? Maybe you want your last thought to be you analyzing your last thought. . . .

Just ahead, Santen stood at the cliff's edge, arms folded over his chest in what might be his last act of defiance. He could throw himself off, and even in the lighter gravity he might die from the fall. At the very least he might suffer a suit breach. Pettengill watched the man for a moment, then ambled toward him, assuming that Santen heard his approach but would not waste a glance on him. He came up next to the captain and took in the view of channel walls and shadows blending into an extraordinary vortex.

And for a few seconds, lengthened by a surge of adrenaline, Pettengill imagined leaning forward to give himself to the channel, to the planet. A simple act. Almost effortless. He would spare himself the horror of suffocation, though a fall might prove even more horrific.

Forget that. You didn't come here to kill yourself. You will die, but do it with a clear conscience.

Out of nowhere, he began speaking. "Last month, I decided to get engaged when we got back. My girlfriend,
she'd been bugging me for months. And she swore up
and down she'd wait for me. I didn't want to do anything
before we left because, well, you know. Actually, I was
just scared. I've never put that rope around my neck. But
then I just realized, I guess like a lot of guys do, that I
wasn't gonna find anyone else like her. So I just made the
decision. I spent a lot of nights up on *Medea* rehearsing
how I was gonna ask her and realizing how much I miss
her."

"I'm gonna miss a lot of girls," Santen said. "And a lot
of girls are gonna miss me."

Clearly, the captain's thoughts lay parsecs away. No
longing had crept into his voice, no sense of impending
doom, just that olive drab stoicism—even in the final
minutes of existence. He scrutinized the depths before
him, then, as though the shadows had permeated his
being to force out the truth, he added, "My flying ability
isn't an issue now. With Hab destroyed, it makes no difference where we landed."

Pettengill took a step back, his face tightening in dis-
belief. "You're out here calculating excuses?"

"There's nothing to excuse. It's moot. No impact."

"What about Chantilas? Your landing killed that man."

"Moot. He would've died here anyway."

"But he would've taken the first step. He wanted to be
here more than any of us."

"Twenty roads. They all lead to the same dead end.
Matter which one you're on?"

"You're amazing. You can't admit failure. Even when
you're about to die."

Santen brought his lips together, and his eyes grew distant.

There. Pettengill had finally reached the man after all this time. Emotions crashed over in waves—joy, sorrow, pain, forgiveness—rinsing Pettengill's soul clean and lifting him on wings. Months of evil thoughts directed toward Santen slithered over the cliff and vanished.

"I come across as abrupt to some people," Santen finally said, his bitter tone slightly defused. "I know that. But technically, I didn't fail."

Wings snapped. Waves withdrew. Pettengill's blood turned cold, or at least it felt so. "I came here to forgive you before you died. To forgive you for all the bullshit you've put me through from the first day we met. The snide remarks, the personal attacks, the embarrassing moments in front of my peers, the shoves, the kicks, the little jabs, all of it. I wanted to say that I forgive you and that I'm sorry we didn't get along."

"Yeah, well, screw you. I don't need forgiveness from an egghead. And I sure as hell never wanted to be your friend." Santen turned to reveal his face, half eclipsed in darkness, the one eye like a narrow breach in a swollen, decaying globe. His lip twisted into a snarl as sunlight flashed off his drool-slick teeth. He hyperventilated through the comm, and then that corrupt face blurred into another face, a thousand faces, the faces that had for two-and-a-half decades haunted Pettengill. Santen did not stand there; every son of a bitch who had ever taunted Pettengill now dwelled in this man's body.

Pettengill should pull back. Let it go. They would both die. Santen's death would be ample revenge. That represented the mature, logical decision.

But what did maturity and logic have to do with this? They were about to die. And now he knew what his last thought would be. He would die knowing that he was a victim. A victim of his own cowardice. A victim to the end.

No. For once in his rapidly ending life he would take charge. He would die knowing that his life mattered, that justice lay within *his* grasp and no one else's.

He shoved Santen.

Hard.

Past the edge of the cliff.

The pilot's mouth fell open. His eyelids flapped in terror. He groped. Nothing but air to catch. Then his military training kicked in, as though he had thrown a switch. Santen craned his head, tread more air, then hunkered a bit as heels dug in. The effort failed him.

More desperate now, he reached back, and a gloved hand materialized before Pettengill, darted, then fingers locked on to Pettengill's suit, near the abdomen.

Still falling, Santen threw all his energy into that hand and spun around. He reached for Pettengill with his free hand, missed, then reached again as Pettengill screamed and slapped the hand away.

But Santen kept on, found an opening in Pettengill's defenses, and nearly latched on before Pettengill wrenched him away. A guttural cry erupted from Pettengill's lips, a cry over the terrifying threshold he had chosen to cross.

Were they struggling in Earth's gravity, Santen would have already gone over the edge, but Mars helped him now, helped him to exact revenge upon a would-be murderer. Pettengill shuddered as Santen lunged in one concentrated effort and arrived back on his feet.

They stood together now on the cliff, the captain a being of sweat and muscle awash in adrenaline, a being radiating with survival energy, and Pettengill, a being of sweat and raw bones chilled to the marrow, a being whose own will to survive lay beneath a heavy tarpaulin of fear.

Santen unleashed a head butt to Pettengill's shoulder, driving Pettengill to the ground. The captain dropped to his knees and delivered one, two, three, solid punches to Pettengill's gut, robbing him of breath as a tremendous ache mounted his throat.

Rearing back, Santen prepared for another head butt.

Pettengill crawled in retreat, but the captain charged on hands and knees.

Sprang.

They butted helmets so hard that a web of cracks formed in Santen's clear dome.

But that hardly slowed him. He seized Pettengill's suit near the clavicle, and even as he drew Pettengill in, about to throw him hard into the dirt, Pettengill grabbed the collar of the flyboy's suit and tugged hard to the right.

They rolled together in the dust, one, two, three revolutions, knees, elbows, and backs crunching.

As they came out of the final revolution, with Santen on top and about to wrest open the latches on Pettengill's helmet, an odd look stole over the captain's face. He took a breath. But it wasn't there.

He rolled his wrist, gaped at his readout. Pettengill saw that he had but two minutes. Santen had used up his O2 supply faster than anyone, and the exertion had overworked his system. The pack could not supply him fast enough.

The captain released Pettengill, crawled off, choking, willing himself away with remarkable strength given his predicament. He thought he could keep death at bay just a little longer, but Pettengill would unlatch the reaper's gate. He stood, and, with goose flesh of rage, crossed to the jock, placed a boot behind his head.

And stomped.

Stomped again. Drove the bastard's helmet into the regolith. Small, sharp stones dug in to the already compromised glass. Another stomp. The dome caved in amid a spatter of blood. Stomp. Stomp. Stomp!

Then nothing. Nothing save for a murderous afterglow. *Breathing. Just breathing. In. Out. In. Out.*

"Don't want forgiveness?" he asked Santen's corpse. "Then how about *this* from an egghead?"

He gripped Santen's shoulders, then dragged him to the cliff's edge. As he forced the captain feetfirst over the side, Santen raised his head. Whether it was an involuntary reflex, Pettengill was not sure, but it shocked him so severely that he screamed and stomped once more on the astronaut's crumpled bubble, driving him over the side.

Santen began the long fall, tumbling slowly until his boot caught on a ledge and kicked him into a faster spin toward grainy jaws of darkness.

How much time? Five minutes. Enough to go back. I don't want to die alone.

twelve

Gallagher had reasoned that he and Burchanel could not just sit and wait to die. They had to do something. So they had paced. Spoke about what they should do. And realized with bitter laughter that their decision to just sit and talk it away had been the best one.

"Italian astronomer Giovanni Schiaparelli drew the first map of Mars in 1877. All he had was a blurry image from a simple telescope. Saw what he called *canali*, which is Italian for "channels." The word was mistranslated as "canals." So in 1894, Percival Lowell picks up on this. He's in Flagstaff, at a high-altitude observatory, and sees what he calls 'the products of an intelligence.' " Burchenal sniggered. "Too bad he didn't have a better telescope."

"Yeah, but then H. G. Wells and Edgar Rice Burroughs wouldn't have kept our ancestors so entertained," Gallagher said, hazarding a glance at his air supply. Ohmygod. Three minutes.

Burchanel stood and walked off, head bowed. "Melt the polar caps with low-order nukes. That releases C-oh-two. And C-oh-two buildup creates a greenhouse effect. Mars starts warming up. Add some algae. The algae grows and emits oxygen. It all tracks. Terraforming should've kept working here. What knocked out our sensors? Why is the algae gone? What happened to Hab? There have to be some damned answers."

"So you go for your yearly physical," Gallagher said, ignoring the good scientist's obsession. "Doc tells you that you got six months. It'll be a quick death. You'll be healthy to the last few minutes. What would you do?"

Burchanel stopped, drew himself to full height, then turned around. "Most people would say they'd travel, right? See all the places on Earth they never got to see. We traveled all right, eh?"

"So that's what you'd do?"

"First thing is I'd make peace with my ex-wives. Tell 'em I'm sorry for not giving them any kids. I wouldn't tell them I'm dying. I wouldn't want the sympathy. Then I'd go off, and I'd meet with each of the great scientists of the world, people like Foga, Ryltala, Gramanzini, and Garibaldi. I'd sit down with each of 'em, and I'd ask, what are the questions you simply can't answer? I'd make a list. And I'd spend the rest of my days trying to figure out the answers."

"From a whorehouse near Vegas," Gallagher added.

"Exactly. And I'd bring my horse with me. You?"

"Guess I'd be pissed off for a long time. I've already seen a lot of the world. There's this little bar down in the Keys. Probably go there. Eat. Stay drunk for a long time.

But I know one thing. I'd wanna leave something behind. Something good. Something people would remember."

"Got your wish right here."

Gallagher closed his eyes. "Guess so."

"Pettengill? That you?"

A lone figure rounded one of Hab's ribs and came forward, his suit a patchwork of dark and light dust, as though he had rolled on the ground and beat his fists against the planet. The glare on his helmet cleared to unveil Pettengill, his face stiff, eyes unable to focus. "Santen's dead." He brushed sand from his arms. "Threw himself off a cliff back there. I tried to stop him." Still the zombie, Pettengill joined them on the reef, drawing Burchenal's curious gaze.

Gallagher turned his trembling wrist, read his panel. "I'm at under a minute."

"I'm not far behind you," Burchenal reported. "Life's too short."

"What's it gonna be like?" asked Gallagher.

"Hypoxia?"

He nodded.

"Remember your paramedic training? Dizziness. Your skin'll tingle. Vision narrows. Then anoxia. Shock, convulsions, acidosis . . ."

"Gonna hurt?"

"Yeah."

Another glance to the panel. Fifteen seconds.

Ten. Five.

A warning tone resounded.

No minutes of life left.

If I can just take tiny breaths. Maybe I can—

Only a hint of air found his lungs. Panic grabbed his chest, squeezed. He dropped to his knees, then onto all fours as he sucked in the very last of his air.

The tingling started. Had it begun at his head? His toes? He wasn't sure, but it needled through his entire body now. The ground lifted and fell, and his head tossed like a buoy on high seas.

He felt so afraid of his own death that he struck out at that fear, using the only tool he had left: his anger. Desperate, mutinous, unwilling to go down without protest, he shot up, turned, and unfastened his visor. The helmet clouded over into its flexible, gelatinous state. He pushed back the hood and with every last bit of air screamed, "Fuck this planet!"

A curse against fate. A curse at the coolness of the universe. A final statement to reinforce that he was better than the damned planet. His own sentience allowed him that much in the end.

As the cry faded, Burchanel and Pettengill grimaced and looked away, unable to watch an interpretation of their own fates played out live before their eyes.

Gallagher had no air left. There would be no final, choking cry. No whimper. His next inhale would bring no relief. How much longer could he hold out? Darkness already gripped the corners of his gaze.

He shuddered. Fought off the desire to inhale. Held it behind a door. But it rammed through, came reflexively, unavoidably, lungs contracting to take in the worthless Martian atmosphere.

Shock now. And convulsions that would send him writhing spasmodically across the dirt as the acidity of his body's fluids dramatically increased.

Gallagher exhaled. Stood there.

Still alive.

He inhaled again. "I'm breathing." He regarded Burchanel and Pettengill, who sat in stunned tableau. "I can breathe."

Beep . . . beep . . . beep. . . . That from Pettengill's oxygen alarm. He panted and fumbled with his latches. The
dome softened. He threw pack the hood. Looked horrified.
Took a breath. And the amazed expression returned.

"I still got six minutes on my supply," Burchenal announced. "Shutting down." He tapped his panel, then de-
activated his own helmet and chanced the atmosphere.

"It's like being at high altitude," Gallagher said
through a shivery sigh. It felt odd to hear his own voice
without the muffle of his helmet. "Air's thin. But we're
not gonna die."

"This isn't possible," cried Pettengill. "The oxygen
was dropping."

Gallagher drew in a long, slow breath. "It's a miracle."
Bud, maybe this is your answer. Air by God. . . .

"Something obviously happened after the biosensors
crashed," Burchanel said, sniffing at something curious
in the air, a faint stench as though from an old, dry closet.
"I just don't understand this. Where the hell would oxygen come from?"

"Who cares where from," Gallagher said, his veins
flooding with a fresh rush of life. "As long as it's here."
Had he a mirror, Gallagher would see the largest shit-
eating grin he had ever produced. And his grin infected
Burchenal, who couldn't help himself despite the unan-
swered questions.

Pettengill gulped, his expression somewhere between
dour and downright suicidal. "I thought we'd be dead . . ."

"If only Santen had known," Burchenal said, his tone
more than a little accusing. "What a waste." He slapped
Pettengill hard on the back. "At least you tried to save
him. Did the best you could, right?"

"It's moot. No impact," Pettengill answered, sounding
strangely like the man under discussion. He glanced off

at Hab. "Supplies are gone. We'll die of starvation in a couple of days anyway."

"There's a reason for whatever's happening here," Gallagher said, hearing Chantilas's words ring out clearly in his thoughts. "We were meant to find something. Maybe this is it."

"So we found it." Pettengill threw back his head. "Now we die."

"I'm breathing," said Burchanel. "And I just erased dying from my schedule." He frowned at Gallagher. "Any ideas?"

"We need communications. We need to contact someone. Bowman."

"If she's still up there," Burchenal reminded him.

Pettengill muttered a curse. "For all the good it'll do us. How's she supposed to get supplies down to us? FedEx? Give me a fucking break."

Gallagher shrugged. "Well, my sitting around days are over."

"Can we modify the taccoms in our suits?" Burchenal asked. "Increase signal strength so that we can get a message to her?"

"Thought of that during the big hike here. Thought of using components from our HHCs. But it won't work. Can't amplify the carrier wave. Our cells just won't do it."

"Come on," Burchenal said, heading back to Hab. "Maybe there's something we can use."

UNITED STATES SPACECRAFT *MEDEA ONE*
MARS ORBIT
MISSION TIME: DAY 182

Bowman squeezed herself farther into the rectangular crawl space and reached propulsion substation panel

#213b4. She cracked on a glow panel and got to work replacing the four melted chips. Though claustrophobia had never been a problem, she felt more than a little uneasy as she hung within the narrow confines of a shaft that chased the gloom for twenty meters above and below her, drawing out pangs of loneliness.

Fifty-six minutes had passed since her transmission to Houston—more than enough time for them to receive it and broadcast a response. Whoever had said that the waiting was the hardest part knew all about it.

She had kept busy, had tried to funnel her sorrow and frustration into positive energy, into restoring her ride home. But God, she wished Gallagher were present to help. With each task that strained the limits of her knowledge and talent, she missed him even more. Occasionally, twisted thoughts would blind her with images of him running frantically across the rocky terrain, choking, hands locked futilely around his neck. She would shudder them off, catch her breath, and mutter, "I gotta get home. I just gotta get home."

A voice woke over the intercom and echoed up into the shaft. "*Medea One*, Houston. We copy you. Transmission to follow in thirty seconds."

The burst startled Bowman so thoroughly that she dropped the chip she had been balancing over its socket. She would find it later. Now she crawled backward out of the shaft, her eagerness making the effort seem nominal. She dropped onto the maintenance deck, then took off running toward Command and Control.

"*Medea One*, Houston. We copy you. Transmission to follow in twenty seconds."

Access tubes wiped by, and overhead lights streamed into glowing bars. Her boot caught on something. Down she went. Cocked her head. Damned debris still lying all over the place. She had fallen over the tattered leg of a lab table.

"*Medea One*, Houston. We copy you. Transmission to follow in ten seconds."

She got to her feet, resumed the jog, more wary of the path. She reached the Flight Deck hatch and hustled by as John Skavlem's voice broke a final time over the comm:

"Transmission in five, four, three, two, one. Welcome back, *Medea One*. We confirm your assessment of proton field upset. Your telemetry indicates orbital failure in thirty-one hours. Mars landing team presumed End Of Mission. We believe we can restore engine function for main engine burn. We're bringing you home. Standby for instructions from PROP and GNC."

It took a moment for Bowman to fully absorb that. She pressed her head on the viewport, closed her eyes, and transported herself down to Mars.

She wasn't abandoning them; they were already dead. Years from now the crash site would become a memorial, a largely ignored testament to humanity's hubris.

How dare we defy the universe?

thirteen

HAB ONE SITE
NEAR ARES VALLIS, MARS
MISSION TIME: DAY 182

"Although Mars' diameter stands at six thousand seven hundred eighty-eight kilometers, putting it at about half the size of Earth and with only about one-tenth the mass, other characteristics bear an uncanny resemblance to our planet. The surface area on Mars measures nearly the same as that of the dry land on Earth. A day on Mars lasts about twenty-four and a half hours, though the planet takes just under two Earth years to complete an orbit of the sun, traveling at twenty-four point one three kilometers per second, slightly slower than Earth's orbital velocity. And just as Earth's axis is tipped at about twenty-three and a half degrees, Mars's inclination comes in at about twenty-four, making seasonal changes visible even through a small telescope."

Gallagher could still see the gangly SEO instructor in

that overwashed lavender dress shirt. The guy had been trying just a little too hard to point out the similarities between Mars and Earth. Make no mistake, the similarities were there, especially now that humans could breathe Martian air. Old purple shirt's heart would trip-hammer when he learned of the discovery.

Still rummaging through Hab's ruins, Gallagher paused to catch his breath and clear his thoughts. The sun shied toward the horizon, its blue halo blossoming by the minute. While the Martian dust usually absorbed blue light and gave the sky its red color, Burchenal had stolen the sunset's beauty by explaining that "the dust also scatters some blue light just around the sun because during sunrise and sunset the sun's light has to pass through the most amount of dust. We get a similar effect on Earth, only the colors lean toward the ROY side of the spectrum."

Explanations or not, the small, near-white globe had been an unappreciated friend to Gallagher and the others. And now that it prepared to set and a chill cleaved the air, Gallagher realized how much he would miss it. He tried to forget how cold it would become, but he knew the numbers, as did the others. No one said a word about it. Denial was yet another beautiful thing.

"Oh, well," Gallagher sighed, lifting a knotted pasta salad of wires and circuit boards. Someone or something had taken a pair of scissors or some other cutting device to the electronics. "Found the radio. What's left of it. We can use it to make some of that hip, electronic jewelry that Russert's daughter likes to wear."

Burchenal stared grimly at the remains. "Sure there's nothing we could use from MEV?"

"Not for communications. Primary system took the brunt of the impact. And the cells got damaged, so there's zip for the redundancies, which, by the way, also sustained a power surge. Not sure if they'd even work. We could've used a cell from Hab to check it out, but they're gone."

The scientist puffed air, then added a long piece of plastic to a pile of debris. Pettengill, who had joined them, added his own section of foam from a mattress.

Like archaeologists carefully sifting through a dig, they continued to probe Hab, examining each piece then tossing it onto the pile. They worked quietly for several minutes, then Pettengill cursed and said, "There's nothing here. We're wasting time."

Gallagher glimpsed the sun, now waning behind the ridge line. "I didn't want to talk about this, but it's gonna get real cold in a few minutes."

"Yeah, like minus one hundred sixty degrees Fahrenheit," groaned Pettengill. "Greenhouse effect or not. I had it all wrong. We're gonna freeze to death before we starve."

"Fuel drums are gone, but I think a lot of it spilled into the soil," Burchenal said. "Here. And here. It hasn't all evaporated. Toss some of this dirt over the pile and see what happens." He pulled out his HHC, then leaned on a rib, intent on the computer's screen.

As Gallagher started for the spill site, a powerful whir overhead gained his attention. An object sliced across the twilight sky, obscured by its own velocity. It shifted quickly to the north, then slowly circled. "Hey, that's AMEE's scout." Gallagher whistled. Listened.

"Thought she was screwed up," Pettengill said, pivoting to follow the satellite.

"Her nanotech repair crew had off-lined. Must've rerouted and repaired her. Damn smart machine. She's out here, somewhere. The drone can't fly without her."

"How'd she find us?"

"Simple visual inspection of our footprints. She also triangulates off me." Gallagher tapped his wrist. "Short-range transmitter in my suit. She'll get here sooner or later."

"She got anything on her we can salvage?"

"Her cell's the wrong size for the comm redundancies back at MEV. She might come in handy for something else, though. Just wish she had a radio."

Burchanel hastened away from Hab, all broad grin and five o'clock shadow. He either had gas or good news. "Gentlemen, gotta think about our problem scientifically."

"How 'bout realistically?" Pettengill suggested darkly. "We need facts. Not theories."

"Want facts? Here's one for you. There's another radio, two kilometers east of here." Burchenal pointed.

Gallagher squinted into the distance, then turned to Burchenal's HHC. "Nineteen point three three degrees north, thirty-three point five five degrees west."

"Exactly," Burchenal said. "We're right over the edge from Ares Vallis."

Now Gallagher wore a grin. "*Pathfinder*. And *Sojourner*."

"That rover we sent up in '97?" asked Pettengill.

"It's still there," Burchenal replied. "Arrived on July fourth. Came in the same way we did, bouncing about fifteen times before stopping about a klick from the first impact. We got about three months of data from the rover and lander before the cold got to 'em."

"Tech's real old, but I bet I can work with it," Gallagher said, before another thought tempered his enthusiasm. "If whatever happened to Hab didn't happen to it . . ."

Burchenal switched off his HHC. "Now who's being negative?"

"If he doesn't want the job, I'll take it," Pettengill said. "And he's right about the tech being old. And even if we get it working, what if we can't patch in to our frequency? It's not like there's some geek in Pasadena who strapped himself to a chair for the last fifty-three years, waiting for a signal from the damned thing."

"You're right, Pettengill. And maybe Bowman's gone. Maybe they can't get a rescue mission to us for another six or seven months. Maybe we're already dead. But before I go, I want someone to know what happened here." Gallagher fixed his gaze on the terraformer. "That's all."

Unimpressed, Pettengill humped off toward Hab.

Stars burned through the rufescent gloom, and Gallagher noticed with a tremor how thick his breath had become. "Look, it's too late to go now."

"We'll leave in the morning," said Burchenal. "After a night around the old campfire."

"The old seventy-five-billion-dollar campfire," Gallagher qualified, picturing himself testifying before a senate subcommittee. "You did what?" the stodgy chairman asked.

"We were cold, sir. So we burned it."

Gallagher smiled inwardly as he and Burchenal returned to the Hab. After fishing out and lighting his cigar-sized torch, Gallagher balanced it near the sandy pile. The debris caught, the flames low and blue at their bases.

The three astronauts huddled around the warmth, and it struck Gallagher how a century's worth of blood, sweat, and tears had put them on Mars so that they could gather around a fire like their ancestors had several hundred thousand years prior. Instead of fashioning hand axes from their environment, they would plunder their own artifacts to build a radio. But how much different was it? Had humanity truly come that far? Or were we just intelligent apes clad in the uniforms of an illusory society?

Gallagher leaned in toward the flames. *Bud, I'm asking some big questions. You'd be proud.*

UNITED STATES SPACECRAFT *MEDEA ONE*
MARS ORBIT
MISSION TIME: DAY 182

The propulsion engineers back at Houston had uploaded forty-one scenarios for waking up the engine ignition. Bowman had carefully and systematically gone through thirty-eight of them without a single spark—or even the suggestion of a spark. With each failure, her breath grew more shallow. The thirty-ninth scenario called for her to lock out subsystems seventeen, twenty-two, and forty. Numbed fingers banged on the touchboard. She engaged the drive. Forty free-flows. Now she held her breath. Held herself against yet another blow.

Two more to go. Forty called for a similar lockout pattern with different stations. She went through the motions, not expecting anything and receiving . . . nothing. One more scenario. This was it. Last try. Last one had to do it. And wasn't that the way irony worked? It always had to be the last one. Lockouts programmed. Engage drive. And . . . And . . .

She bounded from the chair, raised her fist at the touchboard—

And smashed the mirror above her pretty white dressing table. Her teddy bear, "Groomsburrow," toppled to the carpet as Mom stormed into the room. "What are you doing?"

"I can't do it! I just can't get the answer!" she cried, waving the geometry book.

Mom tugged the book out of her hand, then led her back to the bed, where Kate sat, sobbing into her hands.

"It's just a math problem, honey. You can't destroy your room over it. You're father's going to be so pissed when he sees what you've done."

"I don't care. I don't care!"

"Honey, maybe you can't get all the answers. So what? Get as many as you can. Sometimes we learn more from the ones we can't figure out than the ones we can."

"I can't learn anything. I'm just stupid."

"Trust me on this one. You're not stupid. Do all those trophies downstairs say you're stupid?"

"No."

"Then why don't you just rest for now? Take a break. Come back to the math later. We'll clean up the glass and have a snack. Okay?"

"Okay."

Bowman lowered her fist then shrank back into her seat. She thought of the chocolate-chip cookies down in the kitchen sphere, then cleared her throat. "Houston, *Medea One*. No joy on all scenarios for engine ignition. Double-checked all replacement chips. Multiple free-flows continue. Please advise. *Medea One*, out."

And I wish I'd hear from you sooner than forty minutes from now. . . .

USS *PAUL REVERE* (SSBN-1928)
TRIDENT IV NUCLEAR SUBMARINE
SOMEWHERE IN THE SOUTH CHINA SEA
1450 HOURS ZULU TIME

"Sir, encryption code has been accepted and verified," Lieutenant Commander Rick Hardeson cried, marching away from the comm station toward Command and Control, where Captain Joseph Brama stood, staring into nowhere as he read data from his PIM. The solidly built man in his late forties acknowledged Hardeson with a curt nod. "Very well, XO. Put it through."

"Aye-aye, sir. Comm station, conn. Direct encrypted Emergency Action Message to command staff PIMs."

Comm Officer Nayfeh repeated the command and promptly initiated the transfer.

Hardeson scanned the data, and when the transmission ended, he flipped up his monocle and gazed soberly at the captain.

"I'll address the crew," said Brama, then plugged a command into his control watch, switching his headset to ship-wide intercom. "Attention. This is the captain. We have just received an Emergency Action Message and have been ordered to set DEFCON Four. Seems our bosses at the Pentagon are responding to accusations that the Chinese might have sabotaged our Mars expedition. I know all of you have been following the reports since our own Robert Gallagher is up there. I'll say this: don't believe those End Of Mission reports. If there's a way to survive, Mr. Gallagher will find it. I'll continue to make available everything I can. But for now, initiate DEFCON Four. This is the captain."

"Initiate DEFCON Four. This is the XO." Hardeson turned to the captain, his voice dropping to church depths. "Sir, you really believe he's still alive?"

"I do. I'll never forget that seaman. A wiseass with incredible gifts. Never bought into a military lifestyle." Brama's eyes misted over as he reflected for a few seconds. "So we were off the Ross Ice Shelf, up at McMurdo. Thermal systems went down. We were going to freeze to death before we made it back to Scott Base. I had twenty-one sailors working on the problem. Gallagher went below, and I swear to God, true story, he fixed the damned thing with foam coffee cups and duct tape. And that wasn't the first time he hot-wired his ass out of trouble. Like I said, if there's a way to stay alive up there, he'll find it."

"Just hope he packed duct tape."

Brama smiled wanly, then faced forward and assumed his familiar impassive expression. "Chief of the boat, make your depth one-five-zero-zero feet, smartly. Rig ship for ultraquiet. Weapons, conn. Set condition One-QRXZO. Spin up missiles nineteen through twenty-two and twenty-eight through thirty-one. This is the captain."

fourteen

Gallagher had to snicker the first time he had been intro-
duced to *Medea One*'s "hygiene sphere." Leave it to an
engineering team to concoct a fancy name for a bathroom. The hygiene sphere, aka the Self-contained Cleaning and Waste Processing Environment, aka the SCWPE,
came equipped with a sundry of mirrors on plastic goose-
necks; sinks, showers, and toilets with powerful suction
drains; and a lovely antiseptic white motif unsullied by
Aunt Tanya's shag bowl cover and the pastel-colored
soaps and towels that you were not allowed to use. Instead, utilitarian instruction placards hung from the walls,
indicating the proper use for each piece of sophisticated
equipment. One Gallagher particularly enjoyed read
thusly:

PROPER AND SAFE USE OF ONBOARD TOILET

1. PLACE GLUTEUS MAXIMUS FIRMLY ON SEAT

2. BE SURE TO ALLOW PROPER AIRFLOW BETWEEN INNER TOILET ATMOSPHERE AND SURROUNDING STALL, AS CREATING A VACUUM COULD RESULT IN SEVERE INJURY WHEN FLUSHING

3. SHOULD GRAVITY FAILURE OCCUR, FLUSH IMMEDIATELY TO AVOID DEFACING U.S. PROPERTY, WHICH IS A FEDERAL CRIME

4. AVOID READING WHILE ON TOILET, AS THIS MAY CAUSE USAGE DELAYS AND UNDERMINE CREW MORALE

5. BE SURE TO READ THE PROPER AND SAFE USE OF ONBOARD TOILET BEFORE OPERATING THIS PIECE OF EQUIPMENT

One enterprising young engineer had managed to sneak the placard onboard, though Bowman and Santen had initially accused Gallagher of putting it there. Creating his own plausible deniability had never come easily to Gallagher, so for a week he had taken the rap until the engineer had folded under the spotlights, the beatings, and the loneliness of the deprivation tank. All of which was to say that Gallagher would give the kid a Mars rock in exchange for the laughs.

Presently, he padded into the sphere, fully educated in the proper and safe use of the onboard toilet, and suddenly realized that his timing was at once good and bad.

Bowman stepped naked, dripping, from the shower.

And all the frustration of staring at her cotton shirts and imagining what lay within was satisfied in a single glance. My God. His imagination had not done her justice. Why she hadn't become a model, he would never know. Any agency would have scooped her up in a heartbeat.

And her damned intelligence made her even more achingly beautiful, as did the devilish and submissive fantasy of lusting after his own boss.

Gallagher stood there, mesmerized, a teenaged virgin staring at his first naked lady.

"Hand it to me?" she asked.

What was so interesting over his shoulder? He glanced back. Oh, her towel. He pulled it from the rung, thought of holding it back for just a second more, then surrendered.

She wrapped up calmly, as though he hadn't seen her. "Just pretend I'm your sister."

"I have two," he said, examining the magic she performed on the towel with her hips and breasts. "One's got a kid. Neither is this fine."

"It's just a body, Mr. Gallagher. It'll get old, wrinkled, wither away. It's just a shell."

"I'm sorry, ma'am. It's . . . well, some of us can't turn it on and off like that."

"And you're turned on?"

"Uh, no, I didn't say that, ma'am. I just mean—"

"Look, the only way this works is if we both believe it doesn't matter."

"Like you could be Burchenal?" he asked innocently, wild thoughts tacking a thick layer of stubble on her face.

"Well, I'd prefer a little more credit than that."

"In terms of credit, I'd say you qualify for the prime interest rate."

"Trouble is, I'm not shopping."

"Have you ever shopped?"

"Mr. Gallagher, I'm not in the mood for one of those coy little conversations where we talk about shopping but what we're really talking about is relationships. If you wanna know, yes, I've shopped before. Returned my purchases. All I got back were bad memories."

"Sorry."

Her bitterness vapored off. "Look, I'm sorry, too. I didn't mean to make you so nervous. It was just an accident."

"I'm not nervous, ma'am." Gallagher shifted his weight between legs and repressed the desire to grab his crotch. "I gotta go." He hobbled past her. "Could you step out for a sec? If I know you're listening. . . ."

"Okay. And hey. Thanks for the . . . just thanks."

HAB ONE SITE
NEAR ARES VALLIS, MARS
MISSION TIME: DAY 182

"You ever accidentally walk in on a woman while she was getting out of the shower?" Gallagher asked Burchenal.

"How I met my third wife." The scientist held gloveless hands close to the fire. "I was at a convention in Seattle. My buddy gave me his room key, told me to wait for him there. Forgot to tell me that his girlfriend was also there. I go in. She's in the bathroom, hears me come in. Calls out my buddy's name. I think about answering, but I know my buddy's taste in women, and I already know I'm a pig and figure I'll cop a quick look. So I go in. And she's in there. She's finished the shower. Her hair's all done up. Makeup on. High heels. And nothing else. You wanna talk tan lines? Jesus Christ . . ."

"She kick you out?"

"Oh, yeah. She had those heels on. Used 'em. But as crazy as it sounds, we shared something in that moment, a kind of weird intimacy. A month later it brought us back together. Why do you ask?"

"I don't know. Just thinking . . ."

"How long can that drone stay up there?" groaned Pettengill, his gaze skyward.

"Until AMEE's cell runs out—a couple years from now." Gallagher tossed a look over to Hab. "Still driving me nuts what happened here. Could a dust storm have done this? That might account for a lot of missing stuff."

Burchenal used a thin, titanium rod to poke at the fire. "Hab was built to withstand them. Winds get up to a hundred kilometers per hour. Vents were designed to automatically purge dust." He swore at the fire. "There's so little oh-two. It's gonna burn slow."

"Feels hot to me," said Pettengill.

Though Burchenal had not mentioned it to Gallagher, his expression clearly conveyed his mistrust of the terraformer. "Had to be hard watching Santen jump. After trying to stop him and all."

Gallagher watched Pettengill's face for a reaction. "All bullies are cowards in the end," the terraformer said impassively.

"And what are cowards in the end?" Burchenal asked. "Bullies?"

"No. Victims."

Faint at first, barely conspicuous above the occasional crackle of the fire, a scraping and crunching sound birthed from the darkness. Rocks tumbled, and the unmistakable whine of servos finally resounded.

Gallagher whistled. And as his whistle reverberated toward the hills, AMEE whistled back. A few seconds later, the bot shifted into the dim firelight, her frame coated with dust, one of her legs dangling uselessly. "AMEE, way to get here, cutie." Gallagher switched on his suit's light and examined the robot as her drone buzzed by. "How you doing? Kind of banged up, huh? Why'd you tell me your nanotech repair crew was off-line? You didn't lie to me, did you? Nah. Guess we're all pretty messed up. Just good to see you."

As Gallagher examined her damaged limb, she suddenly recoiled and hunkered down like a wild cat ready to spring. "Whoa. Take it easy. You seem a little outta whack."

"I don't like this damned thing," said Pettengill. "And unless we can find a use for it, I say we lose it."

"What's wrong with her?" Burchenal asked.

"Don't know." Gallagher crouched beside the bot and began a diagnostic with his wrist control. "Let's check out your insides. Roll over, sweets."

AMEE complied, hitting the dirt with a slight *clunk* and extending her limbs in the air like a metallic dog begging to have her tummy rubbed. Gallagher keyed open the small, octagonal service panel and shined his light deep into AMEE's innards. He spotted the burned out chips that accounted for her broken limb. He aimed the light at her CPU and IDed three more scorched chips and a number of frayed wires, though her bus and e-source appeared intact. "She got whacked pretty good. See evidence of flare emissions. Some chips wasted. Nanotech did what it could, but her systems are still damaged."

Burchenal squatted for a look himself. "Can we still use her?"

"Until she breaks down for good."

"We wait till she breaks down, that drone'll crash," Burchenal concluded, cocking a thumb skyward. "And with my luck, it'll drop on me like pigeon shit. Let's take out her MPS system now."

AMEE's legs twitched.

Gallagher consulted the wrist panel, which now displayed the results of the diagnostic: damage to CPU and AI central processors. He pouted at the results, then regarded Burchenal. "Her hard drive's modular. It's self-powered. We could run it through an HHC." He gestured to the sky. "We'd have command of the drone then. But that'd be killing her."

AMEE's legs twitched more violently.

"What do you want me to do?" Burchenal asked.

With a deep sigh of resignation, Gallagher shook his head. "I'll do it." He opened a second panel just below the first and reached in to unclip the bindings on a thin, silver box the size of a business card. He released the first binding, felt a terrific blow to his chest, and suddenly found himself hurling through the air.

Even as Gallagher fell, AMEE's hind legs telescoped out, her claws elongated, and she seized Pettengill's waist. The terraformer shrieked through a curse and gripped AMEE's talons, trying to pry them off. No good. He wailed again. The bot increased her grip. "She's gonna squeeze me to—"

AMEE threw Pettengill, his words wrenched off as he tumbled through the air, then smashed supine to the ground with a half-strangled cry.

Burchenal reflexively lifted his palms, but as he straightened, AMEE cuffed his wrist. Twisted. Burchenal cried out as his legs went flaccid and his free hand darted to the talon. AMEE dropped him like a martial artist, maintained her grip, and held him there, drawing back her free leg to deliver a death blow.

Gallagher frantically pulled up the powerdown menu, set off the sequence. SYSTEM ERROR. *Shit!* "AMEE, stop!"

With sensors either damaged or muted, AMEE rolled over, dragging Burchenal as she did so. "Get it the hell off," the scientist begged, his face a mask of torture.

"AMEE, no!" Gallagher ordered, a last ditch effort before he would grab the titanium rod Burchenal had used to poke the fire.

The bot ceased activity. Legs locked. Servos hummed down, giving way to a faint clicking from somewhere within her bowels.

"She's loosening her grip," Burchenal reported. "I can almost get my hand—"

AMEE drove her free leg into Burchenal's chest, her talon shrinking to the size of a human hand. She dug into his suit, found a rib, and turned it. Gallagher thought he heard the bone snap as Burchenal made noises that only the damned would find familiar.

Then, with the unaffected grace that reflected her programming, AMEE discarded the damaged rag doll called Burchenal, then scampered off, a nightmarish bug fleeing the campfire's light.

After a few surreal strides, Gallagher reached Burchenal, who lay supine, gripping his chest, and flinched with every meager breath. Tears of intense pain clogged his eyes.

"What the hell's going on?" Pettengill asked from somewhere behind them, his voice thin as a reed and shaking in the breeze.

"Get over here," Gallagher shouted. "Let's get him near the fire."

fifteen

HAB ONE SITE
NEAR ARES VALLIS, MARS
MISSION TIME: DAY 183

Burchenal swore to the midnight Martian sky as Gallagher and Pettengill lifted the scientist and carried him to the fire. AMEE's drone hummed over them like a menacing sentinel, noting their every move. They found a level spot near the flames, and Gallagher winced in sympathetic pain as they lowered Burchenal to the ground.

"That's good," the scientist whispered. "Right there. Yeah, right there."

"Why she'd turn on us?" asked Pettengill, ever wary of the hills toward which AMEE had retreated.

"Crash must've flipped her into military mode. We tried to take her eyes. That made us the enemy."

"Great. Now we got a bot on a Green Beret mission. That's number three on the list of ways we'll die. Guess she would've greased us already if it weren't for the lower G's. She'll account for that during her next attack."

Dismissing the prophet, Gallagher opened Burchenal's environment suit down to his waist, then unzipped the thermal suit beneath. He delicately touched the red, swelling band on Burchenal's chest. The man bit back a scream. "Triage comp's at the MEV site, but there's obvious signs of local tenderness, deformity, and crepitation," Gallagher said, hearing the scrape of the broken rib as he touched it.

"Tell me something I don't know," Burchenal managed. "Hurts when I breathe, so I don't breathe deeply and I suffer atelectasis or alveolar collapse. I wanna sigh to relieve this, but the pain won't let me, so my respiration sucks. If I don't heal right, I'll get pneumonia or a respiratory infection."

Gallagher smiled weakly, awed by the man's quick and accurate prognosis. "Guess you paid attention in paramedic class."

"Yeah. And this isn't the first time I've broken a rib. At least it's just one. That bitch could've given me a flail chest, then I'd really be screwed. She could've also broken my wrist. Damn burn still hurts, though."

"Get me some of that leftover foam," Gallagher told Pettengill. "And something to secure it to his chest."

"On it." Pettengill glanced over his shoulder, then slipped around the fire.

Burchenal closed his eyes and shook a little as he waged a counterassault on his pain. Gallagher leered in AMEE's direction for a few moments, then Pettengill arrived with the foam and several long strips of canvas he had cut from an undamaged sheet. Gallagher lifted Burchenal, while Pettengill slid the strips under the man's back. That finished, Gallagher tied the foam tightly in place as Burchenal's eyes narrowed to slits, and he bore his teeth. Gallagher zipped up the man's thermal suit, sealed the e-suit, and responded to Burchenal's motioning that he wanted to sit up. The act brought on a fresh round of groaning.

In the meantime, Pettengill fetched Burchenal's fire pole and beat it into an open palm. "Next time, I don't go down without a fight. We should all carry something."

Gallagher nodded resignedly.

"So why'd she let us live?" asked Burchenal. "She had us."

"Yeah, I guess so," Pettengill chipped in. "Maybe she did account for the lower gravity. You can't override her?"

"I tried," Gallagher told them. "She won't respond. And our problem's much bigger than a simple malfunction."

"I wouldn't call trying to kill us a simple malfunction," Pettengill snapped.

"Yeah, whatever." Gallagher matched the terraformer's tone. "Fact is, she's playing war games."

Pettengill opened his mouth, then shambled away from the fire. "You're fuckin' kidding."

"She's running her military codes," Gallagher went on, his gaze now falling on Burchenal. "Breaking your rib a version of an old Viet Cong trick. Wound one of the enemy. The others help him, and it slows them down."

"Well, it won't slow us down," Burchenal promised. "I've been skiing with a broken rib. And I sure as shit can take a little hike with one."

"I believe you. But sooner or later AMEE's gonna play search and destroy. And then she'll come and kill us."

UNITED STATES SPACECRAFT *MEDEA ONE*
MARS ORBIT
MISSION TIME: DAY 183

Bowman awoke. Lifted her head. Felt the chill surge. Shit. She had fallen asleep on her touchboard. Not since her college days had she done something like that. She felt the board's touchpads still pressed into her cheek.

How long had she been out? Nearly an hour. She had set the comm to record all incoming transmission. Checked it. None. *C'mon, guys. Where are you?*

Nothing to do but kill more time. Wait. Run the scenarios again. Maybe she had neglected something. She rubbed her eyes and began.

By the time she reached number twenty, her headset beeped, followed by the welcoming tones of John Skavlem, who made his transmission countdown, then cut right to the chase. "*Medea One*, Houston. Revised engine scenario uploading now. Suggest you lockout all primaries and attempt snap-fire ignition."

"And Kate?" another man broke in, "we're all pulling for you." Flight Director Matthew Russert's infectious smile, sensitivity, and eternal patience had always inspired Bowman. He paused, and Bowman imagined him choking up. "Truth is, there's no one else I'd rather have in that seat. And standby. There's someone else who wants to talk to you."

Bowman frowned. Panicked. No, it couldn't be her ex-boyfriend.

"Commander Bowman?" came a musical voice tinged with a South Carolina accent. "This is Joan Calhoun. I'd like to take this opportunity to say that the hopes and prayers of the American people are with you. Every eye is turned up to that red planet, and every heart wishes you a safe return home. God rest the souls of your fellow astronauts. God keep them forever."

Although Bowman had previously met the president of the United States, the honor of being directly addressed felt no less stunning. And to think that all over the country, all over the globe, people hoped and prayed that the farthest woman from home would return.

"*Medea One*, Houston," said the capcom. "Please advise on revised scenario. End of transmission. Houston, out."

Freshly inspired, Bowman set about decompressing the revised scenario. Once she had the program in place and the primary propulsion systems locked out, she checked a data bar: secondary systems ready for simulated snap-fire ignition. The engine ignition indicator flashed red. She tapped a button. Program executed. Red light . . . red. . . . Green.

She whooped. Cupped her face in her hands. Tried not to cry tears of joy, of pain, as she glimpsed the planet. "Houston, *Medea One*. Engine ignition is green. Repeat, I am go for engine ignition." She read the data bar marked orbital decay and made a decision that could end her career. "But guys, we still have some time on the clock. I know we've assumed End Of Mission for ground crew, but I won't give up the search. Not yet. I'll try again at daybreak. If there's still no contact, I'll initiate the sequence for Earth return. *Medea One*, out."

HAB ONE SITE
NEAR ARES VALLIS, MARS
MISSION TIME: DAY 183

"Gentlemen, welcome to mission day one-eighty-three, Sol Two on planet," Burchenal grumbled. "And oh, yeah. Morning."

Sunrise nicked the corners of the horizon, and in that poor light Gallagher sat, rolled back his hood, and forced a deep, cold breath.

They had divided the night into three watches, each of about two and a half hours. Pettengill had taken first, Gallagher second, and Burchenal had felt well enough to take third, though Gallagher had volunteered to stay awake.

Somewhere out there, under the tenuous, blue ice clouds that had amassed in the night, AMEE lurked, interpreting her scout's data flow and calculating her next assault.

Gallagher activated his wrist pad and selected for AMEEvision. Static. A diagnostic reported all systems nominal. *She wouldn't be intentionally jamming me, would she?* He shrugged off the thought and stood, more pressing business guiding him away from the smoldering fire toward a trio of knee-high boulders. AMEE's drone tracked him and descended to about three or four meters. "Yeah, well, screw you," he told the sentinel. "I'm taking the first piss on Mars."

After deactivating the suit's catheter and vowing not to use it again, Gallagher opened his e-suit, undid the thermal, and shivered as icy air struck bare flesh.

Burchenal found his own spot near another throng of stones, and after a few moments his quavering voice pierced the wind's faint howl. "Damn. You sure get some arc in this low gravity."

"How you feeling?"

"Still hurts when I breathe. Don't remember if I thanked you for the help."

"Yeah, well now I'm going back and trying to remember everything from those classes," Gallagher revealed. "I went into them with that it'll-never-happen-to-us attitude. Well, it happened."

"And then some," added Burchenal. "Sun's breaking. Let's haul ass to *Sojourner.*"

Gallagher zipped up and gestured to Pettengill, who lay near the embers, crunched up in a fetal position and clutching the titanium pole. "What about him?"

"I don't see Santen throwing himself off any cliffs," Burchenal said. He sealed his suit, then stared gravely at Pettengill. "Trained with him. And he went through the same psych exams and interviews we did. But you take a man with the usual hang-ups we all have, you put him in a place like this, and you tell him he's about to die. He might just crack. I don't care what they say. There's no way to test for something like this. We'd better watch him."

No doubt Gallagher would comply. He scuffled back to the terraformer and nudged the man's leg with his boot. "Pettengill."

"Shit," cried Burchenal.

Gallagher thought his heart had skipped as he swung to face the scientist.

"My HHC's down," Burchenal said, holding the computer.

A quick check of Gallagher's own handheld confirmed the same.

"Mine's out, too," reported Pettengill, who had sat up and spoken through a heavy yawn.

"Tried to pull up AMEE on my screen. Thought she might be jamming me. She must be jamming everything."

Pettengill slammed his computer on his hip. "Jesus, how do we find *Sojourner* now?"

"Best guess," Gallagher answered. "We can follow the ridge line, maybe spot it from high up. We know the distance and general direction."

With an arm draped across his ribs, Burchenal hurried to the wreckage and withdrew one of the titanium crossbars. "Get your pole," he told Pettengill. "And run. Toward the sun."

"Why?"

"Do it."

After a huff, Pettengill obeyed, jogging slowly at first, then evolving into a sprint toward the rising sun.

Burchenal fetched another crossbar and jammed it into the soil nearby. "Stop!" he directed the terraformer. "Left. Left. Little more. Right. There. Mark it."

Pettengill drove in the crossbar, checked its stability, then loped back. "What'd we do?"

Gallagher grinned his approval. "Built a directional."

"Now we know where something is," Burchenal said, his eyes vague as he considered something else. "We've marked the ecliptic. Now we calculate the basic trig. And we'll make the rest of this crap good for something. Come on."

Under Burchenal's guidance, they laid out a triangle of scavenged wires and poles, one side running parallel to the directional, the other pointing east toward the pock-marked uplands.

After taking a last sighting, Burchenal gazed uneasily

at Gallagher. "Well, this one *is* about the math. Let's see if mine's any good."

A shadow wiped over them, and Gallagher palmed away the glare. AMEE's drone glinted about ten meters off. "All right, campers, we go. But remember, AMEE'll be using guerilla tactics. She'll pick off any easy prey. Don't fall behind."

sixteen

Resolution came to within thirty meters through the scope, and Bowman considered firing maneuvering thrusters to adjust her oblique orbit and gain better pictures, but she needed every ounce of liquid hydrogen to get home. She slumped in her chair, battling a vacuum inside, a sense that she had somehow still failed. Indistinct images of the MEV crash site scrolled on the main viewer and underscored that failure. Bowman just sat there, an empty shell, waiting minute after minute until the Hab wreckage finally reached the upper corner of her screen. Nothing new to see. Just another cold tomb rearing up in the wind.

Something caught her eye, a faint outline that seemed unnatural against the meandering troughs and channels. She worked the board. Locked on the site. Brought it into as much focus as possible. It looked like . . . no, it couldn't be.

What am I doing. I'm just wanting to believe too damned much. They're gone. And I'm sure I'll be asked to speak at their funerals:

Ted Santen represented the best interests of not only the space program, but of the American people.

Quinn Burchenal's exhaustive research will help us continue our quest to create a new home for humanity.

Chip Pettengill not only represented the best of the best in his field, but he never lost touch with his soul.

Bud Chantilas's aspirations took him to places few humans dare to travel, and those journeys make him one of the twenty-first century's greatest Renaissance men.

And Robert Gallagher. I wish . . . I just wish. . . .

She dragged herself up and went to the scope, her finger poised over the pad. A tap. No more reason to hope. All the reason to hurt. She went to her touchboard, opened a channel. "Houston, *Medea One*." She paused, braced herself. "No sign of ground crew. Initiating Earth return sequence. Main engine burn in T-minus ninety minutes. Mark. *Medea One*, out."

MARS *PATHFINDER* LANDING SITE
ARES VALLIS FLOOD CHANNEL
MISSION TIME: DAY 183

Though AMEE's drone had tailed them during the entire two kilometers, the warring bot herself had not made an appearance. Her absence had gnawed at Pettengill, whose paranoia kept his teeth gritted and his head shifting so much that Gallagher swore the man would pull a muscle. Burchenal kept to himself during the entire march, issuing neither word nor groan. He even kept the

excruciation out of his expression. Like Santen, he
needed very much to have answers and be in control, and
at the moment, Gallagher would wholeheartedly ride the
coattails of his determination, a determination that had
led them directly to the landing site.

They stood marveling at the dust-laden *Pathfinder*,
then Burchenal gave them a thirty second walking tour.

Three solar panels, circular with their tops squared off,
lay flat on the soil, attached via hinges to the lander's
hexagonal base. A small instrument electronics assembly
designed not unlike a miniature Quonset hut sat at the
base's center; served as home to the unit's accelerometers,
which helped calculate its entry; and supported a thin,
straight low-gain antenna, a camera mounted on a fold-
ing square tower, and a disk-shaped high-gain antenna.
At the top of one solar panel rose the lander's Atmospheric Structure Instrument and Meteorology Package: a
pole with a cylindrical wind sensor mounted on its tip.
Below that sensor hung windsocks attached between
thermocouples to measure temperature.

"They only thought they'd get a month out of this
baby," Burchenal said, "Remarkable feat of engineering,
given their budget. She paved the way for new exploration technology and for our very own terraforming program. All right, they made a few mistakes over the
years—forgot to use the metric system during one mission and lost a one hundred twenty-five million-dollar
probe—but they did all right. Now, where the hell's that
rover?"

"Over there," Pettengill said, pointing at a boulder
about nine meters away that Gallagher knew had a funky
name like "Moe" or "Wedge" or "Chimp." Two of *Sojourner*'s six wheels strayed from beyond the rock.

Gallagher withdrew a tool pack from his suit's hip

pocket as he rushed to the little rover, the shadow of AMEE's drone leading the way. When he got there, he saw that the rover had driven up over a smaller rock, had probably received a traverse error, and had sat where it was for half a century. "Sorry about this," he told the little machine, then withdrew his tools. He power-screwed off the solar panel that gave the rover its flat, skateboard-like top, then thought he might need to disassemble part of the rocker-bogie mobility system, a sophisticated suspension assembly whose pieces seemed borrowed from a kid's erector set. No, he already had access to the digital and analog circuit boards, the zero point five watt heater, and the rest of the rover's rectangular chassis. "Get the panels off that electronics assembly," Gallagher called back to the others near the lander. "Everything around the aerials. Should be a UHF radio in there, powered by a twenty-eight volt source. And look what we have here," he began, eyeing the rover's internals. "It's a fifty-three-year-old, off-the-shelf UHF computer radio modem relying on frequencies we're not using for this mission."

"Then why are we trying?" asked Pettengill. "I mean this place . . . we're defacing it. It's a memorial to Carl Sagan. Didn't they call it the Sagan Memorial Station?"

"It's gonna be the Pettengill Memorial Station if you don't shut up," Burchenal barked.

"We gotta do this," Gallagher urged, his tone far more diplomatic than Burchenal's but still trenchant. "It's slightly more sophisticated than shouting for help."

Even as Gallagher removed the rover's circuit boards, the rest of the radio's assembly came to him in an surge of inspiration he thought was reserved for poets. He would use the lander as the power source and/or utilize its UHF radio modem if the rover's failed. Of course, he would need help angling the solar panels, and he would have to adjust the system to handle voice transmissions; it had been programmed to transmit short bursts of digital symbols called packets, each consisting of two thousand eight-bit bytes. If he managed that small feat, he could wire up the microphone in his suit. Hell, a bit of old-fashioned soldering, and the damned thing might work.

Then came the hard part: reaching someone who might be monitoring the frequency. Deep Space Network might have their dishes pointed his way, and thousands of geeks back home still kept the SETI project alive. There had to be someone somewhere listening.

Twenty minutes and two burned index fingers later, Gallagher had to his own mild astonishment cobbled together a contraption that could be mistaken for a radio. He had even borrowed an LED light from his HHC so that he could monitor power and signal strength. He sat cross-legged near the lander, the rover's circuit boards wired together and lying across his lap, mike held to his lips. "Testing . . . testing . . ." Nothing on the LED. He adjusted a tiny potentiometer near the modem. "Testing . . . testing . . ." Now the LED brightened and dimmed as he spoke.

"Does it work?" cried Burchenal as he and Pettengill tilted the lander's solar panels toward the sun.

Gallagher lowered the mike. "The little green thing lights up. We'll know it works if someone calls back. But we got a lot working against us. See, as the modem's temperature gets warmer, the transmit and receive frequencies increase. As it gets colder, the frequencies drop. We're operating at center frequency now, but that could change. Other thing is, our high-gain antenna back there needs to look horizontally three-hundred and sixty degrees, so rocky structures and ground reflections can cause null zones that screw up reception."

"Yeah, but think about it, Gallagher. We're dialing long distance, and we ain't payin' a dime." Burchenal winked.

Gallagher took a deep breath and crossed mental fingers. "*Medea One*, ground crew. Come back? *Medea One*, ground crew. Do you copy? If anyone's listening, please respond."

MEDEA ONE MISSION CONTROL
JOHNSON SPACE CENTER, HOUSTON
MISSION TIME: DAY 183

"What do you got for me, Cap?" Russert asked, nearly leaping over his desk to get to John Skavlem's station.

"Guy in Australia claims he picked up a signal from our ground crew."

Russert swore away the false alarm. "What's it gonna take to get rid of these nuts? You tell him we're using restricted, encrypted frequencies? He'll do time for this."

"No, he's legit. Part of DSN. We still have all those radio telescopes pointed at Mars. Maybe this guy heard something. He's still on. I'll route him to you."

Russert slid on his headset. "Hello, this is Flight Director Matthew Russert."

"Right, good to hear," the man said. "This is Hank Osterbee in Canberra. Deep Space Network, mate. About ten minutes ago, I intercepted a signal from your ground crew. Four hundred and fifty-nine point seven megahertz. Recorded it, if you'd like to listen."

"Go ahead."

Five seconds into the recording, Russert pulled

Skavlem away from his desk. "Time on Bowman's main engine burn?"

Skavlem referred to his monocle. "T-minus twenty-two minutes, fifty-one seconds."

"Shit, we got a two minute window to stop her. Hank? You copy?"

"Here, mate. What do you think of the—"

"Hank, we're in comm blackout right now, but you're not. I need you to contact Commander Bowman aboard *Medea One*. Our capcom'll upload our freq. Tell her to abort main engine burn and contact the surface immediately. You give her that frequency. You do it now."

UNITED STATES SPACECRAFT *MEDEA ONE*
MARS ORBIT
MISSION TIME: DAY 183

T-minus one minute and forty seconds. Engine ignition indicator still in the green.

I'm going home.

Bowman strapped herself into the pilot's chair. Mars, in all of its bleeding fury, lay below. Her awe for the planet died a few moments ago. Father Mars had punished them, and it felt good to get out of his sight.

But the voyage home. God, it would be the longest ride of her life.

The communications data bar lit up: incoming transmission.

"What?" She piped it through her speakers.

"Commander Bowman, this is Hank Osterbee in Canberra, Australia. Deep Space Network. Flight Director Russert instructs you to abort main engine burn. Seems I've picked up an urgent call for you—from the surface of Mars."

Bowman began to laugh as he told her the frequency, then the tears burned through. She sniffled and began the abort sequence, and damn it she would have to play back the message for that frequency. She chuckled again, wondering if she hadn't fallen asleep in the chair and awoken in the middle of a hopeful dream. After all, how could anyone still be alive? How could anyone have survived without a miracle?

MARS *PATHFINDER* LANDING SITE
ARES VALLIS FLOOD CHANNEL
MISSION TIME: DAY 183

"Come on, you piece of shit."

"You've been swearing at it for what, nearly an hour now?" Burchenal asked Gallagher.

"Yeah, long enough for our signal to reach Earth and for someone to send a reply," Pettengill interjected. "Only no one's responding. 'Cause no one's fuckin' listening! 'Cause we're using a glorified walkie-talkie, for God's sake!"

"Know what? You're right," Gallagher said, his voice coming in a growl. "Well, it was worth a shot." He rose, held the circuit boards in one hand, and wound up for the pitch—

"Ground crew, *Medea One*. Gallagher?"

He barely caught the boards before they tumbled to the rocks. His hand shook as he jammed the microphone to his mouth. "Bowman?"

"You're alive?"

"Ha!" Gallagher cried, gaping at his comrades. "It worked! It fuckin' worked! And she made it, too. Bowman, you there?"

"Who's with you? What's your situation?"

"I'm at the *Pathfinder* site in Ares Vallis. Pettengill and Burchenal are here, too. No food, no water. AMEE's gone mustang. But there's oxygen down here."

She paused, probably blown away by the statement. "How's that possible?"

"Don't know. And Commander? Bud and Santen didn't make it. We lost Bud near the MEV."

"I saw a body there."

"Yeah. I'll give you the details later. Right now, we gotta get some help. We won't last much longer down here. Burchenal has a broken rib. We're all getting dehydrated. And I don't know what we'll do tonight. Our suit torches are rated for about an hour. That's it. We burned debris from Hab last night to keep warm, but there's nothing left."

"Let me get with Houston. We'll work on it. I'll get back to you."

"We'll be here. And the next time you try to contact us, account for a five kilohertz frequency shift—just in case."

"Five kilohertz. Got it. I don't know how you did it. But way to go. *Medea One*, out."

Burchenal swung an arm over Gallagher's shoulder. "With my math and your space janitorial skills, we could go places."

Gallagher raised a brow. "Warm places, I hope."

seventeen

Cheers and rounds of applause thundered through the ficker as Commander Kate Bowman informed the group of controllers that three of the five ground crew had survived.

Flight Director Russert gripped the back of John Skavlem's chair and hollered his own cry of relief, despite having listened to the message before routing it to the intercom.

The jubilation fell into whispers, though, as Bowman added, "Ground crew reports breathable atmosphere. Source unknown. Repeat. Ground crew reports breathable atmosphere. Houston, we need scenarios for getting them off planet ASAP. Please advise. *Medea One*, out."

"If they can breathe, can we live there?" asked Skavlem.

"No," Lowenthal answered, swiveling his chair to face them. "Ninety percent of the algae's gone. It's some kind of freak anomaly. Mars is a dying planet. Just like Earth."

"Freak anomaly or not, those people are breathing," Russert said. "Dammit, maybe somehow it did work."

Lowenthal's voice sobered. "Well it doesn't matter. They'll die come nightfall. Bowman said they built a fire the first night. Can't do that again. They have nothing left to burn but their torches, and their thermal batteries are already dead. Those suits were designed to get them from MEV to Hab, not to spend an extended period on the surface. The real activity suits were at Hab."

Russert gazed thoughtfully at the controller. "Couldn't they sleep now and keep moving all night?"

"They could try. But she said Burchenal's got a broken rib. He'll hold them back. If they stop moving, they'll die. Maybe they could find shelter, but how will they keep it warm?"

"And while we're here trying to figure that out, Bowman's orbit is decaying. We need to buy her more time."

"We analyzed Bowman's recordings," Lowenthal began, his expression growing more dour. "The MEV is trashed. We're talking beyond repair because everything they'd need to repair it was at Hab. There's no way to get the ground crew off planet. They'll freeze tonight. Now, Flight, we can get a free return trajectory right now. Bowman's got enough fuel, food, and water to get her home. This isn't what you wanna hear, but if we waste time on a lost cause, we could lose her, too."

"You're right, Andy, that's not what I wanna hear. You've always been my voice of reason, but we got an unreasonable circumstance that requires unreasonable solutions. Now PROP? GNC?" Russert called into his headset. "I want your teams working on scenarios to buy Bowman more time in orbit." He narrowed his eyes on Lowenthal. "What does our ground crew have, eight or nine hours of daylight left? I want everybody on this. Everybody. There has to be a way." Russert started down a long row of desks, about to consult with Ms. Mod, who had twice asked to speak with him in the past fifteen minutes. But an idea had him whirling back. "What else is on Mars?"

Lowenthal shrugged. "Rocks? Sand?"

"Come on, Andy. Gallagher just built a radio out of a fifty-three-year-old rover mission. What else is up there?"

The science officer returned to his desk, issued commands into his headset, then Russert's PIM snapped on to show a relief map of the region, glowing letters spelling out CHRYSE PLANITIA in the west, while other labels identified Wahoo, Yuty, Shawnee, Bled, and other craters north of Ares Vallis. Four red blips pinpointed the landing sites of previous missions.

"Well, I found our terraformer scouts," Lowenthal said. "Just more junk there. Nothing flammable."

More craters, chaotic terrain, valleys, and ridged plains shifted into focus as Lowenthal zoomed out.

"Got the old *Viking One* at eighteen hundred and fifteen klicks from *Pathfinder.* And we're still out of business."

"Andy?" Russert cried. "Slap your forehead."

"Why?"

"Because we're not the only country with an interest in Mars."

"Right . . ." Lowenthal rattled off three more commands, and a series of color-coded overlays rose out of the map. "Okay, got everybody on there, but most of the stuff in that grid was sent up during the twenties. Basic sample return missions. Everyone wanted to bring back a bucket of Mars rocks. I'm looking at that Euro-Malaysian sample return mission of twenty-eighteen. See it? It's about a quarter klick from Hab. And nope . . . looks like it blew up on attempted return. Just a whole lot of garbage waiting to be picked up."

Russert ordered his own monocle to zoom in on another site about one hundred kilometers north-northeast of *Pathfinder*, up near McLaughlin Crater. He called up and skimmed the report. "Hey, Andy? It's not close, but there's an Uzbecki SRM that failed to launch."

"See it. Probe called *Cosmos*. Would've launched in twenty-two. It's got a sizable payload container."

"Is it viable? Can we get plans?"

"Checking. It was built at none other than the Cosmos factory in Gagarin in twenty-one. The factory closed eight years later. Then it burned down."

"Well that's that," Russert said. "What else do we got? Come on . . ."

"Wait a minute. That SRM was designed by Alexander Ivanovich Borokovski. He was the last of the greats in the Russian space program."

"He still alive?"

"Running through our database now. There's no closing data on his bio. He'd be in his seventies."

"Get a line to Kazakhstan. Find him. Or his obituary."

"You got it, Flight. Course you know this is insanity. A thirty-year-old lander built in a factory that doesn't exist anymore, a lander designed by a man who's probably dead."

"Wouldn't call it insane," Russert said. "More like unreasonable."

"Holy. . . . Oh, this is nuts." Lowenthal threw his head back, dumbfounded. "Ran a local search for the hell of it. Borokovski's alive, all right. Emigrated. He runs a deli in Brooklyn."

MARS *PATHFINDER* LANDING SITE
ARES VALLIS FLOOD CHANNEL
MISSION TIME: DAY 183

With only about five more minutes of patience left, Gallagher resigned himself to building a backup radio from leftover parts. At least the effort would distract him. He tinkered, occasionally lifting his face to the sun and whispering, "We've come this far. Don't let us die. Don't let us die." He tried to remember a story of survival that Bud had read to him, but the details would not come.

Ten meters ahead, Burchenal stalked the environs, inspecting boulders and rocks, his expression knotting a little tighter each time Gallagher regarded him. After twenty minutes of exploration, the scientist wandered back. "What could've removed the algae?"

"Someone else'll have to find out now," Pettengill answered from his perch atop a boulder. He crossed his legs, tapped his forehead with the titanium pole, then rocked to and fro, his eyes clouding over.

Gallagher forced his gaze away from the terraformer, but Burchenal offered an equally disturbing sight. The man stood there, mumbling to himself like the planet's first residentially challenged researcher. "Look at you," Gallagher told the man. "You hate not knowing, don't you?"

"Given time, believe me, I'll know."

"The universe might be full of surprises. Maybe this is one it doesn't want you to have."

Burchenal lowered himself gently to the ground, took a moment to steady himself against the pain, then his wince loosened into a smirk. "The universe, you say? You talking about God, too?"

"Maybe. Maybe God's trying to teach us a hard-assed lesson."

"God? You spent too much time with Chantilas. But hey, if you want to take the easy way out like the rest of the ignorant, the weak, and the hopeless. . . ."

Gallagher switched off his power tool. "The easy way?"

"Falling back on God to explain things. It works. It's weak. Why not just confront your own mortality? Confront the unknown?"

"I bet you don't believe in Santa. And you're no fun at Christmas," Gallagher teased to no avail. "Y'know, not everything has an explanation or a formula."

"Mr. Gallagher, I'm a bioengineer and a geneticist. I write code. Just like a hacker. Four elements: A, G, T, P, in different combinations. I hack the genome. I choose what, I choose where, and your kidneys work or you grow a sixth finger. I line up unconscious atoms, and they give rise to conscious beings. It's like I stack up a bunch of rocks in the right order, and they became a dog. *I do that.* And I just don't hold with mystical explanations for science, with organized religion, with theories like the Bible code. You spot God, you let me know. Till then, I'll trust my Ph.D.s."

Gallagher looked in Pettengill's direction. "Thought *he* was the pessimist."

"Hey, don't get me wrong," Burchenal said. "I think life's an amazing thing. You have to seize it with both hands and live it large—which is why I'm not happy about maybe spending my last hours on this ugly planet."

Whether he appeared as rueful as he felt, Gallagher was not sure. After a moment or two, he returned to his work as Burchenal closed his eyes and worshipped the scientific processes of the sun.

MEDEA ONE MISSION CONTROL
JOHNSON SPACE CENTER, HOUSTON
MISSION TIME: DAY 183

Russert read his watch. Bit his lip. Checked the time again. "Has he even landed yet, John?"

Skavlem winked into his PIM. "Landed on the grounds. Pilots from Fort Hamilton conferring with MOD right now. They say he's a little shaky and a lot pissed off. New York to Houston in two hours? I'd be shaky and pissed, too."

"Ten minutes to coax him. Nearly an hour till he was airborne . . . damn, this had better be worth those three hours."

"It *has* to be," Lowenthal called from his desk. "Because this is it. There's nothing else up there those guys can reach in time. And this old man better have a good memory."

"There he is," Skavlem said.

Alexander Ivanovich Borokovski marched through the doorway and ripped off his rebreather with a vengeance. A shock of snowy hair fell in the bearded man's face as he spotted Russert, nodded curtly, then came forward, trailing his two flunky escorts. Unabashed, the old Russian had stuffed his six foot, two hundred sixty-five pound frame in a decades old, houndstooth check Versace suit two sizes too small and as wrinkled as the man.

After giving the ficker a quick once over, Borokovski finally paused a few steps away, eyeing Lowenthal, then Skavlem, then steadying his gaze on Russert. "All right. I am Borokovski. I am here."

Russert proffered a hand. "Doctor Borokovski, you don't know what a pleasure it is."

"For you, maybe. On airplane they try to give me peanuts. I hate peanuts."

"Sir, we promise we'll feed you anything you want. Caviar. You name it. Just tell us about *Cosmos*."

"I think about it on plane. We have problem. No one uses operating system anymore. They called it Win Twenty-twenty. This was back when you could actually own software and didn't have to rent it from satnet. I think maybe they have copy of software at Smithsonian Institution. Can you call?"

"John, let's get a hold of someone there. That doesn't work out, we check the satnet auctions. Somebody's gotta be cleaning out an attic. And we'll need a courier. I don't care if we gotta land a stealth jet in the parking lot, I wanna copy of that OS in my hands."

Borokovski hoisted a stubby index finger. "Also, I will need computer with one thousand megahertz processor, fifty gig hard drive, CD-ROM drive, and minimum two hundred fifty-six megabytes RAM."

Lowenthal stifled a laugh. "He might as well be asking for one of those old wireless phones or a DVD player."

"It was all state of the art in Kazakhstan," Borokovski argued. "I still have DVD player at home. Can't find disks. But I have player."

Russert leaned back to speak discreetly to Skavlem.

"John, if you get someone at the Smithsonian, see if you can't have 'em throw in a computer with that order."

"Yes, with computer and operating system, we can troubleshoot probe from here," Borokovski rasped. "Maybe reprogram launch sequence or ground crew can do so. No computer? No operating system? I go back to Brooklyn."

eighteen

"Think she's coming down to check it out," Pettengill cried from his worktable in the laboratory sphere.

Gallagher hightailed for the entrance—

And nearly ran head on into Bowman.

"Hi," he said.

"Hi."

He smiled coyly. "Hi."

"Hi." She pushed up on her toes, trying to see over his shoulder. "My flight deck instruments check out. Temp's still up in here. About three degrees."

"Uh, Fahrenheit or Centigrade?"

She saw right through his lame attempt to stall, blew past him, and stared slack-jawed at the assembly of glass tubing, Bunsen burners, and filtration tanks—a mad scientist's skyscraper towering over Burchenal and Pettengill.

"They're teaching me about biology," Gallagher said. "I've developed an interest in—"

"Fermentation? Billions of taxpayer dollars in this mission, and you're using lab equipment for a still? Didn't I see this on a rerun somewhere?"

"We're sterilizing it."

"Nice try."

Burchenal stepped from behind the iridescent conglomeration. "Commander? It's my fault. We were playing cards, and I was telling these gentlemen how much I miss a drink at the end of the day. You know, those damned hard-asses at Houston screwed up my routine."

"What's the fermentation base?"

He faced the still, awestruck, hamming it up. "Now there's where the real genius comes in. We're using freeze-dried taters."

She rolled her eyes. "Tell me, Mr. Burchenal, how do I explain to Houston that half of my crew has gone blind on moonshine vodka?"

"With well-chosen words?" asked Gallagher, wanting immediately to pull back his own poorly chosen words.

Unadulterated anger etched Bowman's face. For a second, Gallagher thought she might spin and wallop him.

Then she looked hurt. "What? This establishment doesn't serve women?"

"Why, it certainly does," Burchenal replied in a singsong. "And you're in luck. It's ladies' night. First drink's on the house." He fetched a cup and opened the tap.

Bowman accepted the drink, studied it, studied them, then tossed it back. *Woof!* Now the burn . . . but she held tight, her eyes growing only a tad reflective. "Making booze or jet gas?" she croaked, then swallowed once more to clear her voice. "How much have you made?"

"About three liters," Burchenal confessed.

"You're done. Dismantle this. Offer equal rations to all of us except for Santen. The captain doesn't drink or approve of those who do. Since he's on duty and on the Flight Deck, what he doesn't know won't hurt him." She spied her empty glass. "How much're you cutting this?"

"It's about seventy-five percent alcohol," Burchenal told her. "Can't believe you took it in one shot standing up."

"I learned to drink in the navy, boys." Bowman crossed to the still, poured herself another snootful, and raised her glass. "Anchors aweigh."

Fifteen minutes later, Gallagher, Chantilas, Bowman, and Burchenal lounged in the kitchen sphere, and Gallagher could not remember the last time he had copped such a decent buzz. He sipped slowly on his moonshine, body tingling, Bowman looking more and more radiant as she tossed her hair and brought her lips together on the rim of her glass.

"Can't figure out what went wrong on Mars," Burchenal was saying, bunching his words. "But we'll get there. And I'll fix it. Then humanity'll build burger franchises and breed like guppies and destroy that planet, too. Then we'll move on to Venus, and when it's gone that's really good-bye 'cause there aren't anymore friendly ones. We're buying another millennium, tops."

"Yeah, but maybe we've learned a lesson from what happened on Earth," Gallagher said.

"Nah. Man's a party animal. If we're doing okay, nothing else matters. Kill half the life. So what. Long as I still got women and booze and expensive toys. That's not gonna change."

A curious grin played over Chantilas's lips. "And what if life's more mysterious than you think, Mr. Burchenal?"

The drunken scientist reached for the beaker of moonshine. "If we're gonna talk God now, I need another pop."

"Not God," said Chantilas. "Faith."

"Faith?" Burchenal asked, then downed his pop. "Had a girlfriend named Faith. She cheated on me—with a girl named Chastity."

Even Chantilas could not contain his smile. "You rode into outer space in a rocket ship built by, as the old cliché goes, the lowest bidder. Nobody does that without a little faith."

"Can't argue with that."

"Works that way with life, too."

"You saying God's the lowest bidder?" Gallagher asked, trying to lighten the mood. He felt too good to be alienated by their oncoming philosophy.

"What I'm saying, Robby, is that we often have to surrender to things beyond our control. To do that and still keep moving forward requires that we believe in a good outcome."

"Gotta have hope, right?" asked Bowman.

"Hope's just a way of postponing disappointment," Burchenal said with a huff.

"Hope is the only way we can realize the very best in us," Chantilas countered. "Which, by the way, also happens to be a pretty good definition of God."

"Forget that for a moment," Burchenal hollered, miscalculating his volume. "I got an idea. Hell with humanity, all right? When we get to Mars, I say we take it over for ourselves."

"What?" Gallagher asked. "Radio back, say it sucks and don't bother coming?"

Burchenal bought that with a nod. "Whatever keeps out the riffraff. Then Chantilas here can handle the religion thing, and Gallagher can keep the space john working. We'll make Santen a cab driver, Pettengill the royal terraformer, and I'll handle pretty much everything else. Y'know . . . *king*."

"Yeah?" said Bowman. "And what about me?"

The king smiled drunkenly. "Propagation of the species."

Chantilas stood. "Okay. With that, I suggest we follow Pettengill off to bed."

"Think I'll take your suggestion," Burchenal said, squirming now under Bowman's heated stare.

Gallagher hung back, whispering inside for her to remain. Ever since their encounter in the hygiene sphere, she had carefully avoided being alone with him.

She didn't budge. Amazing.

"Heavy stuff," he said idly. "Smart people."

"Little too smart. But how 'bout you, Gallagher? Never heard you express your opinion. You ask a lot of questions, but they don't really say what you believe."

"Like Burchenal said, I'm just here to keep the toilets flushing. But actually, yes, I do have an opinion about something."

"Whoa." She raised a brow, set her elbows on the table, and stared intently at him. "Yes?"

"You should wear a bra."

She pushed away from the table, about to fold her arms over her chest. But curiously enough she abandoned that plan and just straightened, even arched her back a little. Then, with a sigh of exertion, she stood, waited for the breaker of alcohol to wash over, then staggered to the exit. "Bras are designed to support your breasts on Earth, where there's real gravity. We shift between micro and artificial a lot. Why would I need one here?"

He closed his eyes. "Because it's very distracting. But not as distracting as seeing you step out of the shower."

"Seems like that happened a lifetime ago. And you haven't said a word since. You've exercised incredible restraint."

"Thanks," he answered, loathing the compliment and getting to his feet.

"Of course, I've done my part. I make sure to lock the door now."

"Yeah, I know."

"You do?"

"Tried walking in on you by accident a dozen times since then," he said apologetically, held the somber look a few seconds more, then unhooked her with a broad grin.

She inched toward him. "You know, at first I thought you were—"

"Don't know if I wanna hear this."

"Well . . . you're not who I thought you were."

"That an insult or a compliment?"

"An observation."

Her azure-flecked eyes, the way she spoke to him in that wonderfully sexy contralto, and the dizzying musk of her perfume presented a potent invitation. To hell with social conventions. To hell with mission priorities. It was all about a moment. Two people just a breath away from each other. Two people who were—

Very drunk.

But that should not matter. He read the longing in her gaze. She obviously read his. A bead of sweat sluiced down his forehead. He lost his breath. Had trouble meeting her gaze. Wanted to reach up, stroke her cheek, home in for the kiss. *She's waiting for you. Come on. Yield.*

Bowman flushed, withdrew, then hurried into the access tube. "Good night," she called back softly.

Gallagher cursed himself, held up his palm, then made a fist. What had he done? She had been right there, *right there*. All right, she had been drunk, but she knew what she was doing. He didn't need to back off. Then why had he?

Had he folded under the pressure to succeed? Was he doing his father's work and punishing himself? Was he just scared of failing with her—or falling for her?

Either way, they had lost the moment, a moment they might never get back. And he had blown it. And this wasn't something you fixed with a wisecrack or a roll of duct tape.

MARS *PATHFINDER* LANDING SITE
ARES VALLIS FLOOD CHANNEL
MISSION TIME: DAY 183

Gallagher adjusted, tweaked, fiddled, and readjusted, but his backup radio would not function. At least it had served one purpose: distraction. He shoved the circuit boards aside, checked on the primary radio's system, then an echo and blur in the sky lured his attention.

Pettengill picked up another rock and hurled it toward AMEE's drone. He swore as the metal vulture veered effortlessly out of the way. He found another rock. Went for the strike. Missed again. Swore again. But now he had the drone banking away in retreat, and he fled after.

"Hey," Gallagher shouted. "AMEE's nearby. Don't get too far out there."

But the terraformer had already strayed out of earshot.

"Like I said, you take an average guy with normal hang-ups. You put him in a situation like this, and sometimes you get that," Burchenal said, tilting his head toward Pettengill.

"I don't trust him, but I still think he'll be all right," Gallagher answered. "He just hasn't figured out his defense mechanism yet."

"Why should he?"

"When I was up in McMurdo, the COB told me stories he'd heard from his brother. The guy was a marine. Fought down in Brazil during the forties. Buncha guys in his unit all had these little mechanisms to keep sane. One guy just turned the whole war into a paintball game. He refused to believe that people died. He even kept score."

"Yeah, kinda like me lookin' around and seeing this as that trip I took to Coober Pedy in Australia. Had to go out to the Woomera Rocket Range for research. We're not stuck on Mars. I'm just performing experiments right now."

"Exactly. And the COB's brother talked about this other guy who started collecting photographs off enemy bodies. He was piecing together this weird family tree, and he turned the whole war into this quest to get more photos. He fought like an animal; he fought harder than anyone in the squad, not because he wanted to kill the enemy. He just wanted their photos. He'd become a devout collector."

"Sorry, Gallagher, but I didn't bring along any photos of my ex-wives."

"No, but don't you see, we've already got our defense mechanisms. You keep busy trying to explain what happened here, and I play with radios. We have to give Pettengill something to do other than chasing AMEE's drone. He's on the edge. We gotta pull him back."

"We know why he's on edge—because he probably

threw someone over one. But if it'll help us, I'll try to get his mind focused on something else."

"Ground crew, *Medea One*," rattled Bowman's voice. "Gallagher?"

He scrambled for the mike. "Here. Go."

"I think we got something. But you should sit down for this. . . ."

nineteen

"So let me get this straight," Gallagher told Bowman. "We walk a hundred kilometers to a thirty-year-old Russian rock probe that failed to launch and try to jump-start it. Huh. Couldn't make it tough?"

"The probe's called *Cosmos,*" she went on, unfazed by his sarcasm. "Houston located the designer, guy named Borokovski, who, get this, now owns a deli in Brooklyn. Anyway, he's gonna try to reprogram the launch sequence. If he can't, he thinks I can help you do it on site."

"If not, maybe he can send up a couple salami-on-ryes," Burchenal scoffed. "And some of those garlic pickles."

"Listen. Here's the big thing. You got twenty-three hours to get there and get off the ground."

Gallagher's shoulders slumped. "I take back what I said about not making it tough."

"PROP and GNC have asked me to ditch B tank and burn more fuel from A tank, just to hold orbit that long. After that, the ship'll only have enough fuel to get home. Now, I'm looking at you through the scope, and I'm wondering why you're still standing there."

Gallagher hollered for Pettengill, then returned to the mike. "Which way we going?"

"North-northeast of your location. You're eleven. Turn a little more. There."

"This battery recharged?" asked Burchenal, leaning down to tap a knuckle on the cell.

"Think so. Silvered thermal blanket should help it hold the charge. But it usually uses internal heaters to maintain temperature, so it could die on us."

"I have work to do here," Bowman interrupted. "Then I'll be in comm blackout. Call you when I come back around."

"And don't panic if we don't answer," Gallagher assured her. "Could be ground clutter or our radio could die. That happens, just track us on the scope. And if the *Cosmos* has a radio, I'll see what I can do with it."

"Understand. Wish I could do more."

"Hey, it's something. And it's nice knowing you're still up there."

Nice? Gallagher had used that word in deference to Burchenal. Words like "relieved" and "overjoyed" felt more appropriate but might come out wrong and reveal his feelings for her.

"You know, I don't mind dying," she said. "But I hate the idea of being alone. Get your asses in gear. *Medea One*, out."

Gallagher tucked the microphone between the circuit boards, then hoisted the electronics box with the battery mounted inside. He held the radio in the crook of his arm, then shouted once more for Pettengill.

"Bastard. Maybe AMEE got him," Burchenal said.

A few seconds later, laughter echoed in the distance. More laughter. Then a figure sprinted into view. "I got it," Pettengill cried, a crazed lilt in his voice. "I got it. Hit that fuckin' drone dead on."

"No way," Gallagher challenged.

"I'm telling you," the terraformer said, fully winded in the thin air. "Threw it and bang! Got her. No damage, though."

Burchenal raised a twisted grin. "I'm happy for you. But we're moving out. I'll explain on the way. And you and me? We have a lot of work to do." The scientist lifted a brow at Gallagher.

MEDEA ONE MISSION CONTROL
JOHNSON SPACE CENTER, HOUSTON
MISSION TIME: DAY 183

It had taken nearly three hours for the package to arrive from the Smithsonian, and while Russert bemoaned every minute they had waited for it, he could not deny the air force's outstanding job of express delivery. The package had been whisked from D.C. by way of VTOL nuclear stealth fighter and dropped right in Russert's lap.

As Borokovski and Lowenthal huddled over the notebook computer with what the Russian called "very good active-matrix screen and useful all-in-one design," Russert lingered behind them, his thoughts orbiting wildly. He had, after all, placed the lives of everyone up there on an old Russian sandwich-maker and his ridiculously out-of-date equipment. At any moment, Russert expected Ms. MOD and her bosses to parade into the ficker and remove him.

If that were not enough, Russert's ex had called to say that Jessica had wanted to go home early, had already packed her bags, and was en route to Galveston as they spoke. Jessica had promised to spend an entire week with Russert, but because of her school schedule, she could only come during the busiest week of his life. Russert had wanted so badly to see her that he had consented. And now he imagined her on that shuttle, teary-eyed, damning him to hell, and telling strangers what a bastard she had for a father.

Borokovski smote a fist on Lowenthal's desk. *"Yob tvyou mot!"*

"What did you say?" asked Russert.

"Better I not tell. It involves software engineer's mother." He shook his head at the computer, whose blue screen displayed the message WIN 2020 HAS DETECTED A FATAL ERROR IN STARTUP MODULE 3409028H29H AND WILL BE SHUTDOWN.

Lowenthal appeared nonplussed as he read and reread the message. "Why does it keep crashing?"

"That was part of its charm. You had to buy programs to check why the program you had already bought was not working." Borokovski switched off the notebook, counted to himself, then switched it on. "And every few weeks you also had to upgrade the program you bought because it was sold to you before it was really tested."

"I still can't believe people installed this operating system on purpose," said Lowenthal. "It's as dangerous as some of our viruses."

"The company planned it this way. It was later discovered that they owned all the companies that sold you the products to fix the product they had already sold you."

"I remember reading about that in some class somewhere," Lowenthal related, grinning ironically. "The government had to bomb the factory in the end."

"Yes. Very sad."

The computer's screen abruptly displayed a WIN 2020 logo with pictures of pristine Earths substituted for the zeros and a subtitle that read: WOULD TODAY BE A GOOD DAY TO GO SOMEWHERE?

Russert tensed. "Is it working?"

"It will," Borokovski said. "But first we must input secret product ID code. This was high security measure to prevent illegal copying of disks, but most codes were available on Internet."

"So how do we get the code?" Lowenthal queried. "Has the information been transferred to satnet?"

"No, code is right here on certificate of authenticity."

None of this dead tech made sense to Russert. "Doctor Borokovski, can you give me an estimate on how long it'll take until you're ready to transmit?"

"First I take Win Twenty-twenty tour to refresh memory. Then we install drivers, set up communications. If we have no problem, we be ready in two, maybe three hours."

CRATERED UPLANDS
NORTH-NORTHEAST OF ARES VALLIS
MISSION TIME: DAY 183

Gallagher had never done much hiking in his life, and he vowed that if he survived, he would never, ever, hike again. Despite the lower gravity, the hump over to Hab had taxed him, but now he and the others would trek much farther and with even less energy. His lips had begun to crack, his throat felt sore, and his stomach grumbled for a nonexistent meal.

He led Burchenal, Pettengill, and AMEE's drone up a lazy, thirty-five degree grade whose surface seemed unusually smooth, devoid of the ejecta that blanketed the rest of the terrain. As they reached the summit, a meandering, half-kilometer wide path rolled out like a paved avenue.

"Dust storm track," Burchenal said through the taccom as he finally reached the top behind Pettengill. "Some devils in there. Must've been a hell of a storm."

"We need to walk parallel to it," Gallagher said, leading them once more. "Then veer a little east." He squinted at the sun, which now hung at the zenith, then glanced back at the course they had followed. "Yeah. This is it."

"Sure we're heading the right way?" asked Burchenal.

"Pretty sure."

Pettengill's voice turned strangely dismal. "We all make mistakes now and then."

Gallagher let that hang a second, then said, "Everyone but the king. Isn't that right, your majesty?"

"No, no," Burchenal protested. "There was one time." He broke off, coughed, then slowed his breath.

"One time you say? Whoa."

"Yeah. Cloning potatoes. Spent two years of my life trying to make a better spud. You got your russet baking potatoes, your new red and your new white potatoes, your Yukon Gold potatoes, and a bunch more. I created a variety so hearty, so aggressive that it took another two years to stop it. Almost wiped out Idaho. You remember those news stories?"

"Think I saw a few," Gallagher lied, not wanting to turn the knife. You could not escape all that bad press.

"We screwed up our own backyard. Sad thing is, we've known what was coming for a long time. Two hundred fifty years ago, guy named Malthus wrote that population tends to increase faster than food supply. What did we do about it? Nothing. Continued poisoning ourselves. Waited until we hit the Malthusian Wall, then tried to breed our way around it. We're never proactive because the budget won't allow it. Now look at the price tag. . . ."

"What's that?" cried Pettengill. He strayed back onto the smooth path and lifted a finger toward a ribbon of oxblood red so far off that Gallagher barely discerned it through the blowing dust.

"What?" asked Gallagher.

"Over there. You didn't see it? The ground was moving."

Gallagher strained for a glimpse. "I don't see anything."

"Could've been a dust devil," Burchenal said. "More likely your paranoia."

"I'm telling you I saw something."

"All right," said Gallagher. "But it's not like we got time to check it out."

"It's gone now. But I definitely saw something. I hate this place. I hate it!"

"Well, Pettengill, can't say I have any particular love for it either," Burchenal said. "And we didn't plan on Lewis and Clarking our asses all over this planet. But punchy or not, we gotta do this."

Pettengill screamed, and Gallagher cocked his head to

watch him pitch a rock at the drone flying in a tight loop above him. "Pettengill!"

"I'm okay now. I'm . . . okay."

They reached the lip of a crater about a hundred meters deep and five hundred meters across. Gallagher picked a route along the lip, over gentle hummocks that fell off into a marked radial pattern, and strings and loops of smaller, secondary craters. As they cleared the lip, the terrain grew more dangerous in that one wrong step in those smaller craters could break an ankle. He warned the others to mind their way. Pettengill acknowledged.

"Burchenal? You with us?" Gallagher glanced over his shoulder.

The scientist braced his rib and doddered about fifty meters behind, in the shadow of AMEE's drone. "I'm . . . coming."

"You're too far back!"

"Scout zeroing in on me?"

"Affirmative."

"Watch me get the son of a bitch," yelled Pettengill. His head jerked as he scanned the surface for a stone, found one, then went charging back like a shot-putter.

Burchenal lifted his hands. "What're you doing?"

But Pettengill had already thrown the rock, and even as it arced over Burchenal, the scientist dropped to his knees to avoid getting beaned.

"Ground crew, *Medea One*. Gallagher?"

"Here. Still en route. How 'bout a heading check?"

"You're right on target."

"I'm surprised. HHCs are still down. Can you get a fix on AMEE?"

"Got her. She's about five hundred meters off. Still no luck shutting her down?"

"She's denied me access."

"I'll watch her for you. Just focus on the hike."

"What's wrong? I can hear it in your voice."

After a pause long enough to rattle Gallagher's gut, she returned. "We need to talk."

twenty

Bowman steeled herself. They had to be told. If she let them reach *Cosmos* without telling them. . . . God, she couldn't think about that.

What angered her most was Houston's delay in realizing the problem. They had tracked down the probe's designer and had even acquired the outmoded software and hardware essential for communicating with it. How had they overlooked something so obvious?

"I'm off the taccom," Gallagher replied. "What's up?"

You rarely hesitate in the execution of a command responsibility. You are a professional. You are aware of the facts and have been ordered to share them.

But how will they decide? It can't be like this. It just can't. Not after we've asked them to go so far.

Should I decide for them? Will they even respect my authority? How do I choose?

One day, you will be asked to make a decision that every commanding officer most fears, a decision you will live with for the rest of your life, a decision that will leave you with a sense of remorse deeper than you have ever felt.

"Bowman?"

She spoke rapidly, as though the velocity of her words would prevent their sting. "The only place to ride *Cosmos* is inside the rock sample container."

"Sounds comfy."

"Gallagher, it's very small. Just a box. No G couches. Houston and Borokovski found the schematics, and they've been going over them for the past few hours. They've done all they could to figure out how to cram three people inside that container."

"Hey, when I was in college, we got sixteen people inside a Nissan Torero. I'm sure we'll work it out. Thing is, not only are we strung out, but we kinda smell. Won't be pretty when you pry us out of there, I promise."

"There's only room for two."

"Say again?"

"Only two people fit, Gallagher. Two people . . . barely."

"What if we strip? I mean, everything except helmets and vests. Scrunch up as tight as we can. Whatever it takes."

"Trust me, when you see it, you'll know that won't work. Then there's the question of air supply. There's no air lock, but there's a vacuum hatch. Houston says two people will have about a minute and a half of air. There're hoping I can get to you before brain damage occurs."

"Burchenal still has some reserve. I think it was six minutes or so. We can share that."

"Outstanding."

"Yeah, but someone has to stay behind."

"I'm sorry."

"Yeah, okay," he said distractedly. "I'll talk to you later."

"Wait. I'm the commander of this mission, and I need to make a decision here." Bowman gripped the edge of her touchboard and shivered. "Burchenal's already injured. The launch will no doubt worsen his condition. He might not survive it anyway. Therefore, I order you and Pettengill to launch in *Cosmos*. Gallagher, do you copy? I order you and Pettengill to launch in *Cosmos*."

No response.

She ripped off her headset. "Son of a bitch."

CRATERED UPLANDS
NORTH-NORTHEAST OF ARES VALLIS
MISSION TIME: DAY 183

Even as Gallagher had uttered the words "someone has to stay behind," he had made the decision—a decision that had to be his, not Bowman's. Screw the chain of command. Though everyone had teased him about being the space janitor, he knew deep down that he was as valuable to the mission as any of them. If something malfunctioned, say life support, he was Robby on the spot.

But, he reasoned, you had to think about this longterm. As a mechanical systems engineer, he would not, after the mission, contribute anything that might change the face of humanity. He would report all of his observations, and a few people would be impressed with his cannibalization of *Pathfinder*'s radio. That was about it.

Burchenal and Pettengill would go home, analyze what they had seen, and probably unravel where the algae had gone, why the air was breathable, and set the scientific community on a new course. That had to happen.

Consequently, Gallagher might be considered a "hero" or "martyr," though he had never known what those labels really meant and had always shunned them because of his ignorance; he simply did not want to screw humanity out of its chance for survival because of his own lame fear of dying. Odd thing, though. The decision itself felt more comforting than frightening because he knew Pettengill and Burchenal now had a better chance of making it; he would exploit his expendability to its fullest. And he had already tasted death when his oxygen had run out. This time he would surrender peacefully, let God steal him away to join Santen and Bud.

"How're we doing?" Burchenal asked, his eyes so red from the dust and his beard growing in so densely that Gallagher hardly recognized him.

"We're fine. On track. Making shitty time, I guess, but still making time."

Burchenal nodded that off. "Shoulda asked how you're doing. You look like hell."

"Yeah." He turned weakly to Pettengill. "What about you?"

"What?" the terraformer retorted, his glaze flicking between Gallagher and AMEE's drone.

"Just asked if you're okay."

"I feel great. I'm not the weak piece of shit pullin' up the rear anymore."

"Hey . . ." Burchenal started for his assistant.

"Guys, that sun's chasing us. I'm going." Gallagher pounded off, and for a moment, he didn't care whether they followed. Twenty meters later, he chanced a look

back. Pettengill swung his arms and shuffled along with the face of an automaton. Burchenal trailed him, but his tighter gait put him farther and farther behind.

Two hours later, as they tramped through yet another undistinguished stretch of heavily cratered regolith, Gallagher shrank a little into his collar. Northern winds had dropped the temperature at least fifteen degrees in the past hour, and the air felt a bit thinner. He spied on the others every few minutes and carefully measured his pace.

Rocks, rocks, and more rocks. Rocks like spears, like benches, like columns, like tables, like temples, like barnacles on the back of some enormous red sea mammal. *Get them out of here. Every last one. Clear the way. We're coming through.*

"Shit." That from Burchenal.

Gallagher cringed and looked back. The scientist stood forty meters away, weak-kneed and choking, with that unshakable metal cloud hanging at his shoulder, watching. "Don't stop, Burchenal. You can't stop."

He stammered. "I'm . . . I'm hurt. I'm tired. I need a drink like you wouldn't believe. I can't do this." With that, he fell onto the ground.

"That's natural selection right there," Pettengill said in a monotone, then resumed his pace.

"Get up!" hollered Gallagher.

"Screw it. I'm through." Burchenal cupped his face, then brushed dust from his brow and lashes.

Maybe the scientist wouldn't make it. Maybe Gallagher and Pettengill should leave him. Maybe Gallagher's contributions to humanity weren't so pathetic after all. And living had always been a pretty good ride.

AMEE's drone flew dangerously close now. A faint

dust cloud rose about ninety meters behind the drone, a cloud whipped up by AMEE as she closed in to pick off the weakest.

Aw, hell.

Gallagher covered the distance between himself and Pettengill in a few seconds. "Wait," he told the terraformer, who made an ugly face and halted.

Burchenal kept his head lowered and held his rib as though making a pledge not to get up. He tugged at the thin air, his lips as chapped as Gallagher's. "Just get outta here."

"What're you gonna do?" Gallagher asked. "Stay here and wait for AMEE to put you out of your misery? What kind of weak-ass shit is that?"

"I don't give a damn. And I don't need to make peace with anyone but myself. So go. And let me do that."

"Get your ass up!" Gallagher took Burchenal's arm in both hands, dragged the grumbling man to his feet, then slung that arm over his shoulder. "I'll carry you the whole way there, damn it."

"The air . . . it's . . . I can barely breathe."

"Don't think about it."

Gallagher's angry sergeant routine finally produced the desired effect. Burchenal pulled his arm away and scuffled off on his own. But after just a few meters into his new-found stride, he tripped to a halt.

"C'mon," Gallagher urged, then gave the scientist a solid shove. "Left foot, right foot, hop like a bunny—I don't care. Let's go."

A shadow tinted the rocks to Gallagher's left. He fetched a rock, came up facing skyward. "And you . . ." He threw his best fastball at the drone. Missed.

If the thing had a voice, it would have cackled.

"Don't get Pettengill started," the scientist said. "And you got any idea how far we've come?"

"Yup."

"Mind sharing?"

"Yup. You keep your head low and don't think about it."

"I'm thinking about it."

"Forget about it."

Twenty minutes later, Bowman checked in, though intermittent bursts of static threatened to break the link. "Pay attention. You're still towing AMEE on about a thousand meter leash."

"Copy that. Good news. She's falling farther behind," said Gallagher.

"And now for the bad news. There's a storm coming at you. It's the size of Montana, and it's moving fast."

"What else can go wrong!" Pettengill screamed at the top of his lungs.

"Hey . . . look . . ." Burchenal gestured toward a dense, sanguine haze bordering the northwest plains. "Powerful winds out there. Gets me thinking about that path we saw. Weird getting storms this far north. Most of them originate in the south."

Gallagher stiffened. "Well, Doctor, shall we continue to ponder the storm's origination—*or find out what the hell we're gonna do about it!*"

"Look, shuddup down there," said Bowman. "In a few seconds, I'll be in blackout again. Find shelter now. Any shelter you can."

twenty-one

CRATERED UPLANDS
NORTH-NORTHEAST OF ARES VALLIS
MISSION TIME: DAY 183

"Better stop and look around. Gotta be some shelter somewhere," Gallagher half-sang, the wind raking through his hair. "I'd even settle for the MEV wreckage right now."

Pettengill wrung his hands, wiped them on his hips, then flipped up his hood. "We're gonna find shelter out here? I don't think so."

"Better figure out something," Gallagher said. "Dust and ice particles are gonna start whipping. Probably create the kind of whiteout conditions we had in the Arctic. You didn't want to be caught in a big blow there. You get caught looking into the wind, you could freeze your corneas. And I guess the temperature will drop a lot more. We stay out, we could get chilblains, frostbite, and hypothermia—suits or not."

"And Mr. Bioengineer here has already got the warning signs of hypothermia," said Pettengill. "Tiredness. Reluctance to keep moving. And he's squinting."

"I'll live," Burchenal said, grinding out the words. "If just to piss you off."

"But he's right," Gallagher told the scientist. "Your core temp's down. You still need to keep moving."

"Which hurts, damn it."

"Hey, Gallagher? You ever get caught in one of those big blows up in McMurdo?" asked Pettengill. "Oh, what am I saying? You wouldn't be here to answer that. You'd be dead. Like us."

"Wait a minute," Burchenal said, a dim light burning in his eyes. "What would you do if you were stranded out there, say up on that Ross Ice Shelf?"

"I don't know. If you didn't have a choice? Dig a snow cave, I guess."

"So let's dig one."

"And there's another warning sign," Pettengill groaned. "Abnormal behavior."

Burchenal's gaze focused on a nearby hillock, a mound about three meters high and twice that around. "We're only about fifteen, twenty degrees north latitude, but . . ." he trailed off into a thought as he reached the hillock, then started kicking a shallow hole. "Gentlemen. Come here."

They gathered around him, and Gallagher scarcely believed what he saw as Burchenal slid away his boot. White stuff.

"Water-ice," Burchenal said. "Place is full of the stuff. Most of the water that cut the runoff channels early in Mars's history outgassed during volcanism, but a lot of it got trapped above or below the permafrost."

"That's right," Pettengill said, hope creeping into his

voice. "And water-ice is unstable everywhere except at the poles. This area must be diffusely isolated from the atmosphere, otherwise this layer would've outgassed."

"Looks like snow to me," Gallagher said.

"And you can dig it," added Burchenal, scraping some away with his boot.

"Pettengill, you got any torch fuel left?" Gallagher asked. "Used mine for soldering. I'm nearly out."

"Yeah, I got a little."

"Good. Burchenal? We'll keep your supply on reserve. We'll soften this patch up even more with our torches, then dig the hell out of it. We can use some of my tools."

In just over an hour, they burrowed about two and a half meters into the hillock, the water-ice giving way under Pettengill's torch and the power screwdriver he used as a pick. The terraformer had volunteered as "chief digger," while Gallagher and Burchenal cleared the debris behind him. Burchenal had remarked that he felt like a prisoner of war tunneling to freedom. *That's not too far from the truth,* Gallagher had thought. Mars remained a formidable captor.

As they worked, the winds picked up to about forty kilometers per hour. Gallagher estimated that the beast would hit in less than thirty minutes, and that drove Pettengill into a feverish pace.

"Hey, take it easy," Gallagher cautioned him, lifting his voice over the howling gale. "You'll get hypoxic."

Pettengill eased out of the cave, switched off his suit light, then sat, taking a much needed break. "If the storm lasts long, we could be digging our graves."

Gallagher sighed off the comment, then he and Burchenal took over for the terraformer. They widened the entrance a bit more, then Gallagher worked on the left wall while Burchenal took the right. Pettengill re-joined the effort, serving as debris man, and within an-other ten minutes, they excavated a chamber large enough for the three of them to sit, albeit hunched over. Gallagher left the cave, figuring that Bowman was just now completing her orbit. "*Medea One*, ground crew. Bowman, you copy?" Static. He tried once more, then checked the radio's circuit boards. No damage. As he turned to head back into the shelter, he caught a glimpse of the storm, its great shoulders of dust and ice driving irrepressibly toward them. To the east, a pair of dust devils circled and probed each other like boxers, and to the west, AMEE's drone buffeted violently against the wind. AMEE would probably recall the drone in a few moments, and Gallagher now hoped that the storm would carry off his pet and dump her into the deepest crater it could find.

"Son of a bitch, it's getting cold," Burchenal said as Gallagher handed him the radio, then crawled back to seal off the cave's entrance with a pair of large stones and a pile of water-ice he would use as caulking. Burchenal coughed, then asked, "You reach Bowman?"

"Still in blackout. And this cave'll weaken if not cut our signal." Gallagher rolled the stones into place, then packed snow into the corners, leaving a small air hole at the top. "Can't get over this," he said, dragging himself back toward the chamber, its eerily lit walls stippled by shadows. "We come to this planet with some of the most sophisticated equipment known to human-ity. And what do we do? We build campfires and live in caves."

"Call it primitivism," Burchenal said, rubbing his icy nose and cradling his ribs. "The acquisitions of civilization are evil. The earliest period of human history was best."

"You study that?"

"No. Met this girl in San Francisco who was getting into it. Whole movement. Kinda like the Amish in Pennsylvania, only more extreme. She—" He seized up in pain.

"It's all right. Just rest," Gallagher insisted.

"Even . . . resting . . . hurts."

"Hey, you're not alone. I've never been this tired or hurt this bad." Gallagher crossed his legs and leaned forward, a bone cracking in his shoulder. He massaged his sore eyes, then looked up to find Pettengill watching him. "What? You're looking at me like I'm dinner. Can you wait till I die first?"

"It's melting. You had some water-ice on your forehead. And it's melting. We might not freeze."

"Positive energy. 'Bout time you tapped into some." Gallagher wiped his head and inspected the stain on his glove. "Hey, can we drink this stuff?"

"If you wanna die . . ." Burchenal answered. "Too many contaminants. And even if we could, do you know how much of this we'd have to melt just to get eight ounces? I forget the ratio, but it's a lot."

"Shhh," Pettengill insisted. "Listen . . ."

A familiar whistle penetrated the roaring wind.

Pettengill's lip curled in anger. "Wolf's at the door."

"AMEE's programmed for psy-ops. She's been listening to our conversations, and now she knows just how to push our buttons," said Gallagher. "She's trying to freak us out."

"Well, she comes near us, and I'm gonna freak her out." Pettengill reached for his titanium pole.

"She'll probably go back in her box soon." Gallagher cupped his hands around his mouth. "Get lost!"

Information from AMEE's weather sensors indicated that wind speed now stood at sixty-eight kilometers per hour. Airborne pebbles and alluvia pelted her shell. Visibility through her camera eyes had been reduced to zero. Survival algorithms suggested appendage retraction, but offensive operational parameters dictated that she remain in position to taunt the operator and his accomplices for as long as possible. She whistled once more, then a dust devil flipped her onto her back. Survival algorithms overrode all offensive parameters. Retraction. Vacuum seals in place to prevent dust contamination. Weather sensor still operative. Mission priorities revised. Storm dimensions and speed calculated. Clock set to resume mission.

Gallagher frowned at his watch, wishing he could calculate how far they were from *Cosmos*. If he knew that, then he would know just how much time they could spend in the shelter. But Bowman's last report had been rushed, and his thoughts had been too divided to think about asking her.

Observing him, Burchenal asked, "Any idea how far we've come?"

"Read my mind. And as a matter of fact, I don't have a clue."

"Well, about thirteen hours have gone by since we left *Pathfinder*. So we got ten hours left, not including the time we blow here."

Gallagher weighed that, then pushed forward onto all fours and headed for the entrance.

"Where are you going?"

"I'll put up the aerial. See if we can get off a signal to Bowman." Gallagher wormed his way to the rocks, then shoved the small antenna through the entrance's air hole. "*Medea One*, ground crew. Copy?"

"Gallagher?" Bowman said excitedly, her voice tinny and backed by a chorus of static.

"Pinpoint this location. Calculate estimated walking time to *Cosmos*."

"Give me a sec. How're you doing down there?"

"Storm's passing over. We're dug in good. We look like a damned Everest expedition."

"Okay. Took an average on your walking speed. You're about six hours from *Cosmos*. Now, listen up . . ."

Gallagher glanced to Burchenal, who said, "Leaves us four for the jump-start. And we're chipping into that as we speak."

"Bowman, can you estimate the storm's speed? When will it clear this location?"

Static crescendoed over her reply.

"Bowman?"

"Lost her?" Pettengill asked.

"Yeah." Gallagher pulled the aerial back in, then kneed his way into the chamber.

"I say we give this storm two more hours to pass. That'll give us six to get there, two to jump," Burchenal said. "If the storm doesn't pass by then, I say we brave it and pray that Borokovski's still on his game because I doubt we'll have time for plan B. We've had one about the picture, one about the math. This one's about the time."

"We won't survive out there," retorted Pettengill. "And we don't know how much time it'll take to jump that piece of shit."

"Exactly. So the more time the better. But you know what? Point's moot for now."

Gallagher watched them share a look of disgust, then lowered his head, trying to perform the small miracle of getting comfortable. The shivering came and went, sometimes voluntary, sometimes involuntary. He knew his own core temperature had dropped and the shivering was, in fact, a good thing and his body's way of helping him produce heat.

They sat for a long while, the wind wailing and warbling through the air hole amid the muffled pinging of ejecta on the stone doorway. Gallagher repeatedly checked on his comrades, and now Burchenal caught him looking. "What're you thinking about?" the scientist asked.

"Nothing, really. Just how damned cold I am. Wondering how Bud would explain all this."

"He'd pull something out of Revelations," Burchenal said with a derisive grin. "Tell us God is faith, God is hope, and that the big guy has a plan and that we have to endure this. Hey, Gallagher? If he said that, would you believe it?"

"I don't know. Maybe. But I've always had trouble with that part, you know the part when we justify why God lets shitty things happen to good people? So this guy lives a decent life, contributes to the community, inspires people, the whole nine. Then he wakes up one morning and coughs up blood and finds out that afternoon that he's got six months to live. That kind of shit."

"You know that guy," said Burchenal.

"My grandfather."

"Sorry." The scientist gazed sympathetically at him. "There's a thing, something maybe science doesn't fully explain."

Gallagher's eyes widened. "Is that you talking?"

"Let me finish. This thing, it's an impulse that drives us on when everything else fails, that extends itself to other people—like when you kept me going back there. I don't wanna sound trite, but it's something heroes are made of. It's what'll get us off this damned planet."

A wave of guilt washed through Gallagher, tightening his muscles and streaming its way to his lips. "Only two of us can go."

"What?"

"*Cosmos* only has room for two people. The rock container's real small."

Pettengill's head snapped up. "Sorry?"

"How long have you known?" Burchenal asked.

"For a little while. I wasn't gonna tell you, but I'd rather settle this here and now. Like you said, this one's about the time, and if we make it to that probe, we won't have time for a debate."

"One of us has to stay?" Pettengill asked. "After all this, one of us has to stay behind?"

"Yeah," Gallagher said, his voice bottoming into a resigned whisper. "I'm staying." He looked at them.

No reaction. Just as well.

"So when you helped me back there, you knew?" asked Burchenal.

Gallagher suppressed a shiver and nodded.

"You could've left me. You had the perfect excuse."

Now Pettengill stared emphatically at Gallagher, his face crimped by the same question.

"So why are you playing martyr?" pried Burchenal.

"Hey, we don't know if *Cosmos* will even launch. They couldn't get it to work the first time. And even if it does, hell, it's Russian, and somebody told me they don't translate those Taiwanese assembly instructions very well. The thing'll probably get three meters off the ground and blow up, and I'll still get to live the longest."

A weird, oily light filtered into Pettengill's eyes and rose from the windburned plains of his cheeks. "Somehow," he said, an edgy lilt back in his voice. "I don't believe you."

"What do you mean?"

"I see the way you've looked at me since yesterday. And I know what you're thinking." Pettengill's head swung like a turret toward Burchenal. "You? You might as well have come out and said it. You blame me for Santen's death."

Before Gallagher could stop it, his eyes found Burchenal, and the meeting of their gazes had Pettengill nodding his confirmation. "Don't you trust me, Gallagher?" the terraformer asked. "You watch my back, I'll watch yours?"

Burchenal hissed. "I know *I* don't trust you."

"But you're gonna leave your buddy behind and take off with *me*?" Pettengill fixed his boss with an incredulous look.

"That's right," Gallagher answered. "He is."

"How do I know this isn't part of your plan?" Pettengill spat. "When we get there, you off me and go for the ride. You make it look like an accident. Real hard to prove."

"And you oughta know, right?" asked Burchenal.

That silenced the terraformer until his paranoid gaze found Gallagher. "Tell me something. Why are you staying?"

"I just am."

"Is it because our lives are worth more than yours? Because you know you're just a fuckin' handyman?"

"Enough," Burchenal roared. He set his teeth together as the pain quaked through him.

Gallagher stared pitifully at the terraformer, then spoke slowly, spacing his words for effect. "You and Burchenal . . . you get out of here, you'll make a difference. I'll make mine helping you."

twenty-two

Sleep deprivation, Bowman had once read, has a positive side effect for those who suffer from certain kinds of depression. A half century earlier, researchers had discovered that staying awake for a twenty-four-hour period has marked effects on patients' moods and outlooks on life.

However, Bowman did not suffer from depression, and the only effects she had noted were an irrepressible fit of yawning every fifteen minutes or so, an itchy pain that ringed her eyes, and the occasional fluttering of her heavy lids. She had fixed herself a pot of strong coffee, and three cups into it had felt her heart palpitating so violently that she disposed of the remaining pot and had downed sixteen ounces of water to flush out her system. At least all those trips to the hygiene sphere had kept her awake, moving, and a little distracted.

Still trying to wear off the residual jitters of caffeine, Bowman paced the Flight Deck, her thoughts veering to the ground crew and the storm that she had calculated would take three point five hours to clear their location, leaving them just six hours to get to *Cosmos* and thirty minutes to get the thing working. Bowman's thoughts also turned to AMEE, and she wondered if there were some way to stop her. The bot utilized a taccom system similar to the one found in the e-suits, thus only short-range communications were possible between her and her operator. *Medea One* had not been fitted with weapons of any kind, which ruled out firing at her from orbit.

Bowman flopped into her seat and chanced another link to Gallagher. It had been nearly three hours since she had last heard from him, and by now the storm should be weakening. "Ground crew, *Medea One*. Copy? Ground crew, *Medea One*. Gallagher, do you copy?"

"He can't hear you, darling."

"Why are his eyes closed?"

"Because Daddy's in heaven now. Remember?"

"I don't want him to be in heaven. Why can't he stay with us? Why does he have to go?"

"I don't know, darling. Now bless yourself and go back to the pew. Mommy wants to stay here for a minute."

"Gallagher, do you read me? C'mon, talk to me."

That's just how it is, Bowman thought. *They just step in and out of your life. You need to hold on to them. You can't let them leave until you say good-bye.*

"Gallagher, come in, damn it."

Something squelched the static, then the capcom's voice resonated loud and clear. For the first time since reestablishing contact with Houston, Bowman dreaded a message from them. In her last report, she had relayed her loss of contact with the ground crew, and were she sitting in the ficker and evaluating the situation, she would probably reach the same conclusions as Flight and the rest of them had.

"*Medea One*, Houston. Kate, it's been over three hours since you've heard from them. All of us want to believe those men are still alive, but we know the odds are nil. You're already at risk. We're not going to lose you or the ship. We need both of you back here to help us try again." Skavlem paused, then he delivered his next sentence as though he were reading it off his PIM. "If the crew has not made contact by the time you receive this, you are ordered to return home. We know you've burned off your A tank to buy yourself more time, but there's no sense orbiting for another six hours if there's no one down there. Houston, out."

"But you don't know that," she argued with the comm unit's speaker. "You can't confirm anything. I'm here. I can do that. They're still alive. And you gave me those six hours. Sorry, people, but I'm taking them." She opened the channel. "Houston, *Medea One*. Still no report from ground crew, but the storm is just clearing their location. I feel strongly that communication will be reestablished and am therefore remaining in orbit until degradation warrants main engine burn. *Medea One*, out." She glanced to a navigation data bar. Time remaining on orbital degradation: 06:37:22.

A dangerous thought crackled to life. She could burn some of B tank to buy a few more orbits. Of course, she wouldn't have enough fuel to make it home. Maybe they could send another ship out to meet her. But that would take time. The life-support system already relied on emergency reserves, and she had lost nearly all of the hydroponics during the air purge. Even if she managed to save the ground crew, they might starve or suffocate before that rescue ship reached them. No, they needed to head back with a full duration burn. And that burn would commence in t-minus 06:36:19.

"Ground crew, *Medea One*. Do you copy? Ground crew, *Medea One*. Gallagher, you down there?"

CRATERED UPLANDS
NORTH-NORTHEAST OF ARES VALLIS
MISSION TIME: DAY 184

The dream felt more real than some others, but even as Gallagher experienced it, the icy voice of reality slipped through the crack in his hood and whispered that he was, in fact, sitting in a cave, in a storm, on another planet. To evade that voice, he fully acquiesced to the dream, accepted the science medal, then slipped the ribbon over his neck. Parents and relatives jammed the warm, comfortable high school auditorium, and Gallagher thrust out his chest, grinning with more pride than he had ever felt. He left the stage and returned to his parents, pressing deeply into the well-cushioned seat.

"Can I see that?" his father asked, eyeing the gold medallion inscribed with the words FIRST PLACE.

Gallagher removed the award and handed it to his father, who stuffed the medal into his mouth, then pushed in the ribbon as he would errant strands of pasta. His cheeks bloated, and bolts of crimson throbbed in his swelling eyes. He gulped.

"What did you do?" cried Gallagher.

"I ate your fuckin' medal. Problem?"

"Why'd you do that?"

"Because your little ergonomics project sucked. Your buddy Rosenberg, there, deserved it. They gave it to you because they're afraid I might cut off my donations. It's all fuckin' politics, kid. But that's why I'm here. I'm here to teach you about the real world. And if I gotta eat a medal to do that, then I'll do it. That's called goin' the extra mile for your kids. And wipe off that fuckin' look. You know you didn't deserve it. Your work is still shit. And until you realize that, you'll never get better. You're lounging through life. Wake up, Robert. Time to wake up!"

Gallagher sprang from his seat, crawled across his mother's lap, and seized his father's neck, but the skin turned blue as he touched it, and great fissures opened up to mount his father's face. The man's head crumbled into his body as his body crumbled into the seat.

The audience applauded.

Then a powerful, cold breath whisked away the fragments as Gallagher grabbed his chest, searching once more for the medallion and awakening with a massive chill that scaled his back and broke into flanks.

Cold. Why so cold? Feel the wind.

He tried to open his eyes, found the lashes frozen together. He zipped off a glove and rubbed them slowly to free them. There. He blinked his gaze into focus.

The shelter's entrance lay wide open, the rocks somewhere outside, the rest of the shelter coated in hoarfrost. Burchenal huddled next to him, snoring softly.

"Burchenal!" Gallagher shook him.

"What is it? What? Oh, man, can't see," groaned the scientist, his lashes rimed with ice.

"Pettengill's gone. He took the radio."

"God damn it. Bastard's gonna try to take off by himself."

"Yeah, he'll lie to Bowman, say we're dead. Come

on." Gallagher pulled on his glove, then clambered out of the cave.

Stiff as the corpse he might soon become, Gallagher struggled to his feet and stood in the cold night air. He flicked a glance to the sky, not one watt of light pollution buffing away the stars. But he could not appreciate the magnificent view. He noted his heading, the time.

Oh my god.

"Burchenal? You know how long we've—"

"Yeah," the scientist intervened, still on his hands and knees. "Four hours, ten minutes. We're already cutting into our travel time, and we got zero for jump-start." He reached out for Gallagher.

"Bowman'll wait for us. She'll find a way." Gallagher helped the man up, switched on his suit light, then directed the beam forward to probe the ground. "There. Got his tracks. At least he was going in the right direction."

"How do you know?"

"When we were digging this place, I took a basic heading. I just lined it up with the stars. I think he watched me do it the first time and did the same when he got here."

"I don't mean to peddle his brand of pessimism, but I don't think we're gonna make it."

"Tell you the truth, me neither."

"So let's stay in the shelter. I'm . . . freezing."

"We're not back to that weak-ass crap, are we? Come on. You gotta keep moving. Your body's losing heat five ways as we speak." Gallagher launched himself away, arcing nearly three meters.

"Five ways? I remember 'em. Radiation. Respiration. Evaporation. Convection. And conduction," Burchenal rasped over the taccom. "Hey, Gallagher? You hear something?"

• • •

More air. God, why isn't there more air? Run. Don't stop. Focus on the beam. Watch out for rocks. I'll make it. I won't be left here to die. They're the murderers. Not me. Whoa. Don't drop the radio. I'm fucked without it.

So Gallagher? Burchenal? You wanna kill me? Ain't gonna happen.

I'M IN CONTROL.

I wasn't his victim, and I won't be yours.

Blame me for his death?

You don't know how wrong you are. How could I have known the air was breathable? It wasn't my fault. And that fucker deserved to die.

Slowing down. Better not. Don't worry. Nothing else out here. Don't get spooked. And hey, the air seems denser here.

What was that?

Oh, no. No. No! Not a whistle. AMEE! Go find Gallagher. Go find him.

Another whistle. She's closer. Gaining.

Watch out for that rock. Jump. Jump. Now run!

"AMEE's out there," said Gallagher. "Directly ahead." He took another huge stride forward, hit the soil, then rebounded in another leap. His sleeve panel beeped sharply. The screen popped, warmed to static, then switched to an infrared image captured by one of AMEE's camera eyes:

Like some pathetic bipedal insect, Pettengill sprinted away, carrying the radio in one hand, his titanium pole in the other, all the while hazarding glances over his shoulder that revealed his terrified expression. He tried to widen the gap, but AMEE zeroed in on him, slicing through dust and navigating the rocky terrain with five limbs functioning in perfect concert. She fired a ruby laser beam at Pettengill's back, not a beam powerful enough to kill; but one to keep her locked on course in lieu of radar or infrared failure. It would not be long now. "Oh, man."

"What is it?" asked Burchenal

"AMEE's after him. She wants us to see it."

"Oh, yeah?"

"Yeah. And I got access to the panel. Maybe this time I can shut her down."

"Maybe this time you shouldn't."

"I'm not armed. You?"

"Left my pole back at the cave. So why don't you try to shut her down?"

Servos hummed so loudly that Pettengill glanced reflexively over his shoulder.

AMEE sprang on him like a plutonium-fed crustacean, anterior limbs outstretched as her belly served up a crushing blow to his back.

Pettengill dropped the radio and titanium pole, ran a half dozen more steps with the drone clawing at his back, then slammed to his stomach, the wind blasting from his lungs. Whine, snap, crack. One of AMEE's talons squeezed his bicep, rolled him over.

Swearing, spitting out dust but with no phlegm to help, Pettengill drove his elbows into the dirt, arched his back, and tugged against her pincer. "AMEE. Stop."

Whine, snap, crack. Another talon clutched his ankle.

Elbows dug deeper. Heels now. Push. Push. Nothing.

He squealed, craned his head forward, stared into those lifeless permaglass eyes, his suit light brushing a thin halo over the bot. He writhed a bit more, shoulder and rump gaining him worthless centimeters across soil that suddenly felt spongy.

AMEE released his bicep, drew back the forelimb.

Pettengill sighed.

And AMEE lashed out with her talon, driving it into his stomach and straight on through to his spine. Pettengill felt the electricity of the blow, listened with a horrid fascination as his vertebrae crunched like leaves underfoot, then he felt quick-wrapped in bandages of numbness.

He blinked.

Blinked again.

The bot drew closer, tilting toward him, her camera eyes extending, the irises opening.

Pettengill opened his mouth. A scream would not clear his frozen tongue.

AMEEvision burst to snow for three seconds before the screen died altogether. Gallagher lowered his arm, thought of looking to Burchenal, who had paused to watch with him, then thought better of it. Forcing off that last image of Pettengill's closing eyes, Gallagher marched on.

No question about it now. He would ride in *Cosmos*. He should throw a party. Invite everyone. Serve Pettengill's blood in a punch bowl. God, he hated this.

Gallagher narrowed his gaze on the terraformer's tracks, his breath steaming through the shaft of light. The uplands ahead still refused to give up Pettengill's location.

"Now that AMEE's done with him, she'll come for us," Burchenal said in a monotone. "But I hurt too much, and I'm too damned tired to worry about it."

"Right now, AMEE thinks we're angry, vengeful, probably more dangerous. She'll wait until she thinks we're grieving, till we've been thoroughly demoralized."

"We are. At least the last part. Hey, stop. What the . . ." Burchenal peeled off to Gallagher's right, his light sweeping across a carpet of pink algae phosphorescing well beyond the beam's reach.

"So, not all of it died," Gallagher said, lowering his beam to where the algae had been extirpated in a long, crooked line.

"I don't get it," Burchenal muttered. "Why does this varietal survive while the others die?" He reached down and scooped up a handful, the pinkish glow slowly dissipating. "And why's it here and not anywhere else we've been? Look at this path. Why does it break off suddenly?"

"Too late to worry about it now."

Burchenal fished out a thumb-sized glass ampoule from his breast pocket and took a sample of the algae. "We get back, we'll study this."

"Look out there," said Gallagher, shooting his light up toward a far off ridge that waved like an arctic sastruga.

"Oh, yeah. Steel blue. Oxblood brown. Burnt orange. Cadmium yellow. Alizarin crimson. Malachite green. More varietals. So it ain't just this one. Maybe it has something to do with our proximity to the northern plains."

"Maybe you can work on it while we hustle?"

"Defense mechanism?"

"Right," Gallagher replied, turning back for the trail.

Burchenal fell in next to him, his eyes riveted to the algae beds. "Let me tell you something, Gallagher. The universe is *not* full of surprises. Wish I could say the same for this godforsaken planet."

twenty-three

"I know what everybody think. Everybody think Russian probe is dead," Borokovski was saying to Russert, Lowenthal, Skavlem, and a half dozen other controllers who had gathered around him. "But it is not."

Russert shut his red and swollen eyes. "Sir, the probe failed to launch the first time because you said there's a inactive module in the communication software."

"Correct."

"And you've also said that the module can't be repaired from here because you can't gain access to—what was that program?"

Borokovski covered a long yawn. "It is called Doctor Swanson. It takes snapshot of system whenever system fault occurs."

"Sir, I know we've kept you up all night for a longshot.

We're all strung out. But I got an astronaut up there who's risking federal prosecution by disobeying a direct order from us and not leaving until her time's up. If I tell her this probe won't launch, then maybe I can save her career and that ship."

"She is breaking law to save ground crew?"

"Yes. And she's very well aware of the penalties."

"I like this girl."

Russert exchanged a weary look with Lowenthal. "Sir, what makes you think the probe isn't dead?"

The old man swatted hair from his eyes and pointed to the notebook computer's screen, to a slowly rotating 3D illustration of an infrared communications system that looked more like a club sandwich than an electronics schematic. "We can gain access through hardwire of this system. There is infrared maintenance port on probe. Bypass corrupted module and run general and launch diagnostics from there."

"Okay, I get it," Lowenthal said, half buying the plan. "Ground crew sets up the bypass, hardwires their radio into the system, and we filter through them, using their radio as the comm package instead of *Cosmos*'s."

"Yeah, but the whole thing will take forever," Skavlem pointed out. "We have to instruct them how to hardwire, then we have to transmit our commands. Twenty-minute delays on both ends. Bowman won't have enough time. And aren't we forgetting that MOD has already declared the ground crew End Of Mission?"

Borokovski waved off the question. "I will set up commands here. We upload everything to Bowman. She communicates directly with ground crew. No time delay."

Lowenthal looked sold. Skavlem climbed aboard after a few seconds of consideration.

"Do it," Russert said. "John? Inform Bowman. Tell her to standby for that upload."

"And Mr. Russert?" Borokovski called. "Could someone get me something to eat? I know you promised caviar, but I would prefer some of this, what you call, TexMex? We have it in Brooklyn, but I want to taste genuine article."

CRATERED UPLANDS
NORTH-NORTHEAST OF ARES VALLIS
MISSION TIME: DAY 184

As Gallagher and Burchenal descended the third of a series of knolls, Gallagher glanced casually to the horizon. A thin shaft of light originated on the ground and shot straight up toward the stars. "There he is."

Burchenal nodded, and they jogged toward the beam, the algae still sweeping off in an iridescent concourse to the east.

They neared the body, and Gallagher hoisted mental braces for what had to be a gory sight.

"Radio," Burchenal said, focusing his light on the circuit boards, battery, and aerial.

Gallagher jogged over and retrieved his contraption. He checked the power, the mike. "Thank God."

"No, thank AMEE for not smashing it."

"Right." Gallagher started toward Pettengill, and a weird sight met the bouncing beam of his light.

Something moved on Pettengill's body.

Many things. Small things.

Gallagher slowed to a brisk walk as a sight worse than he could have imagined became hideously clear.

Thousands of translucent nematodes swarmed over Pettengill's body. The three-inch-long abominations had wriggled into a hole in the terraformer's e-suit and had attached themselves to his abdomen, their innards darkening as they sucked, chewed, and swallowed bloody human flesh through tri-part mouths jammed with multiple rows of tiny, crystalline teeth. A venous membrane had been woven over Pettengill's face, as though the nematodes had decided to nest in his head. Beneath that filmy sheath, the disgusting worms invaded the terraformer's nose, mouth, and ears, the membrane bulging as they squirmed over one another. A thunderbolt of fear struck Gallagher as he realized just how many of the things chomped on his former comrade. Gallagher dropped to his knees, then gagged as he inhaled a rank scent akin to sulfur.

Burchenal stepped up behind him and gasped.

Then Gallagher realized that dozens of nematodes were swarming up his leg. He wrenched back, jerked to his feet, saw more of the things on his sleeves and dropped the radio. "Get 'em off!"

The scientist tugged on a cluster of the worms beginning to chew into Gallagher's e-suit. "They're stuck on like leaches."

"Got any torch fuel left?"

"Some."

"Then burn 'em off like leaches."

Burchenal ignited his small torch and touched the small flame to a few of the nematodes on Gallagher's sleeve.

The worms detonated in fiery, green-yellow explosions that sent Gallagher blinking hard against the popping. He felt no heat against his flame retardant suit, but the little bombs sent his arms recoiling. "Why are they doing that?"

"Son of a bitch. They're full of oxygen." Burchenal waved the torch across Gallagher's legs, and the nematodes burst into slimy lifelessness.

Gallagher's entire body shook as the willies finally took hold. "You get 'em all?"

"Think so," Burchenal said, inspecting Gallagher's suit in the torch light. "Looks like they just got the first layer. Run a diagnostic for breaches."

Still quivering, Gallagher worked his suit's panel. "No breaches." Then he fingered one of the tiny holes on his sleeve. "Thought there wasn't any life on this planet."

"There shouldn't be."

"What are they?"

"Nematodes. Or something like one."

"Did we send 'em up by accident with the probes?"

"Doubt it. Those probes were tucked in bioshields and sterilized like you wouldn't believe."

"So they've been here all along?"

"I don't think they're indigenous. Maybe they came in on a meteor, but . . ." Burchenal switched off his torch, his gaze returning to Pettengill. "This can't be. It can't be."

"Maybe they did come in on a meteor and were lying dormant here. We warmed 'em, woke 'em up, fed 'em algae."

"You don't understand. The odds of there being any other life in the universe are infinitesimally small. The odds that it could survive on something other than its home planet are equally astronomical. The odds that it could travel to another solar system, let alone one where life already existed, are . . . impossible."

"But it's here. And it looks like we're not alone in the universe. You just discovered life on another planet. Life made by God. That's what's stamped on these things. That's what Bud would've said. He would've loved this."

"One mystery closed, another opened. . . ." Burchenal mumbled. "You know what this means?"

"Yeah. You're gonna be more famous than Darwin. They're gonna name buildings after you, spacecraft, cities on Mars."

The scientist withdrew a metal ampoule from his hip pocket, then fished out a telescoping rod that stretched from the length of a pencil to that of a baseball bat. He affixed the ampoule to the rod and drew daringly close to Pettengill's body. Liquid nitrogen jetted out of the rod's tip, quick freezing a nematode. Burchenal jiggled the worm inside the ampoule, withdrew the rig, and sealed the ampoule.

"Another souvenir?"

Burchenal popped off the ampoule and held it up. "You don't see how important this is?"

"I'm the janitor, remember?"

"These things are the reason why we're breathing. They make oxygen. Out of algae. Out of whatever they could digest from Hab. They make oxygen from junk. We won't have to move to a new planet—if we can save the old one." He waved the ampoule. "And even if this bugger thaws, I'm pretty sure he won't chew through titanium."

"Good." Gallagher lifted the radio's mike. "*Medea One*, ground crew. Bowman?"

"Here, Gallagher," she said, sounding utterly shocked. "Pettengill contacted me. Said you and Burchenal—"

"No time. We lost Pettengill. I got a lot to tell you."

"Okay, okay. But right now you're goal in life is getting to *Cosmos*. You got about five hours left."

"You think we can make it?"

"Houston's got a plan to get that probe back on-line. I'm awaiting the upload. You just go! Go!"

"You heard the woman," said Burchenal, his face scrunching up, his hand going for his broken rib.

"All right, Bowman. We're taking off. Ground crew, out." Gallagher looked to Pettengill's body. "Do we just leave him?"

Burchenal thumbed on his torch. He lit worms on Pettengill's legs, arms, and abdomen. A few exploded, kindling others in a domino effect that spread into the hole in Pettengill's abdomen. Half-muted internal explosions caused the terraformer's legs to expand inhumanly. More detonations ripped through the suit, some even jetting up to penetrate Pettengill's helmet in a grisly display of fireworks and viscera.

With the body still fountaining behind him, Burchenal double-timed back.

They continued north. The algae to their east sliced off in an abrupt, meandering line they now recognized as an eating pattern. Gallagher pulled a little ahead of Burchenal, but never opened the gap wider than a dozen meters.

As expected, AMEE did not launch her drone, knowing that it would only incite them and disrupt their "grieving period." She would remain at a cautionary distance, concealing her location and never losing their tracks. And once her psy-op program ran its course, she would kick straight into attack mode. Gallagher locked that fact away in a mental chest.

A trio of craters unfolded into view, the largest several hundred meters in diameter. They skirted the great impact basins, the hummocks more rocky than those kilometers back. With their footing dicey at best, Gallagher opted to slow the pace as, with ironic timing, Burchenal's boots slid out from under him. The scientist dropped to the ground, rode an invisible toboggan past Gallagher, then flipped onto his side and barreled down the knoll, making ten or twelve low-G revolutions before he slammed face first into talus mounded at the slope's base.

Too tired to holler for his comrade, Gallagher just hurried down the knoll, then dropped to his knees and rolled Burchenal onto his back.

Veiled in dust and gagging, Burchenal finally found his breath. "This is where I get off."

Gallagher circled behind the scientist, dug his hands into Burchenal's pits, then hoisted him to a sitting position. "There's this song my grandfather used to sing."

"Just leave me. I'm fucked."

"It's about partying."

"Gallagher, go."

"He said he studied it in college. It was by a group that called themselves the Beastie Guys, I think.

"Gallagher . . ."

"He said most of the music we listen to today is based on the groundbreaking work they did before the turn of the century."

"I'm gonna give you the specimens. You take 'em back."

"No, motherfucker. You're gonna stand up." Gallagher tested his grip on the man. "Ready. One, two, three!"

The researcher let out a bloodcurdling cry that announced he was on his feet. He flinched a moment more. "I just waved a white flag to AMEE."

"Screw her. Now, according to my nonexistent paramedic assessment, you can still walk. And if you can still walk, then you're not getting off. Not this easily, anyway." Gallagher led the scientist around the talus and back to more level ground. "You ready to sing?"

twenty-four

CRATERED UPLANDS
NEAR MCLAUGHLIN CRATER
MISSION TIME: DAY 184

A still Martian night. No wind tugged at Gallagher's shoulders. No wolves howled at the moons. No aroma of burning wood seeped into the air. He confronted only slope after frozen slope camouflaged in dust-lined shadows; heard only the sounds of his footsteps, breathing, and pulse; smelled only the faint trace of sulfur and soot wafting from his suit.

A still Martian night.

Several times he thought he saw his grandfather standing just beyond the light. Grandpa tugged out his cigar and waved him on.

Some time after that, Gallagher spotted his father, whose eyes grew dark as a snake's as he extended a leg to trip him. The image triggered a memory of the dream and the question of why his father devoured everything good. If Gallagher lived through this, he would sit down with the man, force him to shut up, and ask him that simple question.

"Why do I ruin all good things?" the bastard would reply. "Show me something good, something you deserve, something you should be proud of, and I'll slap you on the back."

"What about being chosen for the Mars mission?"

"Know what? You're right. That's something you deserve, something you should be proud of. Too bad you're the janitor. Why the hell didn't they give you more responsibility?"

"You know what you are? You're a cliché. A joke. And the only reason why you're this way is because your father did it to you. He convinced you that you're a piece of shit and now you just want company."

"What shrink died and left you the practice?"

"Forget it."

Gallagher realized with a start that his pace had dramatically increased. He pushed off and soared in a four-meter step, then bulldozed through eroded rock chips as he landed.

The beam of Burchenal's light bobbed over the hills to the east, the man himself ten, maybe fifteen meters back, shielded by the glare and probably still unwilling to talk, let alone sing. That the scientist remained on his feet testified to another of Mars' miracles. A quarter kilometer back, Burchenal had quipped that he had received the memo about dying in the cave but had simply forgotten to key it into his scheduler. Then he had gone on to voice the grim details of death by way of hypothermia "because you probably forgot, and I want you to know what's happening to me." Once Burchenal's core temperature dropped to about ninety-three degrees, muscle incoordination would become apparent, his movements would be slow and labored, and he would suffer mild confusion. At ninety degrees, violent shivering would persist, he would have difficulty thinking and speaking, and he would exhibit signs of depression. A core temp of eighty-six degrees would end his shivering as his muscles ran out of fuel to leave him incoherent, irrational, and unable to walk. At eighty-two degrees, his muscles would become rigid, his pulse and respiration would decrease, and his heart would probably fibrillate. If he plunged down to seventy-eight degrees, pulmonary edema and cardiac and respiratory failure would be inevitable. "Not so bad," the scientist had said. "I die in my sleep. And they say that when you're freezing to death, it gets real warm near the end."

Gallagher reluctantly tightened his strides. "We gotta pick it up," he called over the taccom.

"I'm trying."

And no doubt the scientist was, slamming his battered frame through the darkness, his breath hard and irregular until the taccom squelched it out. "What was it you said that scientists do?" asked Gallagher.

"We look for unity in diversity. The likenesses are hidden. We try to find them. Order doesn't display itself of itself. We discover it. And, in a sense, we create it. What we're looking at here is just disorder."

"So we found the nematodes. Do they give this place any order? Are you making connections?"

"When I said as one mystery closes, another opens, I meant that now we recognize the cause and effect relationships here, and our recognition brings some order and unity. But what sparked those relationships?"

"God did."

"Tell you what, Gallagher, you're wearing me down. At this point, I'd even entertain that."

Gallagher reached the edge of a headland that dropped off in a sheer cliff for about twenty meters. A sprawling vale below led toward a string of hogbacks about a kilometer off. He followed the cliff line as it turned gradually to the west and abutted two slopes descending into the vale at twenty and thirty-five degree gradients respectively. He waited at the smaller hill, and once Burchenal had reached him, they sidestepped together across rock much looser than it appeared. Gallagher's boot gave way, he began to fall, but Burchenal caught his arm and, with a tight-lipped groan, prevented the fall.

Driven by their own momentum, they covered the distance in a few seconds and came dashing into the vale at a runaway pace. Gallagher fought to slow himself as their boots emitted a peculiar rustling and the ground sucked at their heels.

Burchenal grabbed Gallagher's shoulder and pulled him to a halt. The scientist's beam puddled on soil shrouded in pink, phosphorescent algae. Gallagher panned his light over the vale, revealing an enormous living cloak, slick and glistening in their lights, its collar and hems reaching across the entire basin. He pivoted to their glowing footprints, and for a second it all seemed surreal: the Milky Way's band visible in the night sky; the distant mountains like the spines on some slumbering, otherworldly animal; and those prints, those shimmering prints, marking the infrared passage of two doomed aliens.

"Couldn't find any algae when we landed," said Burchenal. "Fifty-two varietals gone. Now we got more than we want. And it's slippery. Watch it."

"Hear something?" Gallagher asked, pricking up his

ears. Somewhere out there, wind rushed through tall meadow grass, or at least it sounded so.

"I hear it," Burchenal answered anxiously. He swept his light to the east. "Oh, man. Must be what Pettengill saw when he thought the ground moved."

About five hundred meters away, a shudder passed through the algae. Then another. Another. The shivers swelled into wavelets that glided off and crossed one another's paths. More shudders. More wavelets. Some coming in from the northeast, the southeast, the whole cloak now buckling at the seams as the horridly fascinating rollers gathered into a massive breaker reaching for them.

"Look at that," Burchenal said. "Nematodes are out there. And they're talking to one another—which pisses me off to no end. It's unfuckin' believable . . ."

While Burchenal had multiple Ph.D.s, Gallagher did not need a single advanced degree to conclude that the nematodes feasted on just about everything he had seen except rock, sand, and titanium. Trillions of them lay out there, their bodies tinted by the algae they had consumed, their appetites obviously unceasing. "We're outta here," he said, nudging the scientist from his trance.

Sprinting headlong across the algae, with the wave's rush and vroom beginning to reverberate off the hills, Gallagher aimed for the hogbacks, where the algae terminated in a smooth brush stroke. He juked right, left, chanced a look to his side, caught a half dozen worm-clustered waves pursuing even faster than the main one.

Ahead, more worms to the northeast and northwest got the word. The algae shook violently awake and heaved toward them in an effort to seal off the vale.

"My lungs are on fire," cried Burchenal, who now

dragged nearly a dozen meters away, combers of algae extinguishing his tracks.

"You just keep running, damn it. Just keep running."

Gallagher slowed as a long band of algae two meters ahead bulged. He charged left like a wide receiver skirting the sidelines until he had cleared the band and nearly ran straight into a humpbacked trio of waves that seemed more likely produced by that species of whale rather than by the collective instincts of a half billion tiny nematodes.

Jolted by a scream, Gallagher cocked his head at Burchenal, who stumbled forward, the waves now breaking over his boots. His voice came thin and grating. "We won't make it."

"We can try. Just gotta suck it up one more time." Gallagher lunged for the man, intent on carrying him.

A tendril split from the nematode sea, then branched into a score of varicose veins that now cut him off from Burchenal.

"Try to circle around," Gallagher implored the scientist.

But Burchenal would not listen. A look had come over him, an expression Gallagher had seen while serving in McMurdo, the look of a man who knows that he has done everything within his power to save himself but recognizes that the end has come, that the universe is merciless and indifferent, and that it is best to go quietly into the night.

Burchenal almost smiled as he unbuckled his e-suit's life support vest and sloughed it off. "Thought we'd share this for the launch. You'll need it now."

"No! Don't do it!"

The scientist wound up, about to pitch the vest, but temblors rocked his body with a force that brought him to his knees. Nematodes chewed into his boots, slithered up his ankles and hips, and now writhed on his arms. He knelt in a pool of his own blood. "I wouldn't have gotten this far without you. But even you can't help me run around these things. I'm only fit for decoy duty."

"No, you're not!"

"When you get back, there's two women in Missoula, one in Bozeman. Tell them each they were my last words. And make sure my horse gets sold to someone who knows how to ride. And oh, yeah. Bud was right. There's gotta be a reason. All of this wasn't an accident. But you'll still find the answers in science." Burchenal lobbed the vest.

Gallagher's arms stung with chills as he caught the life support pack and blinked off tears. "Burchenal!"

The main wave drew up behind the scientist, who stole a look but otherwise did not move. "Specimens are in the vest. Accomplish the mission. Get them to Earth."

Part of Gallagher wanted to ditch the vest and run to the man, but even as he argued with himself, the wave swallowed Burchenal and knocked him to his stomach. He pulled his head out of the muck and cried, "I'm gonna turn off my taccom now. I don't want you hearing this. Now go, you dumb fuck."

As the main breaker dissipated, more waves grew and surged toward Burchenal, some crashing into one another and kicking up jellylike sprays. Gallagher hesitated. Glanced to the vest, then back to Burchenal, now draped from head to toe in nematodes and flailing like a man on fire.

Gallagher let out a strangled cry and bolted, bolted for all he was worth; every damned bit of energy he had left funneled into his legs and propelled him the hell out of there. *Accomplish the mission. Accomplish the mission.*

More waves targeted him. From the right. The left. Some just off his heels. *Hang on to the vest, the radio.*

Another cry. Not fear. Anger now for the loss of his friend. He wove right, slipped, and—holy shit—caught himself. More of the bastards up ahead, coiling through the algae like nightcrawlers in a bait box. Go. Go. Go.

The algae thinned as he neared the hogbacks, having stitched a path so sinuous that it had made him dizzy. Or maybe that was from the richer oxygen. He sucked in long and gratifying breaths.

Repressing the urge to look back, he dialed up the pace and made a beeline for two boulders spaced two meters apart and towering like stanchions of the night sky. If he could reach them. . . .

Boots crunched. Waves of nematodes resounded in muffled roars, cued by each footfall. He swallowed. Winced over his dry throat. Made the final few steps—

And cleared the algae.

He turned back, leaned on one of the boulders to catch his breath, and squinted at a thin beam of light shining up from the vale. The light flickered, flickered, died.

Gallagher set down the radio and unbuckled his own life support vest. He tossed it away, slapped on Burchenal's, then checked the supply. Six minutes. Radio back in hand, he faced the hogbacks, ready to begin a parallel ascent—

When it hit him.

He had been the first man on Mars.

Now he was the last.

twenty-five

During Bowman's first meeting with the controllers at
Houston, Andy Lowenthal had said that with a surname
like hers, she should be going to Jupiter instead of Mars.
Bowman had smiled politely, but had long since grown
weary of the reference. Yes, she knew all about that char-
acter named Dave Bowman who had disappeared in that
seminal novel by that legendary science fiction writer.
And wasn't it oh-so-fitting that here she was, "another
Bowman," heading into space. One geek reporter had
even asked if she were taking along an electronic copy of
the novel. "No," she had said. "I've already read it and
the sequels. But I will be taking along books by Heinlein,
Bradbury, Zubrin, Bizony, Bova, Robinson, Bear, and
Baxter."

Trouble was, Bowman had never found time to read.

Even after she had completed each day's tasks, she constantly found herself not in the mood. And after the night she and Gallagher had nearly kissed, she had spent nearly all of her free time doing menial jobs in an attempt to stop thinking about him. Santen had twice questioned her actions and had eventually chalked them up to an obsessive command style. He had no idea that she lay awake at night, contemplating a future with a man who was an unlikely combination of reckless dreamer and pragmatic engineer.

Did she love him? Not yet. Of course, she loved the idea of being in love with him. But that night, something had held him back, and she wanted so badly to know what that something had been. Was she responsible? If so, what could she do about it? Should she do anything?

Bowman took a deep breath, blinked her gaze clear, then once more studied the pictures coming in from the optical scope. In thirty seconds, she would be out of comm blackout and slip into the enfolding gloom of the planet's dark side. The scope would automatically lock on to Gallagher's last location, then follow a line forward. She had already called up topographic overlays that marked *Cosmos*'s coordinates on the images. A data strip on the bottom would show Gallagher's average speed and estimated time to the probe once the AI identified him.

Sunlight peeled back from the great T of *Medea One*'s bow to expose the darkness. Now, in the soft light of touchboards, screens, and glow panels, Bowman held her breath. "Ground crew, *Medea One*. Gallagher?"

Come on, be there.

"Ground crew, *Medea One*. Gallagher, do you copy?"

His huffing and puffing cut through a faint hiss and crackle. "Bowman? Yeah, I'm . . . I'm here."

"Thank God." Her gaze darted to the optical scope's screen. Fuzzy green images of the terrain panned across the display until the scope tracked a glowing figure. The data strip showed three boxes of scrolling numbers as the AI made its computations. "I'm locating you now. What's your status?"

"Still . . . still heading for *Cosmos*. AMEE's drone is back on my tail. And . . . and . . . Burchenal's dead." He had almost sobbed the news. "I'm alone now. Burchenal gave his life for me, Bowman. He was . . . a brave man."

"Then you gotta make it count," she said, her voice cracking. "You got three hours to get there."

"I'm on course?"

"Yeah. Your celestial navigation is paying off."

"Then I should have three and a half hours."

"Houston says I need to talk to you when you get there. You need to shave off a half hour, otherwise I'll be in comm blackout when you arrive. I'll burn a little fuel to slow my orbit, but you gotta go a little faster. That's all. Just a little faster."

"You kidding me?"

She scanned the screen, found a reason to change the subject. "Got coordinates on AMEE for you. She's about a hundred meters south of your location."

"I can't do it in three hours, Bowman. I can't go any faster . . . than . . . this. And don't waste the fuel. You gotta get home."

His failing will infuriated her. She slammed fists on her armrests, then leapt from the seat. "You listen to me, you bastard. I'm not going home alone. So you get those boots moving a little faster. Do you hear me? Don't stop, damn it. Don't stop."

"Say you'll leave if I'm not there."

"I can't."

"Say it!"

"All right, I'll do it," she lied.

"I'm going . . . ground crew . . . out."

Bowman pressed fingers into the corners of her eyes. *He didn't sound good. No, he didn't sound good at all. . . .*

MEDEA ONE MISSION CONTROL
JOHNSON SPACE CENTER, HOUSTON
MISSION TIME: DAY 184

"Briefing's in ten minutes," the capcom reminded Russert.

"Hey, Andy?" Russert called to Lowenthal, who still sat at his desk, in the throes of programming with an old Russian who now reeked of chimichangas and hot salsa. "Is the upload away?"

"Uh, we're having a 'little problem,' " Lowenthal answered.

"Define 'little problem.' "

Borokovski glanced up from the notebook computer's display. "There is setup magician to help establish communications. It is supposed to make setup easy, but magician is playing trick and asking for file we do not have."

"And we called back the Smithsonian," added Lowenthal. "No luck finding it."

"And nothing on the auctions," Skavlem tossed in.

"We try manual setup now," Borokovski said, then tightened his lips and belched. "You go to media briefing alone. We work here."

Lowenthal must have read Russert's expression. He crossed from the desk, his face never more intent. "Don't worry, Flight. We'll get Bowman this upload."

"All right," Russert said at last. "Let me go throw myself to the sharks."

"I'm thinking a shower and shave first," Lowenthal suggested with a weak smile.

Russert nodded, then an outburst of Russian epithets stole his attention.

Borokovski pushed away from the desk, shook his finger at the computer, swore again, then faced them. "Mr. Lowenthal? Come here. You must see. I think maybe we have other problem."

"What other problem?" Russert demanded.

"I'll handle this," said Lowenthal. "You go."

CRATERED UPLANDS
EN ROUTE TO *COSMOS* LANDING SITE
MISSION TIME: DAY 184

Another vale lay before Gallagher, and his light faded into the vast, corrugated emptiness. He exploited the lighter gravity as much as he could, now unimpressed by his flying, comic-book-hero steps, his thoughts firmly battened to the course ahead. He plotted each landing to avoid shallow groves and small piles of rocks heaped like garden mulch. The incessant hum of AMEE's scout seemed more akin to a ticking clock than the maneuvering jets that functioned like air foils to keep it aloft. "You're a smart girl," he told AMEE. "You must've kept to the hills. Sorry, but I was hoping you'd meet up with the nematodes."

The scout took no offense.

Gallagher peered at his watch. *Three hours she says. Well, I'm down to two. And I'm a scared son of a bitch, but don't tell anyone. And . . . yeah, cleared that pothole. Martians need to get someone out here from the depart-*

ment of transportation to patch these damn holes. "Isn't that right, Burchenal?"

Don't moan about it, Gallagher. Surface of Mars is more subdued than that of the heavily cratered parts of the moon. Plains and uplands have smaller crater densities.

"You're a goddamned ghost, and I'm putting words in your mouth. You're supposed to agree, not toss me a bunch of geobabble."

But you know me too well. You wouldn't put lies in my mouth. That's what I would've said.

"So, am I gonna make it?"

I think you'll make it there. Whether you get Cosmos *started . . . that's another story. And with AMEE still on your ass . . . well, don't take this personally, but I'd have to bet against you.*

"What about you, Bud? Think I'll make it?"

Oh, don't bring him into this. I don't wanna hear anymore mystic warrior pseudoscience faith bullshit.

"Ignore him, Bud. What do you think?"

Well, from a mystic warrior pseudoscience faith bullshit perspective, I'd have to say that I'll keep you in prayer, that God has reason for this, and—

Oh, man. Here comes another quote.

No quotes this time, Burchenal, because Robby's creating my words and hardly remembers the ones I already told him. But I'll say this, Robby. You've faced a lot in your life, but you never gave up believing in yourself— even when others doubted you. And that thing that inspired you to help Burchenal? You'll use it to help yourself.

He'll use his intuition and his knowledge of physics and electronics systems to save himself.

"Gentlemen. I'll try to use both."

Otherwise, he'll wind up like me. Paranoid. Tortured. Victimized to the very end. And you still think I murdered Santen? I want to tell you I did. But you can't call it murder.

"Then what did you do?"

I don't know. I really don't know. But you can't hate me. You need to understand what happened. And you have no idea what it's like to be me.

After an hour-long conversation, the company of specters vaporized for the evening. Gallagher's vision fogged up as he left the valley and ventured into a pass between slopes. Once he cleared the pass, he emerged on a plateau and glanced to the night sky for another heading. Maybe he was still on course. Maybe not. The stars swirled, and the shields of distant craters closed in. Ignore it, he commanded himself, then vaulted on for fifteen, twenty, forty-five minutes. Another hour slipped by.

Then he fell.

Just like that.

Didn't see the rocks or whatever had snagged his boot. Left knee hit first. Then right. Then onto his hands and knees, the radio held tightly in his hand.

AMEE's scout strafed him, blasted into an eighty-degree climb, then traced an imaginary lunette, coming in for another pass. The drone's tiny camera fed back images of the wounded enemy to the multi-taloned queen herself.

Gallagher remained there, sifting oxygen from the thinning air and realizing the full extent to which Burchenal had struggled against hypothermia's siren song, that damned song enticing Gallagher to lie down and sleep, yes, sleep.

"Ground crew, *Medea One*, copy?"

Her voice lifted him like two powerful arms. Back on his feet and still a little dizzy, he unloosed himself in a quickening jog. "Copy, Bowman. Time?"

"I'll be on the light side in twenty-eight minutes."

"And how close am I?"

"You're practically on top of it."

"I don't see anything. Maybe the angle's screwing up your data. Maybe I screwed celestial nav. Maybe I'm way off course."

"It's there. Keep going."

He reached for his suit light, panned it across the plateau, across an interminable route of craters and rocks so monotonous to the eye that he struggled to focus. Nothing, damn it. No Russian rock collector among these billions of rocks. He swung around, jogging backward, his light scouring the regolith. "What if I ran right past it?"

Nothing there. He turned back.

Something flashed in the corner of his beam.

And there it was. Right in front him, in all of its rock-probe ugliness. "I found it."

"See?" cried Bowman. "And you did it in just over three hours, like I said you would."

"You get that upload from Houston?"

"Yeah, like fifteen minutes and two heart attacks ago."

"Okay. Tell me what I need to do."

twenty-six

As Gallagher neared the probe, three stubby solar panels shaped like isosceles triangles tilted toward his light.

Then he got a good look at the thing.

It hardly inspired confidence.

No, Gallagher had not expected to find a looming spacecraft, but he had imagined something more than a lander assembled from parts bought off pegboards at a Russian Wal-Mart. Six rickety-looking, V-shaped leg assemblies terminated in two-meter-wide landing pads, three of which lay fully buried in the sand. The legs sprang from a heptagonal launching base about three meters wide from which eight rock-collecting arms of varying sizes extended like genetic mutations. High- and low-gain dishes protruded up from one side, their surfaces heavily scored from pebble bombardment. Next to them jutted the usual array of weather monitoring instruments, a conical x-ray spectrometer, and three heavily shielded cameras.

Atop this whole flimsy affair sat the flattened sphere of the launch vehicle, fenced in by four capsule-shaped liquid fuel tanks fastened to the sphere by corroded metal straps.

Gallagher circled the craft and found a half-meter-by-two hatch positioned at chest height. That would be the container's lid. Even without seeing inside, Gallagher knew the folks at Houston had been right. No way would they have crammed three men in there.

"There's an infrared maintenance port right near the spectrometer," said Bowman. "Do you see it? It should be marked."

Gallagher shined his light on a square panel about the size of a mudguard; whether it was the port in question he had no idea. *This is that moment my Russian language teacher would have told me about—if I had studied Russian.* He frowned at the placard:

ИНФРАКРАСНЫЙ ОБСЛУЖИВАНИЕ ПОРТ

"You see it?"

"I got something, he replied. "It's marked in Cyrillic. But all right, I think this is it." He tried the first of two thumbscrews that would allow the panel to swing forward on hinges. They wouldn't budge. He stripped off his gloves, then rubbed his hands in some sand to keep his skin from sticking to the metal. He summoned strength into one hand, but his joints were so stiff that he could barely grip the screw. "I'm too cold. My fingers won't work."

"Use your teeth. *You can do this.*"

He dug into the small tool pack at his hip, found the power ratchet, reached for the button. Damned thing would not turn on. He took up Bowman's suggestion and brought the tool's handle to his mouth and bit down on the power button. He slapped the ratchet's ring over the screw and it automatically tightened and began spinning. Once the screw was out, Gallagher discarded it and began work on the second one. Before the tool had fully loosened the screw, Gallagher pulled it away and began spinning the screw himself in an effort to thaw his frozen hand. The screw gave, and the panel creaked open to reveal bundles of multi-colored wires framing the IR port's small, darkly tinted panel. Above them hung a digital status display and shielded electronics boxes with dog-eared labels:

ПЕРЕДАЧА ДАННЫХ
МОДЕМ С ИЗМЕНЕНИЕМ СКОРОСТИ ПЕРЕДАЧ

Despite the Cyrillic, he had a fairly good idea that he was looking at a data communications modem, though he still could not fathom what Houston and Bowman had in mind.

"How's it going, Gallagher?"

"I'm in. What now?"

"Need to switch your radio back to data communications and hardwire it to the port. We're gonna use your radio to bypass *Cosmos*'s damaged comm system, then I'll upload what you need. Takes about two minutes. Now pull off the optical case. Two wires coming out of it. Schematics don't indicate what colors they are. Borokovski doesn't remember."

"Glad he's not on a bomb team. Give me a minute."

"Make it a quick one. You got only twenty-four left."

After flexing his fingers several times, Gallagher reached inside and wiggled off the IR port's panel. A half dozen copper leads snaked from the unit, and Gallagher began the laborious process of cutting and splicing them back together, his efforts clouded by his breath. All the while, AMEE's drone whirred somewhere above, watching, transmitting.

"Nineteen minutes, Gallagher."

"I know. I know. We got six leads in here. Spliced 'em all. You're gonna have to start the upload while I experiment down here with combinations of connections. I'm guessing that when I hit the right one, we'll get something on this display, providing it still has power."

"Borokovski believes the port's cell will still function."

"Okay. Wait thirty seconds, then start the upload."

"Copy."

It took nearly the entire thirty seconds for Gallagher to prepare the radio. He touched the two main leads to *Cosmos*'s spliced wires, and after several attempts, with the panel rising from the dead then dying like cheap Christmas lights, he finally established a connection. "All right, Bowman. I'm set down here. Ten seconds, then start the upload from the beginning."

"Affirmative. Ten seconds."

Gallagher twisted the two main leads in place, then fell back onto the lander and shrank to the floor. He pulled his gloves back on and shut his eyes. His cheeks and ears felt itchy from the chilblains, but he knew better than to rub them, which would, he remembered, cause more damage to his peripheral capillary beds. He just sat, listened to the wind murmur, to AMEE's drone purring as it gained altitude. He felt completely relaxed now and satisfied that he had at least come this far. He could accept death more easily because, like Burchenal, he knew he had done everything in his power to save himself. But an undercurrent of pain still ran through that acceptance. What was that story that Bud had read to him, the story he had been trying to remember while assembling the radio?

I knew you wouldn't remember half the things I told you.

"Cut me some slack. I'm no scholar like you."

It was "The Open Boat" by Stephen Crane. And do you remember the part we discussed?

"About the rage of those sailors on that little lifeboat?"

Exactly. Remember the lines:

If I am going to be drowned—if I am going to be drowned—if I am going to be drowned, why, in the name of the seven mad gods who rule the sea, was I allowed to come thus far and contemplate sand and trees? Was I brought here merely to have my nose dragged away as I was about to nibble the sacred cheese of life? It is preposterous. If this old ninny-woman, Fate, cannot do better than this, she should be deprived of the management of men's fortunes. She is an old hen who knows not her intention. If she has decided to drown me, why did she not do it in the beginning and save me all this trouble? The whole affair is absurd. . . . But, no, she cannot mean to drown me. She dare not drown me. She cannot drown me. Not after all this work.

And that's what I feel, Gallagher thought. *The struggle between the work bringing peace . . . or anger.*

Something glinted at the corner of Gallagher's eye. He cocked his head toward the display as data zigzagged

down the screen. Something about WIN 2020 LAUNCH PRO-
GRAM STATUS and input chain commands on-line. A cur-
sor blinked. He rolled anxiously onto his knees and
crawled back to the port, removed the leads, and gaped at
the screen. "Bowman? I think it worked. Still has power."

"Good. There's a tray beneath the display. Slide it out;
it's a rudimentary touchboard."

Pinching the little handles, Gallagher complied, and
the touchboard lit as it clinked into place. "I'm on the
board. Of course, it's in Cyrillic."

"All systems are under manual control now. You
should be able to run general sys diagnostics. We'll run
the launch stuff in a minute. Borokovski set it up so you
don't have to learn the Russian alphabet. Just type Y,
yeah it looks just like a Y. Then hit the colon, the forward
slash, then there's a symbol that looks like an A with a
flat top and the left side slanted inward. Hit it four times."

With a finger like an ice pick, Gallagher hunt-and-
pecked Y:/дддд then eyed the screen.

Wouldn't you know, pinpoints effloresced into multiple boxes, each showing the results of individual systems
checks. Flight dynamics, guidance, data processing, payload, propulsion, and electrical systems all flashed NO
ANOMALIES FOUND messages in highly readable English.
The comm system came up with multiple problems, but
they were obviously of no consequence. "Diagnostic
complete. We're in the green."

"Thanks, I can breathe. Okay, this thing only has two
settings: on and off. Right now, On sends it all the way
back to Earth. As you lack food, water, and a long-term
air supply, that'd be bad."

"So what now?"

"We want just enough power to reach geostatic orbit.
I've recalculated for your weight and probable weight

loss on planet, your suit, and your thermal. You need to drain a liter out of each fuel tank. There's a central purge. You'll have to measure it somehow. It's gotta be pretty exact."

"Russians couldn't add a gas gauge?"

"Clock is ticking. Shuddup and figure it out. You got anything down there you can use?"

He thought a curse. "I'll get back to you."

Bracing himself on the lander, Gallagher stood, then walked once more around the probe. *Something large enough to hold four liters. Think two soda bottles.*

A few of the larger rock-collecting arms had rectangular sample containers bolted at their third joints. He slipped an electronic tape measure from his tool pack, thumbed it on, then guided the sensor over one box's dimensions, taking mental note of each. Then he removed his HHC, wondering if AMEE still jammed it. Yes, she did. "Bowman, I need you to do some math. A box forty centimeters by twenty centimeters square and ten high. How deep's four liters?"

"Pop quiz. Hang on. Okay. Okay. Here it is. Eight and three-quarter centimeters."

"I have a sample container that'll work. Now the fun part of unbolting it. Standby."

The box hung from two thin rods about six centimeters long. Gallagher tucked his gloves under his arms, then, with his screwdriver, he dug around the couplings to loosen them, but they had had nearly thirty years to corrode into place. He wasted another few seconds tugging and swearing, then jerked back and booted the entire arm assembly, booted it again, and again, and again until the arm and accompanying container snapped right off the lander.

Thanking God for Russian engineers on tight budgets,

he dragged the amputated arm over to the central purge
valve located beneath one of the tanks. He opened the
rock container, measured the depth, then notched a fill
mark into the steel with his screwdriver's tip. Taking in a
long breath and holding it, he reached for the large wing
nut, prayed it had not jammed shut and would not break
off in his hand, then applied a little pressure.

Out poured the rank-smelling fuel with a wonderful
splashing inside the container. In a dozen breaths, the liquid bubbled up to the mark, and he flicked the valve shut.
Then he dragged the arm and container about ten meters
away and stowed it behind a boulder. If he left it too close
to the lander, he might as well douse himself in gasoline
and light the match. "Bowman? Fuel level is set. What
now?"

"Launch diagnostics. Same input as before, only hit
that letter that looks like an N before you hit that funky
A."

"Got it," he said. Y:/пдддд and Gallagher skimmed the
screen as the program executed.

"And, oh yeah," Bowman added. "Avoid running anything that says ignition."

He made a lopsided grin. "Got that one covered."

More boxes popped on the screen with colorful graphs
indicating fuel levels, heat shield integrity, and a half
dozen other readings that Gallagher could care less about
so long as their bars all rose into the green.

All of them did.

But one.

Ignition power.

The graph said that three hundred volts at six amps
would put him in the green.

He had exactly zero. Secondary cell dead as a doornail.

If I am going to die—if I am going to die—if I am going

to die, why, in the name of the god of war who rules this
planet, was I allowed to come thus far and contemplate
the launch and the return home?

Another box opened in the display's corner:

300V IGNITION CELL #4987YH9H9H9H
REPLACEMENT PART #338J98928YU39
ORDER ONLINE VIA SATNET@GSN.SS.XFT.CELL
ALL MAJOR CREDIT CARDS ACCEPTED

"Gallagher?"

He stood there, the screen morphing into a blue sheet that smothered him.

"Gallagher?"

"Ignition battery's dead," he moaned. "There's not enough power to launch."

"Is there anything else you can use?"

His gaze turned to the barren landscape, and his reply came through a hiss. "Let me look around. Maybe there's a high voltage source here. Nope. Just rocks."

"What about your radio's cell?"

"It's twenty-eight volts. That leaves me only two hundred seventy-two volts shy."

"Let me check the schematic. Maybe this thing's got other cells you can use."

As he waited, Gallagher slumped to the dirt. No way would anything else on the probe rely on a cell as powerful. She wasted her time, but if it made her feel better to check, then so be it.

"Gallagher? Sorry, there's . . . well the other cells won't . . ."

"Yeah, I know." He tossed his head back and clutched the soil. "Shit. I didn't wanna die here."

twenty-seven

Bowman frantically tapped through *Cosmos*'s schematics, her finger keeping time with her racing pulse. *Come on. What did I miss? What did I miss?* She had about four minutes until comm blackout, about thirty until main engine burn. And damn it, she would not give up. That was not her.

Mars had already claimed four souls.

He would not claim another.

But the facts were clear. Gallagher did not have a cell, and without it, *Cosmos* would not launch. What else did she need? A thousand people with bullhorns to remind her?

Then what am I doing? I didn't miss anything. There's nothing to see.

She switched off the schematics and pictured herself

smashing apart the Flight Deck with a steel rod. Sparks showered everywhere; consoles exploded; shattered permaglass and plastic clattered across the deck. She inhaled the coils of toxic smoke encircling her until she died knowing that she had struck out at the helplessness.

I can't go home alone. I just can't. "Gallagher?"

"Know what pisses me off more than dying?" he answered abruptly. "I got screwed out of my last meal. Funny, that's all I'm thinking about. Food. A big plate of ziti. Nachos. Fried rice. Ribs. Hot dogs. Lots of relish. There's this little pizza place in Daytona. I used to get this stuffed pizza thing. And I remember Bud talking about bacon one day. He had us all tasting it. I wish I could do that now."

"Maybe I can help you."

"No. You'll be gone. What do you got, couple, three minutes till comm blackout?"

"I'm gonna stay. We'll talk till we can't talk anymore."

"Bowman—"

"I'm not cutting out on the last person on my team."

"It's not worth it."

"I'm mission commander. It's worth it to me. I've thought about this. I know what I'm doing."

"No, you don't. If you stay, then all of it dies with us. Who's gonna tell our story? There's so much to tell and so much everyone back home has to learn. You wanna stay 'cause it feels bad leaving. Get over it."

The bastard was terribly right. She gasped his name. "Gallagher . . ."

"How much time we got left?"

"About two minutes."

"So we have two minutes. And here's what you need to tell 'em. First off, the worms . . ."

"What worms?"

"Burchenal said they're like nematodes. Maybe they rode a meteor to Mars and we set off their alarm clocks. Who knows? But they ate most of the algae, ate Hab, and they got Pettengill and Burchenal. Irony is, they eat junk and make oxygen."

"So there's life on Mars?"

"Besides me? Yeah, a whole lot of it. That's why you need to leave. Burchenal thought these worms might help us save Earth. And maybe this mission will be a success after all."

She winced at the clock. "Anything you want me to do?"

"Let 'em know Bud was a hero. So was Santen. And even Pettengill. Tell all of Burchenal's ex-wives that they were his last words. Make sure his horse gets sold to someone who can ride. And make sure he gets credit for discovering the worms."

"What about you?"

"Just . . . I guess . . . tell my father that what I did here I did well. He needs to hear that. And tell everyone else I love them. Otherwise, you can just listen to me babble for another minute."

She closed her eyes to dam the tears. "I'm here."

"So, Bowman, I gotta tell you, I really hate Mars. I didn't come here to be a citizen. I'd never want to live here. I'd miss Earth too much, the way I do now. The way I miss a lot of things." His voice grew heavy with regret. "I should've kissed you."

"Yeah. You should've kissed me."

"*You* could've kissed me."

"I'm old fashioned," she admitted as the first spate of tears broke free. "I like to know I'm wanted."

"Of course, if I *had* kissed you, saying good-bye would be even tougher."

"It couldn't be tougher." Bowman's lips trembled as daylight wedged across the flight deck. "Gallagher? Are you there? Gallagher?"

CRATERED UPLANDS
COSMOS LANDING SITE
MISSION TIME: DAY 184

"Good-bye, Bowman. I'll miss you. Bowman? Bowman?"

She had not heard him, and that was just par for the day. Pettengill had been right—at least about one thing. Life was just like high school, full of math and beautiful women that you're too stupid to tell you love. There had obviously been something there, and now he knew just how badly he had screwed up that night. The alcohol had meant nothing. She had wanted him to kiss her. Now he would die never knowing that moment. He released a cackle that would drive observers cowering from the lunatic who had produced it. She would never kiss his swollen and chapped lips now, never mind his two-day beard and lack of bathing. Was that why he laughed? No. *Have to laugh, laugh at the pain.*

A hint of sunrise woke in the distance, the hills now silhouetted against an ice-blue aura. *Maybe I'll last another day or two. I can climb inside* Cosmos *for shelter, and if Burchenal's torch still works, I can burn fuel to keep warm. Can I eat the algae? The worms? Melt the permafrost for water? Yeah, I'll poison myself. Maybe that's the way to go.* "What do you think?" he hollered at AMEE's drone. "Ain't it a bitch that you and I'll be here forever? Stuck on this big, cold rock? Couple years, you'll be dead, too." He leaned back, took his gaze out of focus. "Here it comes, here it comes, here it comes—"

His sleeve panel beeped. AMEE's infrared point of view snapped on the screen, the image bobbing as she scampered over rocks. Her psy-op program had apparently run its course. She would now eliminate the target and move on with impunity.

Gallagher gritted his teeth at the display. "Letting me know you're still coming, huh? Just remember, your days are as numbered as—"

AMEE had an energy cell.

He cursed himself for not remembering sooner. But the exhaustion, the cold, the hunger. . . .

Yes, she had a cell. He could not recall how powerful it was, but he knew it had to be stronger than three hundred volts. He rolled onto his stomach and crawled under the lander, located a second maintenance port, and pried it open with his screwdriver. Guided by his suit light, Gallagher reached for the battery, a cylindrical cell about the size of a sports bottle and IDed by its 300 вольт label. He unclipped the battery from a pair of copper bindings and pulled it out. Then he scanned the nearby circuit board and found them: voltage regulators, probably the old TO-220s. Even if AMEE's battery were much stronger, these babies would protect the system during the initial surge. Sure, they would probably burn out, but Gallagher would already be in the air. *Damn it, this could work.*

Back on his feet, he hurried around the probe, searching for something he could use as a weapon. Still, a metal pole would only work if he could get in close, otherwise he might as well wave a cotton swab. What he really needed was an old-fashioned diversion, something to keep her busy.

He smashed free another of *Cosmos*'s arms, twisted off

the talon, then gave his makeshift sword a test swing. Easy part done. Now a plan to divert her. . . .

A fire? Maybe. Still enough oxygen to produce a decent burn. But how could he get close enough to douse her with fuel? He needed a way to deliver the fuel to her. What did he have?

He swung back to *Cosmos*'s touchboard and set down the pole. The screen above showed the keys he should press to bring up various commands, including a parts list from the diagnostic program. He pulled that up and waited as the CPU translated Cyrillic to English. Tracing a finger down the list, Gallagher stopped at a pair of words: ПАРАШЮТ (PARACHUTE). And from the corner of his eye, he spotted one of two square compartments mounted on the underside of the launch vehicle. The Cyrillic matched.

Okay. Gain access to the chute. How? Through the diagnostic program. After a few second's worth of trial and error, the chute's command box eclipsed a corner of the screen. He tapped two keys. One of the chute doors popped open. *Yes.* Wasting no time, Gallagher unfurled the huge bundle of white nylon, followed by the smaller drogue chute. Then he jogged back to the severed rock arm and its fuel-filled container. He dragged the arm over to the parachute and carefully saturated the nylon canopy. With AMEE's drone hovering curiously above, Gallagher rolled up the chute, jammed it back into the compartment, then sealed the hatch. He checked the command box once more, memorized the key he needed to press, then sat. Within a minute, a faint rumble lured him away from the probe.

About a hundred meters out, an inhuman shadow picked its way over the plateau, a six-legged Beret who, with the element of surprise, could probably take on an entire platoon. Gallagher checked his sleeve screen. AMEEvision played on without commercial interruption. "Moving in for the kill, huh? Good. Come on over and finish me. Then you can be here alone. Just walking around Mars. Whistling at the wind." Gallagher lowered himself to the soil. "Know what? Screw you. It couldn't happen to a nicer girl."

The bot forged on in three, six, eight meter strides, servos whining in protest.

Gallagher's eyelids grew heavy, and his voice now came in a heavy slur. "Better hurry, AMEE. You're losing your chance to kill me while I'm still awake. Air's thinner. I'm very cold, very tired. So damned tired. I gotta sleep. Gotta put my head down and go to sleep for the rest of my life . . ." Gallagher tipped onto his side and rested his head on the ground, his left eye closed, his right eye trained on his sleeve screen. *Don't cut this signal, you bitch.*

The whine and rumble drew closer. Gallagher's heart slammed against his ribs. He saw himself lying on the ground, drawn and pathetic, haloed in green.

AMEE kept coming, kept performing billions of calculations in order to reach complex, logical conclusions that would, he hoped, exclude her recognition of the gambit. She would deem him asleep and realize that she could dispatch him with minimal effort and with the least risk to herself. Gallagher was the last one. His death would complete the mission.

Despite that strong possibility, Gallagher still clung to an ember of hope that AMEE would pause, recognize him as her primary operator, as her friend, and switch back to techie mode. That would be nice, but he doubted she would reach an electronic epiphany any time soon.

Dust vibrated up into Gallagher's eye as the bot came within two meters.

One meter.

A lithe shadow fell over him.

AMEE raised an arm. Her talon snapped shut into a spike. Then her entire frame reared back for the plunge.

twenty-eight

CRATERED UPLANDS
COSMOS LANDING SITE
MISSION TIME: DAY 184

Gallagher took in a long breath. Held it. Stiffened every muscle in his body.

AMEE's arm dropped like a guillotine even as Gallagher rolled out of its path, landed on his hands and knees, then catapulted toward *Cosmos,* gliding three meters before he crashed onto his stomach. He coughed away the dust, stood, then turned back.

The bot was right there, tipped onto her hind legs as forelimbs extended toward him.

He stabbed the touchboard.

The chute exploded from its compartment, and, with no updraft, it unfurled laterally, falling over AMEE in great waves of nylon.

With the pole in one hand, Burchenal's ignited torch in the other, Gallagher touched the flame to one of the chute lines. The fuse burned back toward the canopy, until with a terrific *whoosh,* the whole thing went up in roiling, orange-blue flames.

AMEE fought wildly against the burning trap, her limbs tenting up fiery peaks as Gallagher circled behind her. He lifted the burning chute with his pole, then dove into the gap and struggled forward through the smoky darkness. About midway under AMEE, he flipped onto his back, the suit light whipping across the panel he wanted. He opened it, then screamed and drove the pole home in a grinding, sparking thrust that penetrated AMEE's CPU. From somewhere outside came a metallic clang, then a snake of current wound up the pole and blew his hands away, leaving the pole dangling there.

Choking, Gallagher crawled crablike toward the chute's edge, kicked it up, then passed beneath it and into the better air. He glanced back at the bot, who writhed involuntarily now as the chute flames died. Her drone lay alongside her, half buried in the sand, and Gallagher thought of retrieving his pole and swatting the dead vulture. Instead, he scooped up the scorched parachute lines and peeled the smoldering nylon away from AMEE.

The bot had fallen forward, her posterior still held high on fully extended limbs. Her camera eyes had gone dark, and tethers of smoke wound up from her belly.

"Robust, real-time response to the environment, my butt," Gallagher muttered, then stole a few breaths before dropping back down and pulling himself under her head. He thumbed open a secondary maintenance port just above her octagonal main service panel. AMEE's e-source lay deep in her electronic entrails, and Gallagher buried his arm to the hilt in order to reach the two knobs that would release it. He pulled one down, then the other, and the silver soda can came free in his hand. If there had been a label identifying the cell's voltage, some anal retentive engineer had removed it. It just had to be more than three hundred volts. Had to be.

With only twelve minutes until Bowman would fire main engines, Gallagher hustled back to *Cosmos*. He tore two pieces of wire from his radio, each about ten centimeters long. He fastened those to each end of the e-source with some electrical tape from his tool pack.

Now came the critical part of attaching the leads and mounting the cell, and since the rest of *Cosmos*'s innards looked as coat-hangered together as some of the cars Gallagher had owned as a teenager, he would have to be careful not to bump anything too sharply. He wound the leads around the contact points, then jammed the e-source sideways between two electronics boxes. Seemed like a snug fit. He twisted free of the port, then returned to the touchboard and ran the launch diagnostic once more. *Come on, you bastard. . . .*

Bingo. Ignition power in the green. Warnings about voltage being too high—and who cares about that?

Launch clock. Could he start it from out here? He and Bowman had never covered this part of the procedure. He selected a box labeled launch command. Simple enough. Start a countdown with no stops. How much time? Say sixty seconds. One press to start the clock.

Now for the launch container. He rolled the handle counterclockwise and pulled. The hatch gave with a hiss of stale air that sent a hand to his nose and mouth. He yanked out three sample trays loaded with rocks and tossed them away. Damn. Barely room enough inside for one, let alone two. And the only thing that would protect him from the scorching heat of launch was the vehicle's thin heat shield. *What did I expect? First class? Champagne? Warm towels after my meal?*

Okay, one other small problem. How to seal himself inside. With the hatch still open, he dialed the lock, then slammed the door closed. Got to love Russian engineering. They had designed the thing like an old style car trunk. No problem there.

"I'm getting off this planet," he said, heading back to the touchboard. Tap. LAUNCH CLOCK INITIATED: 00:00:30.

He hurried back to the collection container, gripped the outer rim, then swung into the cold box that could easily have come from a hospital's morgue. He sealed the hatch.

This should be interesting. . . .

Enveloped in darkness, Gallagher slid his hood over his face, then pressurized his suit. Burchenal's life-support gauge reported five minutes and thirty-four seconds of air left. Bowman would pull up stakes in about seven minutes. Launch in T-minus ten seconds.

Gallagher closed his eyes. He spread his palms across the steel and pressed his back as deeply into the metal as he could. *It just takes faith. That's all I need. Just a little.*

Three, two, one—

Something clicked. Silence.

Then a powerful grinding noise from thirty-year-old motors came so loudly that it vibrated through Gallagher's bones. A surge of warmth moved through him, accompanied by a quake that threw him against the heat shield. As he fell back, the full-throated roar of the main engines kicked in, as did one hell of a g-force, which pinned him hard to the deck.

But he had launched, damn it. He had launched.

More G-forces now. He could not tell how many. Four? Five? Six? If he accelerated any faster, he would suffer G-induced loss of consciousness, known by astronauts and military pilots as G-LOC. The only way to combat it was to take quick breaths and try to force the blood out of his head and back into his extremities.

As he began the effort, his face smeared back against his head. Warm, wet blood dribbled from his eyes and ears. Vision began to narrow. The heat shield glowed bright red and hung within arm's reach.

A jarring bang, and the first stage engines tumbled away—along with the heat shield, which had been ripped off its bindings.

Gallagher's head jerked sideways as the second stage engines ignited. Minute dust particles bombarded his now exposed body for one, two, three seconds before *Cosmos* punched through Mars' upper atmosphere. The probe suddenly accelerated, no longer held by Mars' gravity and atmospheric friction.

I see them, Gallagher thought before the void consumed him. *I see the stars.*

UNITED STATES SPACECRAFT *MEDEA ONE*
MARS ORBIT
MISSION TIME: DAY 184

With eyes still pink and puffy, Bowman regarded her displays, making sure that all systems were green-lined for main engine burn.

I can't go home alone. I just can't.

But you are. You already told them you're coming:

Houston, Medea One. *Ground crew reduced to Gallagher. Reached* Cosmos. *Link established. Probe failed second diagnostics. Ignition cell dead. No joy. No launch. While crew member is extant, mission commander declaring him End Of Mission. Commencing return sequence at zero, zero, zero, zero on orbital degradation clock.* Medea One, *out.*

As a child, Bowman had listened to admonishments like "turn that frown upside down" and "if you keep making that face, it'll get stuck like that." She suspected now that her expression would remain as is for a very long time. She had never hated anything as much in her life. . . .

She remembered a conversation with a former radar intercept officer, Jon "Mr. Potatohead" Potasky, a young man who had been her "backseat" for nearly a year when they had flown F-87s in the Adriatic. Jon had talked about his experience getting shot down in South America. He and his pilot, Captain Francis "Madhatter" O'Malley, had punched out, but O'Malley had broken both legs on impact and had ordered Jon to leave before ground troops swarmed them. Jon had refused. The enemy drew near, and Jon finally made the heartbreaking decision to go. He watched from afar as a bearded trooper jammed a rifle in O'Malley's mouth and pulled the trigger.

Since then, Jon wondered why only he had lived. Bowman had told him that survivor guilt seems like such a clinical term; it's an abstraction until it happens to you. She had been right. Only now could she know Jon's pain.

A navigation screen came alive, its touchboard beeping rapidly. *What now? Proximity alert? There's something out there?*

Fearing a meteor or something worse, Bowman rushed to the optical scope, brought it on-line, then trained it on coordinates behind the ship.

Even as she turned to the scope's display, the image focused.

"Gallagher . . ."

She lunged for her touchboard, switched the ship's AI to voice activation. "Computer. Abort main engine burn. Pause return sequence. Power Orbital Maneuvering System and Retro Control System." She pushed in the corner of a compartment at her knees, and a thick, rubberized joystick lowered into place. "Okay. Nav is manual. I need roll, pitch, yaw. X, Y, Z. Ten millimeter bursts."

"Main engine burn aborted," came the computer's voice. "Return sequence paused. OMS and RCS on-line. Maneuvering will answer to your call."

Still hardly believing what she had seen, Bowman guided the ship around, leaving hydrogen bursts in her wake. She headed back for the crippled probe floating like a metallic raft lost at sea. *Not much time. How much air did he say he would have? Oh, God. C'mon. C'mon!*

Dividing her gaze between the nav system's report and the twinkling speck out there, beyond her viewport, Bowman came up hard and fast on the tiny craft, then fired breaking thrusters in twin plumes that intersected near the bow. "Computer. Hold this position relative to second spacecraft."

"Autopilot engaged," acknowledged the computer. "Coordinates plotted."

"Hey, Commander? Promise you won't leave if we don't like it there?"

"I promise."

"And now I'm gonna keep it," Bowman said, bounding free of her chair.

twenty-nine

Once off the Flight Deck, Bowman sprinted through the first access tube. When she hit the second, she flew forward like a long jumper in zero G. She had forgotten that only three of the spheres and six of the access tubes still rotated to provide artificial gravity. Now she would have to catch the damned wall rungs and pull herself through. *Okay. Got one. Another. Pull. Pull. Just like the monkey bars when you were a kid.*

Her arms burned by the time she reached the maintenance level/MEV deck. She propelled herself through the anteroom, then floated into the MEV deck proper, aiming for the bulky EVA suit across the immense bay. The upper and lower halves of the suit hung high on magnetic grips. Bowman righted herself, then slid down through the pants and into the boots, which automatically conformed to her foot and locked her tightly in place. She pulled up the pants, and as she did so, they too adjusted to fit snugly around her hips. With a jolt of nerves, she pushed off, soaring up and into the EVA suit, sliding arms into sleeves. Her head cleared the neckline, and she glimpsed through the permaglass bubble as automatic fitting systems sealed and pressurized. The Heads Up Display shimmered to life and divided into two data bars running down the sides, a communications bar on the bottom, and a targeting reticle in the center. "Computer. Seal this level. Override primary hatch codes on my voice ID. Cancel lockout sequence for immediate purge."

"Level sealed. Primary hatch codes overridden. Lockout bypassed. Standby for atmospheric venting."

The MEV deck's main doors parted, purging the rest of the debris Bowman had not bothered to clean up. She hung there on the magnetic grips as the last of the air escaped. "Release suit binding." She jerked away from the bulkhead and booted off toward the open hatch. Out there, three hundred meters beyond *Medea One*'s colossal windmill of solar panels, lay *Cosmos* and Gallagher, backlit by the planet's flame-colored aureole.

Bowman drove herself down toward the harpoon gun seated in its wall mount. She gripped one of two U-shaped handles extending from either side of the large barrel, then turned on a palm-sized targeting index and range-finder screen resting on a swivel mount. A rotary chamber below the barrel spooled out retrieval line. As the gun powered up, Bowman's HUD switched to a harpoon overlay, with a targeting reticle linked to the gun's sight. She aimed at Gallagher, then squeezed a secondary trigger to activate the laser sight. Her HUD zoomed in on Gallagher's chest, showing where the laser dot had struck. But the gun's targeting index beamed the grim news: OBJECT OUT OF RANGE.

Shoving the gun aside, Bowman gazed up and across the bay at the huge Spacecraft Remote Manipulator Arm, a sophisticated robotic retrieval, repair, and docking aid manufactured by the Canadian Space Agency and its subcontractors. She had flown up to Saint-Hubert, Quebec, to tour the facility and to confer with the engineers who worked on the system. The SRMA's primary function had been to retrieve Hab after the mission. Well, if it couldn't do that, Bowman certainly had another job for it.

She lunged up toward the arm—twenty meters of alloy folded in on itself like an accordion, with the final two segments remaining in rest position, crooked at an obtuse angle. The entire appendage hung at the starting line of a linear accelerator track that ran the length of the MEV deck's overhead.

As Bowman reached the SRMA, she pivoted and backed toward the jetpack retrieval ball affixed to the arm. About as wide as her back and equipped with tiny hydrogen jets, the ball *chink*ed into the receptacle between her shoulders, locking her to it. "Last acquisition," she told the ship's AI, which would immediately calculate *Cosmos*'s present speed and coordinates. "Line release. Full velocity."

After a triplet of clangs, the arm blasted off down the track, slamming Bowman into her suit and driving her face-first toward the void. No amusement park ride could ever match the sensation.

The midpoint found her bearing teeth as the Gs piled on, the bulkheads smeared by, and the stars hurtled toward her.

Two blinks later, the arm thudded against its braking pad, a surge of deceleration threw Bowman forward into her suit, then flung her into space with the ball still attached to her back and trailing an EVA line attached to the arm.

She sped like a glass-domed bullet toward *Cosmos,* skimming along *Medea One*'s hull and a pair of rotund fuel tanks. Two of the four solar panels lay ahead, fanning out into a massive V through which she streaked.

Open space now. She wouldn't look down. Vertigo big-time here. Fifty meters away from the ship, according to the HUD. Seventy-five. One hundred. Coming up fast on *Cosmos.* One-twenty-five. One-fifty. She needed to get ready. Turn back. Fire the jetpack to slow herself.

But then she did it. Looked down. Swirling hues of red drew her into a whirlpool. A glance to *Cosmos.* Where was it? Gone in slashes of star lines. No more space. Just—

The air blew from her lungs as she crashed into *Cosmos,* rebounded, regained her senses, then groped for the edge of a compartment attached to the launch sphere's remaining half. She pulled herself up, saw the top of Gallagher's helmet, then muscled up and over him.

He lay inert across the pockmarked surface of the sample container. Thin lines of caked blood traced the gaps between his eyes and ears. Ruddy dust matted his short hair, and his stubble-laden cheeks sank toward his blue nose.

Bowman shook him, then pressed her helmet against his, hoping that even the muffled hum between faceplates might bring him around. "Gallagher! Gallagher!" She lifted his arm, checked his life support panel. Zero oxygen. No pulse and respiration. Heart in ventricular fibrillation. "Computer. Retrieve line. Full velocity."

Slapping palms onto the container's rim, Bowman hung on as she became a link in the chain reeling *Cosmos* back toward the ship. Velocity ticked up in Bowman's HUD: twenty kilometers per hour, thirty, forty-five, sixty, seventy-five. They knifed between the solar panels, then *Cosmos* dipped and caromed off one of the fuel tanks with a reverberation that nearly blew Bowman's hands off the rim. Thankfully, the probe's course evened out, and in a few seconds they passed through the bay's gaping maw.

With velocity suddenly up to ninety kilometers per hour and slack growing in the line, Bowman knew she had to do more than just gawk at the approaching bay and the arm that had lowered several segments to drag them in. "Computer. Braking bursts."

The jetpack ball fired twin puffs of hydrogen that snapped the line taut, even as Bowman manually triggered another burst that tipped *Cosmos* onto its side so that its base faced the oncoming arm and shielded them behind it.

"Computer. Braking bursts!"

Three more puffs barely slowed the probe.

An alarm sounded in Bowman's suit. She flinched and held it. They passed into the shadows of the bay. The robotic arm barreled toward them. Closer. Closer. They crashed into it with a breath-robbing thud, followed by a chiseling quake as two pieces of the arm snapped away amid a slow-moving shower of torn conduits ripped from *Cosmos*'s undercarriage.

Blown free by the collision, Bowman immediately swam back toward the probe but noticed that the collision had all but stopped it. *Cosmos* floated slowly through the bay, headed for a gentle tap on the opposite bulkhead. "Computer! Seal MEV deck! Emergency atmosphere now!"

While the doors rolled shut behind her, Bowman

darted for a maintenance kit set into the bulkhead. She tugged open the panel, then pulled out a laser blade the size of a flashlight, an instrument was used to make precise cuts in thermoplastic and other kinds of tubing. She started back for Gallagher as white mist jetted into the bay from nearly a hundred vents.

Shaking, Bowman straddled Gallagher, unbuckled and tore off his life-support vest, then fumbled with the laser's control knob, setting the beam's depth. She burned a jittery line over his helmet's binding, then another from his Adam's apple to his navel. She tugged open the smoldering suit, twisted the helmet away, then seized Gallagher by his thermal, pulling him away to shed his pants and boots. His head lolled back, and his arms bobbed limply at his sides.

"Not after all this, damn it," she cried, feeling the walls of a breakdown tumbling on her.

No. Can't give up. Think. Think.

Okay. Time for her to remember all that paramedic training. She had to get him oxygen and defibrillate, had to get that current into his heart to depolarize the cells and allow them to repolarize uniformly. She needed to restore an organized cardiac rhythm.

Dragging Gallagher by the front of his thermal, Bowman sprang forward. The emergency aid station lay just outside the anteroom. Her gaze narrowed on the pair of pre-gummed heart paddles mounted in their rectangular capacitor. She trembled more violently now as she remembered that it's more difficult to convert ventricular fibrillation in the presence of hypoxia and hypothermia, either of which had probably driven Gallagher's heart into v-fib.

She reached the station, pushed Gallagher down on the deck below, unfastened his thermal, slipped the auto hyperventilator's mask over his face, then powered up the wireless electrocardiograph located just above the capacitor. Paddles in hand, she thumbed a knob to set the defibrillator to two hundred joules and tried to remember the placement of the paddles. Shit. The information would not come. One higher, one lower . . . something like that. No time to worry. She applied firm, downward pressure on the paddles and hit him with a twelve-millisecond shock of direct current. The EKG's screen continued painting the jagged rhythm of Gallagher's heart.

Three hundred joules. Clear. His back arched.

Nothing.

Three-hundred-and-sixty joules. As high as she dared go.

She hit him, felt the current spider into her fingers—

Then blew backward through the bay, the paddles tumbling toward her. The bulkhead came up hard and unforgiving, and Bowman closed her eyes as the aftershock rattled through. She hovered there, her own heart drumming as she sobbed quietly for a few seconds, then booted herself back to Gallagher—

Whose eyes flickered open. He took in a little air, coughed, coughed again, his face slowly pinking. Once his breath had steadied, he blinked hard, trying to focus.

"I'm right here," she said softly, then glanced to a readout. "Your core temp's way down. Have to get you to the infirmary. Ventilate you with warm air. Get some IVs started and tuck you in a hypothermia wrap. God, you look like shit."

He tried to smile, but his lips cracked, and he shuddered.

She caressed his head through the thick glove. "Easy. Close your eyes. Dream. . . ."

epilogue

"Houston, *Medea One*. Strike last communication. You
won't believe this, but Gallagher got that probe off the
ground. He used AMEE's e-source for ignition power. I
recovered him during orbital degradation. He's presently
stable but suffering from severe hypothermia. Request
medical consult. Request recalc and reconfiguration for
return flight home. Sorry guys, but I dipped into A tank
to maintain orbit. We're presently stable but diminished.
More news to follow. Uploading telemetry. Please advise.
Medea One, out."

Russert flipped back his PIM, took off his headset,
then laughed at himself for getting so choked up. That
damned fool had done it.

With a tremulous voice, Russert ordered the message
played through the intercom, and as Commander Kate

Bowman's voice resounded through the ficker, he left his desk and came up behind Lowenthal, who had been staring absently through his PIM. Beside him sat Borokovski, eyes shut, head tucked into his sagging chest as he wheezed in exhaustion.

When Bowman had reported the second diagnostic failure and had declared Gallagher End Of Mission, Russert had told Borokovski that they would fly him back to Brooklyn and that he would be generously rewarded for his time. The old Russian had scowled and said, "I go when fat lady sings."

"Hey, Doctor Borokovski, wake up," cried Lowenthal, elbowing the man's gut. "*Cosmos* launched."

"Wha? Wha? It is dream?" Borokovski asked, eyes narrowed to slits. He jolted awake, craned his head to Lowenthal. "Probe launched?"

"That's right, sir," answered Russert. "Ignition cell was dead. Our astronaut found another cell."

Borokovski's face split open in a wide, gap-toothed grin. "*Molodets!* Celebration then!"

At that moment Bowman's message completed, and it seemed as though the controllers had heard Borokovski and erupted in whoops and hollers.

"This is all a bit premature," Lowenthal said. "I don't even need to see the telemetry to know that she burned up way too much fuel. And her life support took a hell of a beating. We'll need to mount a rescue mission. Meet 'em in transit. Rescue team will need to launch ASAP. Which raises another problem—Lockheed's next Heavy Launch Vehicle won't be ready for another eight months."

"What about the Canadians?" asked Russert. "Thought I read something about their lunar HLV going up next month."

"You did," Lowenthal confirmed. "But now it's been

delayed. The Chinese would've loaned us one if we hadn't pissed them off."

Borokovski waved his hands. "Gentlemen. I know where there is Heavy Launch Vehicle in Uzbekistan. For cheap. A friend of mine has kept it."

Lowenthal gazed dubiously at the designer. "This HLV's command system doesn't use Win Twenty-twenty, does it?"

"I don't know. It is old rocket. Fixer-upper. Maybe. But with notebook computer and copy of software, it's no problem. Also, this rocket can launch from sea platform near Hawaii. I go now. Make phone call." Borokovski got unsteadily to his feet.

"Hey, Miguel?" Russert called into his headset. "I'm sending Doctor Borokovski down to your station. Get him a line out, would you please? And when you get a chance, book me on a flight for Galveston. Get me out of here before dinner."

"Think that's wise?"

"I'm sure I can talk the administration out of half a day—especially after this stretch."

"I meant going to see Jessica. She's really pissed. I spent like twenty minutes on the phone with her yesterday."

"God, does she go around telling everybody?"

"Pretty much."

"Just get me on that flight. And tell Ms. MOD I need to speak with her when she gets a chance."

"You got it."

Russert gazed thoughtfully across the ficker. The PROP and GNC teams huddled over desks and discussed Bowman's request for recalculations. Flight Surgeon Palladino and her staff of six doctors studied 3D cross sections of Gallagher's body. Greg Sudmanski's EECOM team prepared oxygen and food supply projections for posting on the big screen. And all of the activity only confirmed what Jessica had implied. If he left, the whole place would *not* fall apart. Rockets would *not* crash into Mars.

He just prayed it wasn't too late to tell her.

UNITED STATES SPACECRAFT *MEDEA ONE*
MARS ORBIT
MISSION TIME: DAY 184

Gallagher set Burchenal's life support vest down on the only laboratory table that had survived the air purge, then he withdrew the titanium ampoule containing the frozen nematode and the glass one with the algae sample.

"Come on, you shouldn't be up," Bowman said. "And you pulled out your IVs? *Come on. . . .*"

"You kidding? It's been over two hours since I was raised from the dead."

"You need to get back into that wrap."

"Just let me stow this."

"I could've done that for you."

He held up the ampoules. "These are Burchenal's prizes, and I feel responsible for them."

She hoisted a brow. "Whatever's in there will save the world?"

"He thought so." Gallagher turned back to a storage berth built into the bulkhead and withdrew a heavy, metal box used to cache algae samples. He opened the box, slipped the tubes into foam sleeves, sealed the box, then returned it to the berth. "We get back, we'll let someone else handle these." He gazed wistfully at the life support vest. "So, you tell 'em yet?"

"Not yet."

"What're you waiting for?"

"Be honest, once word gets out that we discovered life on another world, our lives won't be our own. I just wanna enjoy a few more hours of freedom before the comm starts ringing off the hook."

"They're gonna ask you why you waited."

"I'll tell them we wanted to have breakfast first."

"I hear that. Lead the way."

"Of course, we still don't have any bacon."

He grinned and followed her out of the laboratory sphere, through the adjoining access tubes, and as they reached the kitchen sphere's entrance, she paused.

Then he saw them, too. The ghosts of missing friends.

As Gallagher padded tentatively into the room, he could still hear the soft music of Bud's voice, the intensity of Burchenal's, the terseness of Santen's, and the halting uncertainty of Pettengill's. So much of them remained.

"We have a long trip ahead," Bowman said weakly.

He met her gaze, came forward, then gripped her shoulders, pulling her close to him. "None of us were ready for this. We all made mistakes. Things we'd take back if we could." He glanced at the empty kitchen. "Four men died. But in the end, we pulled it off. And like I said, that's what people need to remember—that every man down there died a hero."

She traced a finger down his chest, drew circles around his heart. "You kept the faith."

"Yeah. Bud got me through. He got us all through. Y'know, he was the happiest person I've ever met."

"I'm happy, Gallagher. Right now. This minute." She widened her eyes. "That's all you can do—take it minute by minute. And if you're lucky, you get a second chance."

It was a light kiss, elegant and old fashioned; one that would let her know that she was wanted. One that would not tear open his chapped lips. She kissed back. Much harder. Then pulled away, breathless and flushed.

"Go for a walk?" he suggested.

Her smile roused his own. "Sure. But I thought you wanted to eat."

"I can wait."

She nodded, and they crossed to a porthole affording views of a burnt orange stretch of Acidalia Planitia, Mars' great northern plains.

With his forehead pressed to the permaglass, Gallagher listened for the lonely red planet, for a voice he could now interpret.

about the author

Peter Telep received a large portion of his education in New York, spent a number of years in Los Angeles, where he worked for such television shows as *In The Heat of the Night* and *The Legend of Prince Valiant*, then returned east to Florida. There, he earned his undergraduate and graduate degrees and now teaches composition, scriptwriting, and creative-writing courses at the University of Central Florida.

Mr. Telep's other novels include the *Squire Trilogy*, two books based on Fox's *Space: Above and Beyond* television show, a trilogy of novels based on the bestselling computer game *Descent*, four books in the film-based *Wing Commander* series, a forthcoming original novel entitled *Sol 17*, and he is presently writing *Night Angel 9*, a new series of novels about firefighter-paramedics. You may E-mail him at PTelep@aol.com or contact him via the publisher. He is always delighted to hear from his fans.